TRIAL BY CHARM

TRIAL BY CHARM

THE CHARMED TRIAL SERIES - 1

JOLENE BUCHHEIT

Jaedha,
Prepare to be charmed.
♥ always,
Jolene Buchheit

Trial by Charm

By Jolene Buchheit

Elephantine Publishing, LLC.

www.elephantinepublishing.com

ISBN-13: 978-0-9968428-5-3

ISBN-10: 0996842853

Cover design by Berto Designs

Interior Design and Formatting by E.M. Tippetts Book Designs

To Chris, who manages to face an enormous trial every day she breathes, yet never loses her charm.

CHAPTER ONE

"Earth to Julia!"

Taylor stands up from the floor and waves her hand in my face; Lissy laughs along with her. I've clearly been in my own world a little too long for their liking.

We are celebrating our first swim-meet-free weekend since school started with a sleepover. It's true, I wasn't really paying attention, but I am happy to be hanging out with my friends, especially now that I am able to leave the house for a night without panicking. I used to avoid spending nights away from my mom after my dad died and my panic attacks began, and for a while I fell out of the habit of getting together with the girls. Life is better now, partly because Lissy and Taylor understand how to calm me down, but mainly because they never make me feel like my friendship is a burden.

Sitting on Taylor's bed while they were "girl-talking" about the school's biggest heartthrob, I was keeping myself busy by making a list of all the potential things that could be wrong with that popular jock, Vander Thelxinoe—he's a werewolf who can't help being a jerk with each new phase of the moon and that's why some days he tries to flirt with me and I tell him to back off, and other days he tries to pick a fight with me. Or he could be a vampire who's a jerk because he gets tired trying to stay out of the sun and that's why he finds pleasure in flirting with my friends so I have to listen to them go on and on about him, to make my life a dark place, too.

When they bring me out of my trance, I realize they are still singing his praises. I sigh in exasperation. They tease me about this habit of mine all the time, and I tell them I think my heart must be as dark as my skin. I can't help how I feel—I just don't get any pleasure out of talking positively about boys like they do.

"Sorry, ladies," I say, though I'm not, really. Every time they do this something in my brain just shuts down; I'm not at all interested. Like, at all, at all. I once considered the possibility, for a short period of time, that I might be a lesbian, but I ruled that out when I had no attraction to girls, or even a desire to think about them, either. I choose now to believe I am just unique, fully above those basic instincts of attraction, because, somehow, I have control over myself. This feels most like the truth, even if it makes me sound pompous. I can't explain it any better than that.

I had tuned out of their conversation on purpose, for the sake of preserving my sanity—the subject was causing me to lose brain cells at a rapid rate because of their overabundant use of exaggerated adjectives on boys. But I can't avoid it any longer. Taylor flips her long, curly, dark-blonde hair back, revealing her wide caramel-colored eyes, a question waiting on her face.

"Well, what about you? Do you think Wesley has better abs than Vander?" Lissy challenges me. I stare at her blue eyes framed by sea-blue and foam-green-dyed hair, hoping I'd only imagined that she is asking me a boy-related question.

I hadn't. I guess I can be grateful they are fussing about boys our age this time, instead of our teacher, Mr. Daniels, like they sometimes do. Whatever swooning is, these girls do it and they look like morons fanning themselves and crying out "I'm dying" or "I'm dead" all the time. Who actually does that? Not me. That's one upside to being counted out of that mess, because I don't want to ride on that crazy train.

Taylor clears her throat to get my attention.

"Ugh! Vander is always flirting with you guys and is such a jerk to me. Not to mention he always seems to get what he wants. As for Wesley, I hardly even know him, because he's so quiet. So what does it matter who works out more?" Irritated at being reminded about how I'm not like them, I raise my eyebrows and tilt my head, letting them know that if we don't change the subject, I'm going to leave—again. Only this time, I will physically leave the room or just go to sleep instead of mentally checking out.

"Okay, okay, never mind. But for the record, Vander isn't always flirting. He is just polite and he ignores you sometimes because you ignore him," Lissy says to me, with a we'd-better-stop-now look at Taylor. "What do you want to do?"

"I don't know, something fun that involves far fewer boy-focused words. Sleepovers are supposed to be exciting, even if we are seventeen years old and this is our senior year. I always imagined that when I got to high school, sleepovers would be more like they are in *Grease*. You know—climbing out of windows, randomly breaking into song, yelling at dumb boys, and playing in a pool or something."

"Yes! Let's go swimming! That's a great idea!" Lissy jumps up and starts jabbing her thumbs wildly on her phone.

Taylor and I just exchange confused looks. Did Lissy sign us up for a polar bear plunge without our permission?

"Yeah, except that I didn't bring a swimsuit with me. Oh, and there is the minor detail that it is November in Iowa, less than fifty degrees outside, and you don't have a heated pool!"

Lissy reaches in Taylor's top dresser drawer and pulls out last year's red team swimsuit. We all wear about the same size, so now that argument has been nullified. But there is still the major issue of us freezing our butts off. Lissy's phone whistles at her; it lights up with a message from her brother, and after she reads it, she pumps her fist in the air.

"Grant still has his keys to the school, and he's going to let me use them! Of course, I have to agree to do his laundry for the next month, and to confess that I stole them from an unsuspecting teacher should we get caught. But at least we can go swimming tonight. It's totally worth it." She then flings the red swimsuit over her shoulder and skips—literally—into the bathroom, closing the door behind her as if this conversation is over.

"Wait! Are we talking about breaking into our school, like for real?" Taylor asks, darting her eyes between the bathroom and me in disbelief. If I wasn't so busy trying to decipher if this is really happening or if I am having an elaborate dream, I would be doing the same thing. We make our way to the bathroom door and she pushes it open. The door stops after an inch or two, and Lissy's face appears in the crack.

"You said you wanted to do something exciting, and mentioned a pool. Well, going for a swim at school is a two birds, one stone type of thing. Aren't you ready to go on an adventure? Don't you think it's time to see how it feels to walk on the wild side? I know I am." Her tone reminds me of a little kid pulling out the triple dog dare.

"Lissy, what happens if we get caught?" Taylor takes the words right out of my mouth.

Lissy proceeds to change into the swimsuit behind the door, undeterred. "What makes you think anyone will be at school on a Saturday night in November, let alone in the pool area? Our state swim meet was last week, and the men's team doesn't start until next week. We'll be fine. Now, quit being sissies and get your suits on." She walks out of the bathroom and starts to pull her sweats on over her suit.

"How do you know your brother won't send someone there to catch us so that we will for sure be found out?" I have several more doubts to express, but this seems the most urgent.

"Because I reminded him that I still have pictures of him and his boyfriend throwing rolls of toilet paper into our neighbor's trees this summer, and my parents still don't know they did that. And besides, how can something be exciting if there is no risk of getting in trouble for doing it?" She reaches in Taylor's top drawer and throws one of her practice suits at me. It doesn't take me long to throw it back. It's chocolate brown, almost the exact same color as my skin, and I would look naked if I put it on. After seeing the look on my face, she tosses our blue sophomore-year team suit at me. "Now, please get ready."

I turn to Taylor to see if the look on her face is telling me whether we are going to do this or not. Our eyes lock in some kind of showdown. After a series of eyebrow raises and questioning glances are exchanged between us, a smile starts to form on my lips. I never do anything wrong—*why not do this and see how it feels to live on the wild side for once?* Taylor's eyes widen farther at my smile, and then she shrugs, causing her curly blonde locks to bounce on her shoulders. She digs into her pool bag and pulls out our recently retired team suit for herself.

We are so going to do this!

We both turn to look at Lissy, and she's grinning like a mad woman. She already has her mermaid-colored hair up in two messy side buns. Taylor doesn't move, so I take my turn in the bathroom to change first. When I come back out and reach for my sweatpants, Taylor is still frozen in place.

"We're not getting any younger," Lissy teases as she bodily shoves Taylor and her swimsuit into her own bathroom. I give her an encouraging thumbs up before Lissy pulls the door closed.

After five minutes, Taylor emerges with her suit on, but changing her clothes was not all she was doing in there. Her hair is now in two French braids, the same way she always wears it for swim meets. I can tell by the smile on her lips and the mysterious spark in her eyes that she's fully on board with this plan now, despite her initial hesitation.

Taylor looks at me, and then turns her head to Lissy, who squeals like a dolphin. "*Eep*! Let's do this!"

We have to stop at Lissy's house to get the school keys from her twin brother before we hit the pool.

Grant and his boyfriend, Kevin, meet us at the curb as we pull up. Grant relinquishes his keys but not before confirming the deal Lissy agreed to, this time with witnesses. Kevin sticks his head in the window. "Try not to drown, girls."

Lissy pushes his head out of the way as she presses the window button. Right before it closes, Grant leans down and imitates their mom's voice, "Make good choices!"

We laugh as we drive off. Those two lovebirds are always getting involved in some crazy shenanigans, but they never get caught. That's probably what gave Lissy the idea to do this in the first place. Well, that, and the fact that Grant uses the school's keys—passed down to him from the previous football team captain—all the time without getting in trouble.

The school looks different with no lights on, no cars in the parking lot, and no other people around. Much like an amusement park in winter, it feels desolate and a bit sad. We park on a side street in the neighborhood behind the school so we don't draw attention to ourselves and walk stealthily up to the gym's entrance. Lissy holds the exterior door's key up in her fist. Before she places it in the lock, she looks into my eyes. I nod, and then she turns to Taylor for the same look of affirmation.

She slides the key in the lock and opens the door. Our bodies are pressed tightly to the wall as we soundlessly tiptoe down the hall. With the way my heart is pounding in my chest, I swear people can hear it from a mile away. We make it past the gym, and can see the door to the women's locker room a few yards in front of us, when I hear voices.

"Toss it here!" a male voice whispers, and I can't tell where it is coming from.

We rush the remaining few feet to the locker room door, open it, and file in. Then we all jockey for position to look out the window in the door to see if we can find whom the voice belongs to, as well as to whom he was speaking. After a few minutes of craning our necks to try to catch a glimpse of the culprits, we hear a low rumble of laughter coming from behind the privacy wall. My heart starts to beat wildly and my palms start to sweat at the thought of being caught, maybe even arrested.

I knew this was a bad idea.

We turn around to find it's not security or any off-duty teacher, but the ab models in the flesh: Wesley and Vander, co-captains of the men's swim team, standing there in black sweats and hoodies. They don't look as surprised to see us in here as we are to see them. It's obvious that Vander is the one who spoke because his hands are empty, and Wesley's are hidden behind his back.

"What are you doing here?" we all ask at the same time, like some Scooby-Doo cartoon moment.

No one offers an answer. Wesley's dad is a science teacher in the building, and my heart sinks when I realize they might actually have permission to be here. But before it dips too low, it occurs to me that nobody would give these boys permission to be in the women's locker room. A grin breaks out across my face at the sudden realization.

"I think you should explain why you are in the ladies' room before we say anything."

Lissy looks at me, and seeing my determination gives her the confidence to put her hands on her hips and add, "Yeah, boys, what do you think you're doing in here?"

"Aww, aren't you ladies happy to see me or are you just in shock because my being here makes all of your dreams come true?" Vander must really think he's something special. I mean seriously, could he be any more full of himself?

The sly grin on his face reeks of smugness, and when he offers what I assume is supposed to be a playful wink, it makes my skin crawl. But one look at my girls, and I can see why he seems so confident: they are nodding, smiling, and—*Santa, save me*—they are even batting their eyelashes!

The whole scene makes me roll my eyes. "I think I'd rather see the dentist for a root canal, but I will ask you one more time before I lose my shit and call security. What. Are. You. Doing. Here?"

"The way I see it," Vander starts in a low hiss-like whisper that sounds like a growl, running his hands through his straight, dark hair to sweep it out of his face. He tilts his head down, the move revealing a blue-eyed pendant around his neck, and peers at us from the top of his eyes. "None of us are *supposed* to be here. But we've got what we came here for, and we can leave now without you remembering that you even saw us."

Taylor and Lissy both nod at him as if they are stuck in some weird trance, but I am above agreeing with doing whatever he says. *Who does he think he is?*

"What the hell are you talking about, Vander? Why would I forget I saw you here?" I ignore the shocked look on his face and turn to his partner in crime. "And what the hell are you hiding behind your back, Wesley?"

As if on auto-pilot, he starts to move his hands and I lean in for a better view.

"Don't show her, Wes!" Vander shouts, but it's too late. I've already seen the red, lacy bra, laying in his hands like an offering to me. I recognize it instantly as belonging to Maddie Tucker, the captain of our swim team.

"What do you think you're going to do with that?" I reach for it, sure that whatever they plan to do will not be anything good.

Vander grabs it before I can, puts it behind his back, and locks his gaze with mine again. In the strange whisper he used before, he says, "You never saw anything. You never saw me, you never saw Wesley, and you certainly never saw Madeline's bra."

"I sure as hell *did* see you and Wesley with your paws all over Maddie's bra!

And if you don't stop with that creepy growly voice shit, I'm going to kick you in the balls so hard, you will taste the scum on the bottom of my shoe!"

Vander's blue-green eyes are now as wide as I have ever seen them. He seems thoroughly thrown off by my threat. I turn to see why the girls aren't backing me up here, but they are both sitting on a bench with their heads together, whispering and giggling. This is no time to act so ridiculous! *What are they thinking?*

Vander reaches up, pushes Wesley's dreadlocks out of the way, and covers his ears for him. Wesley's dark eyes show confusion, but Vander nods at him reassuringly. Then Vander starts to sing, "Goodnight, ladies, goodnight, ladies—" like a scene straight out of a musical.

My first thought during this is that they must have been eavesdropping on us at Taylor's house when we made plans to come here and somehow overheard my desire to break out in song. That is a totally ridiculous notion, though, so I let it go. My second thought is concerning how my knees are giving out from beneath me, and I am about to go down—*hard*. My eyelids get so heavy I have to blink and I struggle to open my eyes again, as my body starts to tip over. Suddenly, Vander stops singing, lets go of Wesley's ears, and grabs me before he lays me down on the floor.

The tile feels cold and refreshing against my cheek. The floor of the locker room gives me a vantage point I've never seen before—*how lovely everything looks from down here*. The lockers are getting blurry and dancing around a bit.

Vander's spinning face comes into my view. "You look tired, Julia."

"Yeah, I'm just going to take a little nap."

His smirk is the last thing I see before my eyes flutter closed.

CHAPTER

TWO

O*uch!*

My head is pounding, my face stings like I've just been slapped, and my mattress feels as hard as a board. *Why am I wet—did I take a shower before bed?* I can hear a strange faraway voice yelling or maybe crying—could be both, I suppose.

Everything hurts; was I in a fight? Am I in the hospital?

The voice is suddenly not so distant, and it doesn't belong to a stranger. It's Lissy and I think she is sitting on my chest.

"Please wake up, Julia!"

The panic in her voice opens my eyes. I try to take in her tear-stained face and her open hand reeling back to take another blow. She grabs my shoulders instead, pulling me up to her, and crushes me with a hug. "Taylor! She's awake."

Even in my sleepy and painful state I manage to turn my head to Taylor and see tears running down her face as well. She rushes to embrace me as I notice the lockers beyond her. What the hell am I doing sleeping in the locker room?

On top of Lissy slapping me, it looks like Taylor is getting ready to wring out a soaking-wet towel on my face. That explains the sogginess.

"What do you bitches think you're doing?" I ask as I push them away so I can assess the damage done to my sore cheek.

The sighs of relief from both of them is concerning. Lissy wipes her face with the backs of her hands before I can ask why she was crying; I hate to see people crying, it makes me feel like crying myself and I'm afraid once I start, I won't stop.

Between her sniffles, Lissy says, "You've been out cold for ten minutes. I was just about to call an ambulance! I know you like to sleep and all, but this is not the time."

It's all coming back to me now.

"Where did Vander and Wesley go?" I ask, sitting up and feeling my head for lumps. Now that I'm awake, the only thing I'm worried about is whether those punks got away with Maddie's bra.

"Vander?" Lissy repeats, frowning.

"Yes, Vander. And Wesley. Did you see which way they went?" I ask, wondering if maybe they hit their heads too. Their confusion is not helping.

Taylor exchanges a glance with Lissy and then turns to me, brows wrinkled. "I haven't seen Vander or Wesley. Are you okay?"

"What are you talking about?" They exchange concerned glances, which warns me they aren't convinced that I'm okay after all. I'm starting to agree with them. *Could I have dreamed all of this? Did I fall, hit my head, and suffer a hallucination?* Maybe I *do* need medical attention.

"Tell me everything that happened, from the minute we entered the building until now! Don't leave anything out," I demand, the urgency in my tone evident despite my effort to stay calm. I climb to my feet and investigate Maddie's locker, which had been left open a tad, and I can see that her red bra is still in there. My head is spinning with questions: *Did I dream all of this? Were those guys actually here? Did I slip, or did something happen to me? Why did they leave her bra here, to confuse me further?*

What the hell actually happened here?

"We came into the locker room," Taylor explains gently, like I'm the one who has lost her mind.

"But, why?" I interrupt her, because she skipped the important part.

"Because that's how we get to the pool, and we wanted to go swimming." She's petting my back like I'm some kind of dog. It irritates me, so I shrug her off.

"So, why aren't we in the pool already?" I ask, hoping to hear any mention of Vander and Wesley.

"Because you passed out as soon as we got in here, and just now woke up?" Lissy gently suggests. It's plain to see they have no recollection of what happened with the guys. It's like Vander told them that they would forget, and now they have. Or maybe they are pretending to. I don't trust this guy further than I can throw him, though I'm certainly not going to get close enough to even attempt that. And besides, I am their best friend, whom they love and trust. *Why would they listen to him?*

"Y'all are pissing me off, for real. I can't believe you would pretend that you didn't see them, just because he told you to!"

"Who are you talking about? Julia, you're not making any sense. We haven't spoken to Vander. Do you need to go to the hospital, or something?" Taylor has stopped the waterworks, but her eyes are red and she's still concerned. I shake my head at the ground.

"I'm going to go and splash some cold water on my face." Slamming Maddie's locker shut, I step toward the bathroom area. Their eyes are burning a hole in the back of my head as I go. They are watching me as if I'm a fragile vase about to crack apart. *Surely, if I had hit my head, the sound of a slamming locker would have hurt, right?*

The water is already running in the sink when Taylor and Lissy walk into the bathroom behind me. Feeling their eyes on me, I look up in the mirror, and watch them flinch when I hear the locker room door open. Shooing them into the stalls, I motion for them to hide and be quiet while I check it out.

Stepping out of the bathroom, I fully expect to give Vander and Wesley a piece of my mind, but come face to face with Coach Winter instead. Her name suits her well at this moment, because the look she gives me is definitely chilling.

"Oh, hey, Coach." I say it louder than necessary to give my friends a head's up. "I was just getting something from my locker."

"Would you like to tell me how you got into the building?" My hope that she'd just let me go is dashed immediately by the tone of her voice.

"The door was open?" That might have worked if I had said it less like a question, and more like a statement.

"I'm afraid not, Wright. Do you want to try again?"

Deciding that it may be best to plead the fifth in this moment, I simply shake my head and keep my focus on the pattern of the cold floor's tiles. She steps into her glass-walled office and grabs a jangling key ring off of her desk. Figures, *she* has an excuse to be here.

"Tell you what—I'm going to give you a choice." That makes me lift my eyes to hers. "If you promise not to ever break into this school again, I will choose your punishment. If you don't, I'll turn you over to Principal Ralphman, and let him decide. Make no mistake, this infraction will go on your record, but nobody else needs to know about it for now."

"I promise," I croak out as quickly as I can. I don't care if I'm stuck on towel duty until graduation day; I just want to put this night behind me.

"Great! I was hoping that's what you'd choose. Report to the pool on Monday, immediately after school. You are the new men's swim team manager." With that horrible pronouncement, she walks out of the locker room and holds the door open for me to follow. It takes some effort, but I manage to exit without a single glance back to where my friends are hiding.

When we get outside, she shuts the door behind me, and I finally get the nerve to ask, "What exactly does a swim team manager do?"

"You will be the go-to person to assist me with whatever I need—scorekeeping, lap counting, making ice packs, towel duty, putting kickboards away, et cetera. You will also help the captains of the team with pep duties. You know, decorating lockers on meet days, mixing oils for rubdowns, stuff like that. You are going to be a vital member of—and a real asset to—the team."

"Oh, great." I don't even try to suppress the sarcasm in my tone. I'm so salty about this situation, she might as well call me Pretzel.

That's just what any *other* girl would want—the chance to be Wesley and Vander's pool girl. But I am not just any other girl, and, therefore, this is going to suck so hard.

"If you've changed your mind, just say the word and I'll call Principal Ralphman right now." She holds her phone up, as if she is actually about to dial. Part of the reason I love my coach so much is because she doesn't mess around. She gets right to the point, and always follows through on what she says she will do. I'm well aware that this is not an empty threat.

"No, Coach, I haven't changed my mind. I'll see you Monday." I force a smile as I walk off toward the neighborhood where I parked my car, and turn around only twice. Once, to watch Coach climb into her car, and then a minute later to see Coach Winter eyeing me. She isn't going to go anywhere until she is sure I'm gone. Putting my head down, I keep walking as I pull out my phone and send a text to Lissy.

Me: Coach is sitting in her car watching to make sure I drive away. Go to the church across from the North lot and when it is clear, I'll pick you guys up.
Lissy: Thank you, Jules. I can't believe you got caught!
Me: You'd better believe it. I have the worst punishment ever.
Lissy: Oh no!! Towel duty?
Me: Worse!!!!! I'll tell you when I get there.

When I drop the girls off at Taylor's house, I decide to pick up my stuff. The mood has sufficiently soured, and it's probably best for me to go home to sleep. I think we've all had enough excitement for one night.

Against my wishes, Momma enters my room before noon. In fact, it's before 10:00AM, and I am *not* a morning person, to say the least. Our two-person household has many rules, but letting me sleep in on the weekends is the only one I got to make. This must be important—maybe Coach ratted me out after all. My heart is racing with anxiety as I slowly sit up.

"Julia, Coach Winter called a few minutes ago to thank me for supporting your desire to help out with the men's swim team this year. To say I was confused would be an understatement. Last I knew, you didn't want anything to do with boys." She raises her eyebrows at me, her hopeful face asking if maybe that had changed—she doesn't understand why I'm so different from other girls my age either. I control my expression and otherwise remain still, trying to think of the best way to play this situation off. "And now I've been told that you want to spend your afternoons playing in the pool with a whole scantily-clad group of them?"

Okay, that last bit was intended to get a reaction out of me, but I could see it coming, and I am prepared. My anxiety is gone and sleepiness is starting to take over again.

"As far as I am concerned, it could be a swim team of dogs. I just don't want my high school swim experience to be over yet. Coach offered me the position, and I told her I thought you would approve of me helping out. Was I wrong?" I implore her to disagree.

Momma smirks at my statement comparing boys to dogs, and it quickly turns into a full-on smile. "I'm proud of you, Julia. I know you'll be a great asset to the team. Try not to fall in love with any strays in the process, though," she says sarcastically while I try not to cringe at the sound of Coach's words coming out of her mouth. Then her comment about the strays sparks a sarcastic reply that I choose to keep in my head. *I'd be more likely to put those guys on leashes and train them to behave.*

"That would take an act of God, Momma," I reply instead, snuggling back down under my blanket, finished with this conversation.

"That's exactly what it was with me and your daddy, you know. An act of God, to be sure," she reminisces. "It could be that way for you, too. Crazier things have happened."

"Momma, please. I'm sleeping here." I point toward the door. My head is already drifting back to sleep.

"Before I forget to tell you, I've invited my coworker and his son over for dinner tomorrow night." It sounds like mumbling to me in my sleepy state.

"Momma! You know I love you, but pleeeease *get out*!" I throw my spare pillow at the door to emphasize my point. It misses its mark, but I hear the door click behind my mom as she exits my room. The silence hanging in the air makes my mind drift back to what happened—or didn't happen—last night. *Ugh, sleep come take me now.*

CHAPTER THREE

On Monday, I tell Taylor and Lissy I have to stay behind to finish an English assignment and send them to lunch off campus without me. Lying to my best friends sucks, but I need to find Maddie Tucker—alone. Mostly so I can figure out if I'm actually going crazy. I'm hoping she knows why the captains of the men's swim team would be so interested in confiscating her undergarment that they would risk breaking into the school to do it. Going straight to the source and questioning Vander or Wesley would be more direct—but I can't bring myself to face them until I know what happened. Instead, I head to the cafeteria and find Maddie at her usual table.

"Hey, Maddie." I slide my tray onto the table and take the empty seat next to her.

"Hi, Julia. What's up?" She's nibbling on a baby carrot, freshly dipped in ranch dressing. Her long, straight, black hair is tied back neatly, and her almond-shaped eyes show her uncertainty about why I'm sitting down next to her. It is warranted. We've swam for four years on the same team, but we aren't exactly close friends.

"Do you know if there is a rivalry or some kind of dare going on between the men's swim team and the women's?"

She looks over my shoulder, then behind herself before she leans in and asks, "Why? What have you heard?"

"I haven't heard anything, but I may have seen something on Saturday night. What's going on?"

Her darting eyes have me checking my surroundings, though I have no idea what or whom I'm supposed to be looking out for.

"We are supposed to raise the other team captain's undergarments up the school flagpole. Captains of the losing team have to do something even more embarrassing than having their underwear flapping in the wind for the whole school to see. There are two rules, though. Captains can't take their unmentionables off school grounds, and we can't capture the garments during school hours. Want to help?"

A chuckle bubbles its way right out of my mouth. *Oh, this is rich!* What a perfect way to embarrass Vander and Wesley for what they did the other night. I pull myself together and wipe the disbelieving smile from my face. Maybe Lissy was right when she said it's time for me see how it feels to live a little closer to the edge.

"Yes, I do want to help. But, first of all, I think it would help if you moved your red bra to your school locker, instead of your locker room locker."

"Wait, how did you know which bra I had in there?"

"Because Wesley and Vander almost took it Saturday night, but I caught them in the act and made them put it back." *Yeah, that's exactly how that happened—in a roundabout way. Truthfully, I don't know why they didn't just take it. It's not like I could have stopped them from my position on the floor.*

"Oh no! I would have died if I came to school today and found my bra flying around up on the flagpole. We *have* to win." She looks desperate, her dark eyes pleading with me, but somehow it looks like an act.

"Well, I am the men's team manager now, so I will see what I can do to help."

"Wow!" she exclaims, pressing one beautifully manicured hand to her lips. I can't tell if she feels sorry for me or if she is jealous like my friends. "What did you do to get stuck with that job?" I don't want to answer right away, but it only takes her a second to put it together on her own. "Oh, Saturday night. In the locker room. With boys. Yeah, sorry about that." I don't really believe she's sorry at all, since she says it while her shoulders bob up and down with laughter.

"Thanks." I shrug. There really are worse punishments ... though none are immediately coming to my mind.

I walk into Coach's office after school, and she hands me a clipboard. "Keep this with you at all times, and stay close to me unless I tell you otherwise. Got it?" Her rushed words make me give up any hope of having time to read the book I brought. I'm starting to think it's going to take a lot of energy to stay on top of things.

"Yes, Coach." I take the clipboard and pen she hands me. The paper on top has a list of names on it. I recognize a lot of them as swimmers from last year's team. There are plenty of empty lines, as well.

"Wright?" she says quietly, which is so out of character for her that I immediately look up from the clipboard.

"Yes, Coach?"

"I know this wasn't your idea, but I really do appreciate your willingness to help out. Thank you." Like a weight off my shoulders, her sincerity lifts away some of the annoyance about being the manager.

"No problem."

I follow her out to the pool deck. A group of twenty or so of my male classmates are standing around in their swimsuits, waiting. Coach blows her whistle to get their attention, and they all stop talking and look in her direction. I turn to her also and find her hand out, no doubt waiting for the clipboard. I pass it to her, and she starts taking roll.

As I look around at the team I have now unwillingly become a part of, I can tell that some of these guys spent a lot of time during the off-season in the gym, and some of them didn't. Unfortunately, there is no way to gauge who the fastest swimmer will be until they all get in the water. I can't help but think of how much Taylor and Lissy would love to be in my shoes right now. It almost makes me wish I could see things from their point of view, but not quite.

As roll call wraps up, only Miles Udell from last year's team is unaccounted for. Wesley speaks up to tell Coach about Miles being on a college visit, but that he does plan to be on the team. She makes a note before handing me the clipboard and pen.

"Everyone whose name I didn't call, line up in front of Wright, here. She will take down your name and number."

"And what if we don't want to give her our numbers?" Vander interjects.

I turn to glare at him, but I'm surprised to see that he's grinning at me. The blue stone necklace he's always wearing catches my attention yet again. I have a violent moment, fantasizing about grabbing onto it to bring him down to my level, so I can watch his reaction up close and personal when my knee meets his swimsuit at a fast rate of speed. But Coach speaks before I can form a sentence.

"You are already on my list, Thelxinoe, so that is not an issue you need to be worried about." She draws him closer by lowering her voice to just above a whisper, and if she wasn't standing next to me, I wouldn't have been able to hear her at all. "Not to mention, that was a jerky thing to say for a team captain. I expect you to set a better example for your teammates, and to show respect to your new manager."

She mock salutes him and motions for him to start leading the stretches. I mentally add a point for Coach on my tally sheet. If I were five years old, I may have stuck my tongue out at Vander; he just won't leave me alone. But as I'm now seventeen—for a few more weeks, at least—watching the transformation of his face when he realizes that I will be here at every practice and every meet is enjoyable enough. His jaw tightens, as do his abdominal muscles as he turns to walk away. Some girls may truly enjoy this view, but the sight makes me throw up in my mouth a little.

Once I've collected all the information from the five new team members and the team has finished their stretches, Coach starts to explain the warm-up she's written on the pool's whiteboard. She takes the clipboard from me and assigns a practice lane to everyone. I watch the new swimmers on the team looking uncomfortable in their swim trunks, trying to cover their bodies up with awkwardly crossed arms. They also can't seem to figure out how the lanes are numbered. I point to the lane closest to the locker room and hold up one finger, to let them know where to start counting.

Vander mimics me, pointing to the first lane like I had and then holding up one finger at me. However, the finger he is holding up is different than the one I used. I give him a wry smile and ask, "Your IQ or your age of maturity, Vander?"

Wesley laughs, and it earns him an elbow in his ribs. Vander never looks away from me, though. It's like he's trying to figure something out about me. I won't give him the satisfaction of winning this stare-down, so I refuse to blink.

"That's enough horsing around, gentlemen. Save your energy for the water, which you should be getting into now!" Coach blows her whistle, and it finally makes Vander look away with a shake of his head.

What is his deal?

There has got to be something majorly wrong with him. I spent most of yesterday trying to figure out how he could have hypnotized my friends and made them forget what they'd seen. No matter how many times we went over the events of Saturday night, Taylor and Lissy kept skipping what happened from the moment we entered the school all the way until I passed out, with no recollection of anything in between. I tried to explain what I had seen, and the girls just accused me of trying to get back at them for talking about Vander and Wesley so much earlier in the night.

"Wright!" I jump. The tone of Coach's voice makes me think she has said my name more than once.

"Yeah, Coach?" I walk over to her position near lanes seven and eight, where most of the senior swimmers are assigned.

"I'm going to need you to get the water bottles filled."

"Coming right up." I head out of the pool deck to get the basket of bottles from the training room. I walk through the women's locker room to get there, and cross the hall. When I gather the ice water and start back toward the pool, I see Vander standing in the hall, his arms at his sides. There is no hesitation in his posture, despite the fact that he's not wearing the knee-length suit like the freshmen, preferring last year's tiny team suit instead. He's smiling at me like I should be interested in that kind of thing, and sweeps his nose-length locks out of his face, splashing chlorinated water all over me and the floor.

"Why did Coach let you leave the water during practice?" I ask, rubbing the water off my arms. He shrugs.

"Were you drinking Saturday night?" His accusation is ridiculous, has no basis in reality, and hurts, to be honest.

"Shut up."

I was going to ignore him no matter what he said, but he was able to get under my skin with that question, and the two-word gem slipped out while I yanked open the locker room door with my one free hand.

Vander grabs my wrist, sending heat up my arm, and looks me in the eye as he asks, "You remember, don't you?"

"Let go of me, asshole." I yank my arm back, but Vander slides between me and my destination. "Get out of my way. If you're looking for someone to swoon all over you because you are choosing to give her some of your precious attention, I'm not that girl. Move on."

I don't know if he doesn't believe what I'm saying or if he is just stupid, but either way he doesn't move. I know he is used to getting what he wants and the way he is cornering me is pissing me all the way off. I hold the basket at waist level and thrust it toward him. Bingo! He backs up, stumbling into the women's locker room just as Coach comes in from the pool deck.

"Thelxinoe? You're in the wrong place, Captain." She does not seem amused, but I sure am. He's finally going to get in trouble for being the butt-nugget that he is.

"Coach, you didn't see me in the girl's locker room today," he creepily whispers at her. And with just that said, he walks back out into the hall. The uncharacteristically dreamy look on Coach's face tells me he somehow convinced her, like he hypnotized her or something. Her tilted head reminds me of how my friends looked on Saturday night. When the door closes, she snaps out of it.

"Let's go, Wright. There is a lot more to do."

I stand blinking at her, thinking that I must be living in the Twilight Zone. This shit can't be happening ... *again*.

"Okay, Coach," I say with a sigh, because I can't believe this is my life. I make a plan on my way out to the pool to ask Wesley what he remembers. We aren't friends, and he has no reason to tell me the truth, but there was something about the way my besties and Coach all looked when they tried to remember. I'm hoping I can see that in Wesley when I ask him.

"Hey, Wesley, here's some ice water." He looks to see Coach engaged with the freshman near lane one, then pulls himself out of the water to sit on the deck. "Do you remember seeing me Saturday night?"

"Oh yes, he does," Vander interjects from behind us. I turn around to see him twisting his stone necklace. "We were hanging like bats from Taylor's roof, eavesdropping on your little slumber party. Weren't we, Wesley?" Vander lets a laugh escape his lips as he pats Wesley on his shoulder. Then they both ease back into the water. When Wesley turns around, he has that faraway look in his eyes, and I see the tilted head telling me that he's trying to remember something that Vander made him forget somehow.

"I *knew* it!" I shout too enthusiastically, while pointing at Wesley's face. Wesley just shakes his head, as if trying to clear it, before taking off with his kickboard down the lane. Turning to Vander, I lower my voice so only he can hear me, "I know what you can do, but too bad it doesn't work on me."

He raises his brows at me and slides into the water. "I know. I'm going to have to figure out why."

I squat down to get on his level. "Why don't you just leave me alone?"

"Your friends seem to like me well enough."

"I am aware," I scoff, while rolling my eyes, "but believe me I'm not interested."

"You're just jealous."

Laughing out loud, I stand, shake my head, and begin to walk away. "Hardly."

Coach is making her way over to us. Vander glances at her before preparing to swim backstroke.

"We'll see," Vander says, then stares at me for a few seconds before he kicks off from the wall. He's flipping me alternating birds with every stroke he takes. I blow him a kiss in response, with a cute wave at the end.

What a self-righteous dingleberry! Two can play this game.

CHAPTER FOUR

Throughout the rest of practice I keep eyeing Coach, looking for any sign that she remembers what Vander did. If she does, she's good at hiding it. Her dark gaze is not any different from her regular practice-focused look and there is no shade being thrown at Vander. At first, I think she is nervous about trying to figure out how to handle the fact Vander was in the wrong locker room, but she doesn't take her brown hair out of its ponytail and put it back in at all, like she does during nerve-wracking swim meets. It's as if it never happened in her world.

At the end of practice, Coach instructs me to make sure all of the deck towels get into the laundry cart, and all of the kickboards get stored back in the closet. I have to do a full lap around the eight-lane pool to collect all of the randomly dropped towels, most of which are soaked with pool water. Tomorrow, I will bring the cart with me so I'll end up far less wet myself. The kickboards were all left on one side of the pool, so those were easy enough to pick up. *But would it kill Coach to remind these guys to put their own kickboards away?* Though, now that I think about it, I don't recall ever putting my own kickboard away either, in any of my four years on the team.

I check my phone, and see that I have several messages from Taylor and Lissy, but they all amount to the same thing: *OMG! You have scored big time, you get to watch all the guys in nothing but a swimsuit, every day after school. You're so lucky! Take stalker pictures, please!* and so on. I roll my eyes and make my way into the locker room. It should be empty now, unless Coach is hanging out.

Instead, I see Maddie is waiting there for me.

"Oh hey, Maddie. What's up?" I open my locker to get my book bag out and sling it across my shoulder.

"Turns out, you were right. Vander texted me a picture of my red bra in his hands during seventh period today with a message about how I'm going to lose if I don't make it more of a challenge. I was so embarrassed when Mr. Daniels walked by and caught me looking at it. He took my phone, and threatened to read my text to the class. I felt my heart skip a beat before he decided to just keep my phone until the end of school today. I mean, I thought this would be a fun game, but I never thought I would lose. I could just die!"

"Okay?" I reply as gently as possible, because I'm not sure what I can do to help that situation now.

"Well, it must have been a picture from the other night, because it's still here, but I need to move it to my other locker without them seeing me do it." She's whispering now. She seems paranoid about them eavesdropping, and I can't say I blame her.

I'm starting to catch on to what's happening here. I volunteered to help at lunch, and now I get to be in charge of a bra transport. *Is this real life?*

"Give it to me, and I'll put it in my bag." I unzip the outside pocket for her.

"Just remember it has to stay at school." She hands me the familiar bra and I stuff it in my bag, making sure to zip it back up securely.

"I understand that, but does it have to stay in one of your lockers?" I whisper back, as quietly as I can.

"Let me check the rules." She starts scrolling through the messages on her phone, while a plan begins to develop in my head.

"According to the rules, 'I must not ever take my undergarment out of the school.' So, no, it doesn't need to stay in my own locker, per se."

"Maddie? According to that wording, *I* can take it out of the school, because I am not *you*." I watch as she rereads the rule again, and a smile breaks out across her face.

"You are an absolute genius." She gives me a hug, and starts bouncing up and down at the same time.

"Wait, do you think they've figured that out, too? Because this seems too easy." I hesitate for a moment while I run different potential scenarios through my mind. "What if what they *want* is for someone to take it out, so that they don't have to sneak around the school to get it?"

Maddie's smile fades, realization dawning. "You know, for someone who doesn't like to talk about boys, you sure do seem to understand how they think. So what should we do?"

A shoe squeaks out in the hall, and I turn.

"Give me a minute," I whisper, and grab her arm quickly. I motion to my ear in a silent signal for her to listen, then tiptoe to the window on the door, totally reminiscent of Saturday night, and watch as Wesley's dreadlocked head creeps back toward the men's locker room. As he turns to open the door, his shoe squeaks again.

"They are playing dirty." Maddie seems surprised by this, and she doesn't even know about Vander's hypnotism trick.

"Well, we can play dirty, too." I lift my eyebrows twice in a playful gesture to show the mischief that we are about to get into on our own, and Maddie's smile slowly returns.

CHAPTER FIVE

"Tell me *everything*!" Lissy squeals at me. I make a show of checking my ears to see if my eardrums are bleeding.

I haven't made it out of my car, and she is already pumping me for information. *Give me a break.*

"Back away from the vehicle, and nobody gets hurt!" I honestly can't even open the door because of where she's standing—unless I want to drop her on her ass.

"Only if you promise to tell me all the deets about practice for two minutes at least." She's moved and is leaning against my door. Now that I want to knock her down, the window of opportunity has passed.

"No." Glaring at her doesn't usually work, but I give it a try anyway.

"*Two* minutes?" She's pleading, but I'm not signing on for two minutes of solid torture, no matter how much I love her.

"How about I answer two questions instead?" I have no idea what she wants to know—nothing I saw at practice stands out as important to me.

"Deal." She steps away while rubbing her hands together and I get out of the car. There is a sign of hope in her eyes; she must believe I'm changing. *Maybe this wasn't a good idea, after all.*

Before she can ask me the first question, my phone rings. I fish it out of my bag, my fingertips already chilled by the time they close over it and pull it free.

"Hello?"

"Julia? This is Wesley." *Why is he calling me?*

"Okay—how did you get this number?" I can hear the annoyance in my tone.

Lissy mouths, *Who is it?* to me, but I wave her away.

"From Vander. Anyway—"

I don't need to hear any more of this garbage. I cut him off immediately, as that doesn't even remotely begin to answer my question. "Don't sit there thinking it's okay for Vander to have my number, either. I never gave it to either one of you, and I'm not in the mood to be playing games. Now, how did you get this number?"

I can hear Wesley talking to someone before he responds. Lissy starts to mouth something at me again, but I look away.

"Vander asked Coach for it, and since you are the team's manager, she gave it to him. Anyway—"

Regretting the fact I accepted the manager job, I cut him off again swiftly. "Put Captain Mindgames on the phone right now. I know he's standing there next to you, so just get him on the line." I think I hear Wesley start to say something else, but then there is some commotion, and I hear Vander on the other end. Meanwhile, Lissy is having a minor heart attack, only hearing my side of the conversation. I roll my eyes at her antics—twice for good measure.

"Hello, gorgeous. It's been half an hour since our last special moment together. Do you miss me?"

What a major tool without a single clue! He's so frustrating!

"Shut your lip-hole, you clownlicker. Cut to the chase here, and tell me what you want."

"I want the bra that you have in your bag." I can't help the victorious smile on my face. He fell for it.

"It's really too bad that you can't hypnotize me and make me forget that I gave it to you, huh? I guess you'll just have to play fair like everyone else."

"Hypnotize you? Do you realize how insane you sound right now?"

He actually laughs at me. This boy must have a whole bucket full of nerve.

"I don't know how things usually work out for you, but let me fill you in on how you make me feel." My anger refuses to let my jaw unclench as I spit the words out at him. I try to avoid him and yet he keeps popping up in my life.

"Let me guess, I make you weak in the knees?"

He's teasing me, but I don't miss the subtle hint to the fact he not only made my knees give out, but he made me fall down the other night. I growl in frustration, and then take a deep breath.

"You are an overrated jock with a superiority complex and a sense of entitlement that should lead you straight to jail before too long. If you never call me again, it will be far too soon. To be perfectly honest, I think you're a freaking pervert for even suggesting a contest to see who can run someone else's underwear up a pole first. But since I seem to be the kryptonite to your crazy voodoo powers, I can guarantee that you won't win." I look over at Lissy, and her eyes are as wide as DVDs, with her mouth agape to match.

It's quiet for a second and I start to smirk in victory when he replies, "We'll just have to see about that. In fact, I will see you soon."

The call disconnects, and while I'm still fuming mad, Lissy asks, "Did you really just say all of that to Vander Thelxinoe?"

"Yes I did, and if given the opportunity again, there are a few things I might add." None of them are appropriate, to say the least. I yank my bag from the car and head for my front door.

Lissy hurries behind me. "That was harsh. I know you have something against the fine people of the penis, but are you actually insane?"

"I didn't think so before Saturday night. I still don't know what happened for sure."

"OMG, Taylor is going to lose her shit when I tell her about this."

"Have fun with that. I have to go in—are you staying for dinner? Mom's coworker and kid are joining us tonight." I open the front door, and the smell of Monday's meatloaf greets me. Momma is nothing if not a creature of habit.

"I can't, but I still need to ask my two questions about practice." Her eyes shine with anticipation and it almost keeps me from bursting her bubble, but not quite.

"By my count, you've already asked two questions." I stick my tongue out at her playfully while I watch her go over our conversation again in her head.

"That's evil, Jules. Pure evil." She backs away while giving me the sign of a cross with her two index fingers. After a few steps, she turns around and tells me to text her later, sending me an air kiss. *That's the Lissy I know and love.*

"I love you too, Lissy!"

CHAPTER SIX

"Hey, Momma. I'm home!" I shout as soon as I cross the threshold and throw my bag to the floor. I drop my keys into the bowl on the hall table, glancing in the mirror hanging above it, and kick my shoes off into the basket underneath.

"Hi, sweetheart, we're in here." I slow my roll to try to sneak a peek into the kitchen, so I know who the "we" refers to. I turn the corner, and come face to face with someone whose dark hair and blue-green eyes look familiar, but I can't quite place how. I watch the man sitting next to my mother as she is typing on her laptop. I continue to watch them for a minute, and see her turn her laptop to him so he can read it.

"Are you designing a city brochure or something?" She works for the marketing department for Cedar Rapids, the City of Five Seasons. My dad used to say our great city would probably go back to having only four seasons like everyone else in Iowa, if it weren't for my mother's brilliance at marketing. Momma would shake her head and explain that the fifth season was simply time to enjoy life, but he would always disagree and say it meant something a little different to him.

Momma looks up at me, extinguishing my memory. "Yeah, I'm collaborating with the Department of Fish and Wildlife." She nods to the man next to her and the motion causes him to look up, too. He stands to greet me, so I stick out my hand.

"Hi, I'm Julia." I smile at him.

He also smiles and shakes my hand, but doesn't respond. Instead, he turns to Momma. *Um, what?* That's weird and borderline rude, but I'm giving him the benefit of the doubt, since Momma obviously thinks highly enough of him to invite him into our home for a meal.

"Julia, this is Gunnar Thelxinoe."

Wait, did she just say Thelxinoe? Time is suddenly standing still and racing forward, all at once.

"You may know his son, Vander. He goes to your school."

Dear sweet cheeses and all the rice in Asia, please let this be a nightmare. I pinch myself and yelp. Suddenly, Gunnar's unusual behavior makes sense, since everyone at school knows that Vander's dad is completely deaf.

"No way!" I shout to no one in particular. My mother has invited my enemy to dinner! *She actually expects me to eat a meal with the monster?*

"Julia!" Momma admonishes me. "Don't be rude."

I feel like I've been blindsided. *Oh crap—is it horrible to think the word "blind" in front of a deaf person?* OMG, that is *so* not the issue here. *Focus, Julia Wright. Just focus.*

"You're Vander's dad?"

He nods in response, then leans over and casually types on the laptop, like my worst nightmare isn't coming true. While he's typing, the doorbell rings. I turn to the door as panic takes hold. I look back at my mom, begging for it not to be real. Gunnar shows me the laptop, which reads, ***He should be joining us any minute.***

I'm sure my reaction is not what they were both hoping for. My hands are clenched into fists so hard that I wish I had been holding coal, because it surely would have turned into diamonds by now. There are flames shooting out of my ears, and I wouldn't be surprised to feel daggers flying out of my eyes at any given moment.

Totally channeling Lissy and Taylor, I say, "I can't do this."

I turn to walk out of the kitchen, but Mom stops me. She's turned so that her back is to Gunnar, but she still talks without moving her lips. In fact, I can hear her teeth grinding over her whispered commands.

"You most certainly can and *will* do this, Julia. You aren't going anywhere. If you don't have anything kind to say, then you will not say anything at all, but you will not. Be. Rude. Have I made myself clear?" Her nostrils are flaring—she means business. No amount of explaining how much I hate him or how much of an ass he is will change her mind. The Wright household has expectations of behavior where guests are concerned and I will abide by them.

I don't trust my voice, so I simply nod. She puts a smile on her face before she turns around to face her coworker. If she wants me to be pleasant, I can do that. She never said anything about being sincere, though...

The doorbell rings again, and I go to answer it. I take a deep breath, and before I open the door, an idea comes to mind. I unbutton the top two buttons on my blouse, and bend over to readjust and accentuate my, err—*assets*. Then I take a few seconds to get my 'do together in the mirror. I'm going to be nice, per my mom's request—really, really, *really* nice.

I open the door with grand flair and greet Satan—I mean, Vander. I hit him with as much sweetness as I can muster while fluttering my lashes as often as possible. "Hello, handsome. I beg you to forgive my delay in responding to your beckoning. Please don't be mad for keeps."

I finish with a full-on curtsy, bowing my head and everything. When I finish, he is still standing at the door, staring at me. Or, to be more precise, my cleavage. I shimmy a little bit and tilt my head, giving him the fakest smile I have ever plastered on my face.

Vander puts his hands up and drags them down his face. He groans a little bit, as if he's as frustrated as he usually makes me feel. Suddenly, his eyes focus on something behind me. I look and find that our parents have come to see what's keeping us.

I hold out my hand to encourage Vander to enter our home, and he finally steps through the door. It occurs to me, on my list of all the things that could be wrong with Vander, that at least I can cross vampirism off. I never actually invited him in. He's no Edward Cullen, which is good, because now I don't have to wait for him to start sparkling like a freak in the sun.

He sticks his hand out to my mom and introduces himself. So far, he's making a better impression on her than I did on his dad. But there is no time like the present to start to remedy that.

"Could I please help you set the table, Mother?"

Mom does a double-take from Vander to my chest and back again. I'd like to think that she's caught him staring again, showing her the kind of guy he actually is, but I'm careful not to let the smile slip from my face when I see he's not. He is signing something to his dad without mouthing the words, so we have no clue what's being communicated between them.

"Uh, sure, darling." The use of that word reminds me that I'm not the only one putting on a show here tonight.

We step into the kitchen, and I pull the plates out of the cabinet, setting them on the breakfast bar next to the laptop. I also pick out four matching glasses, and then open the silverware drawer as well. Momma walks over to her laptop and vigorously taps out a message. I pretend that I don't know she's typing something for me. I reach for the placemats and cloth napkins on the top shelf in the pantry, and when I turn around, Momma is holding her computer up to my face.

Button your shirt up! A red bra doesn't work like a red stoplight does... It has just the opposite effect, really. LOL I'm all for you dating if you find the right guy, but this is NOT how Wright women do things. :-)

I proceed to waggle my eyebrows at her and it makes her laugh. I refasten one of my buttons, convinced that if my mom noticed which bra I was wearing, then there is no doubt Vander did, too.

Good luck capturing this flag, bucko!

CHAPTER SEVEN

As I place the last piece of silverware on the table, the Thelxinoes enter the kitchen. Mom has been bustling about, putting the finishing touches on the mashed potatoes and making sure the meatloaf is thoroughly cooked.

"It smells delicious, Ms. Wright." Vander signs as he speaks, to keep his dad in the conversation, I suppose. "Is there anything I can do to help?"

"How about taking drink orders? We have ice water, orange juice, or milk." It's just like my mom not to mention any sugary drinks, knowing Vander is in swim season.

"I can do that." He turns to his dad first, and after signing back and forth, Vander turns to me. "What would you like to drink, Julia?"

His eyes stay level with mine, and I'm sure it's because I've buttoned my shirt back up. I give him a dazzling smile. "Milk always tastes so good with Momma's meatloaf. I'd like that please."

"Sure thing." He smiles back with the most genuine smile I've ever seen on his face. *Oh brother, he's actually buying this charade?*

Or is he just playing along?

"What will you have, Ms. Wright?" He passes my mom on his way to the refrigerator, while she is heading out to the table with the meatloaf.

"I'd love milk with my dinner, Vander. Thank you." She turns to me and asks, "Could you please get the mashed potatoes from the counter and bring them to the table?"

"I'd be happy to," I reply over my shoulder as I head around the breakfast bar. I should have been watching where I was going. Vander could have been watching where he was going, too. But a handful of *shoulda* and a bag full of *coulda* weren't available at the moment. Had they been on hand, they might have been able to prevent the full-frontal body collision that occurred moments later between us.

I find myself pressed firmly against Vander Thelxinoe in my kitchen. We are so close that I can literally feel those abs Lissy loves looking at so much. Vander has a gallon of milk in one hand, and the other is wrapped around my back to keep me from falling to the floor. My own hands are grasping his T-shirt in fists at his chest. I take a calming breath in through my nose, and am surprised when I don't smell chlorine on his skin. Instead, I detect a rainy spring-day scent, which gives me a brief feeling of peace, like on Easter morning.

"Are you okay?" Vander pulls away enough to look me in the eyes.

Please don't let me call him Bunny, or say something else equally as dumb.

"Yeah, I'm fine. Um, sorry for running into you." I bite my lip so nothing else slips out. Then I let go of his shirt and smooth out the wrinkles I squeezed into it. *Wow! Those are* some *pectoral muscles I'm rubbing on.*

Gah! What's wrong with me? Back away, Jules. Back away from the boy.

I take my own advice and find I've backed into the breakfast bar, hard. The jarring sensation in my lower back causes me to bend forward—right into Vander, again. My nose is in his armpit, and before I can tell myself not to, I breathe in, and the scent of fresh rain assaults my senses again. Images of how Easter used to be when Dad was alive fill my mind, unbidden. My eyes flood with tears, which I refuse to let fall. I stand upright and twist away from him. The last thing I want from him is pity. This situation is so awkward, it's beyond ridiculous at this point.

"Um, sorry again. Maybe you should go first this time?"

He puts a finger under my chin and gently draws my face back up to his. "Are you sure you're okay?"

"Yeah, I am. I think the fumes from your cologne just got into my eyes." I use my palms to dry the moisture.

"I'm not wearing any cologne." I'm expecting him to follow that up with a cocky wink or another smart remark. Instead, all he does is softly squeeze my shoulder with his free hand before he heads to the table with our milk. I take a minute by myself in the kitchen to collect my thoughts, but I still can't figure out what game he's playing here.

With mashed potatoes in my shaking hands, I return to the dining room to find my mom sitting next to Gunnar on one side of the table, the laptop between them. They are both engrossed in whatever is on the screen. The only empty seat is on the other side, next to where Vander is standing behind a chair. I try not to look annoyed as I take the seat, but I'm not sure if I'm successful. Vander seats himself after I do, and for a second, I contemplate the possibility of him being an actual gentleman. However, I suddenly feel self-conscious and intimidated, so I go ahead and button my shirt up all the way when his head is turned.

When I look up, Mom is typing something to Gunnar, who is reading as her fingers tap across the keys. I look to Vander next. He's biting his fingernail, obviously lost in thought from the blank expression on his face.

"Would you like some mashed potatoes?" I offer, trying to break the silence. He's a bit startled, but after a few blinks, he jumps to action.

We dish out our food and then return to an uncomfortable silence, except for the taps of fingers on keys across the table. I have no appetite, but I take a bite anyway. Then I try a sip of my milk. My stomach is not excited about this—

too many butterflies flying around in there or something.

Vander puts his hand on my arm. I look up and see sympathy on his face, as if he understands my current struggle. We look at each other for a few moments, and finally he says, "Sorry."

Wait, what? Sorry for what? Then he stands abruptly. He lowers his head at my mom and says in that creepy voice, "Please forgive my rudeness."

I know what that voice means—he's hypnotizing her. I wonder if it will work on her, or if it will fail, like it does on me. Before I know it, he's out of the house and across the lawn, getting into his own car by the time I make it to the door. *What actually happened here?*

A small part of me is wondering why I even care. I'm not hungry, so I don't return to the table, and Mom never comes to ask me to. I turn my phone off and decide to go to bed early. Mondays always suck, but this one has taken the cake.

When Tuesday morning rolls around, I don't think I can handle the twenty million questions game from Lissy and Taylor, so I don't tell them about dinner last night.

When Lissy asks, "Was the coworker's kid a major brat, or what?"

I smile, nod, and simply offer, "You could say that."

Luckily, Lissy drops that subject and quickly starts another one. "Have you guys seen Wesley's latest post on Instagram? He looks so adorable, snuggled up with his dog. Maybe he would volunteer to walk the dogs at the animal shelter with me on Sundays."

"You should totes ask. Is Andrew in that picture?" Taylor asks as she opens the Instagram app on her own phone. She has had the biggest crush on Wesley's big brother, Andrew, since middle school when he picked up her lunchbox for her when she dropped it on her way to school.

Lissy shakes her head.

"Sad day," Taylor replies.

And so my day resumes. I don't pay much attention to Mr. Daniels when I get to my European Literature class third period. But that's nothing new for me. All of the other girls feel compelled to rush to his class before the bell rings and stare at him until they have no choice but to run to their next class. But his appearance and slight Southern accent don't appeal to me. I really like the material he teaches, so I usually pay attention for that reason. Today, however, the fact that Vander is in this class has my full attention.

He hasn't looked at me or otherwise acknowledged my existence, and combined with him bolting when he was supposed to eat a meal sitting beside me—well, it hurts a little bit and I don't understand that feeling at all. *I mean, I was trying to be nice, and everything!* I ache to tell him what I really think of him at this point—he's a stage four asshole.

I'm staring at the back of his head during the lecture, daydreaming about seeing my foot arrive there at a high rate of speed. My grin is removed from my face with the buzzing sensation of my phone vibrating two quick pulses in my pocket.

Unknown contact: I'm glad you are enjoying the view today.

I don't recognize the number, but I already know who *that* message is from. He turns and the cocky grin on his face gives it away. Just like that, jerky Vander returns. I guess he just couldn't handle acting like a human being for one minute longer last night. I look around the front of the classroom near where Vander is sitting and find just the person I need.

Me: Thanks, I AM! I can't help but look, her hair is so beautiful in braids like that.

I watch as he receives the text, and then looks around. I know immediately when he finds Kenzie-Grace and her braids. They dated for all of last year. I remember because Taylor and Lissy always went on and on about how they wished they were Kenzie-Grace. I wasn't there when it happened, but the two of them had a very public breakup in the cafeteria right before prom. It was the news of the day/week/month, and my friends were sad for Kenzie-Grace, only for as long as it took for them to get back in line to be his next victim—I mean, *girlfriend.*

It dawns on me that maybe she was able to resist his creepy voice the same way I can. Otherwise, why would they break up? He could just convince her he was the perfect boyfriend. *Huh, makes me wonder...*

My phone buzzes again before I can finish my thought, and I make sure to save his number so I can ignore him in the future.

Vander: Why ya gotta be so rude?

I try to keep that song out of my head and return my attention to Mr. Daniels. He's holding up a copy of Homer's *The Odyssey,* which is scary, because I tried reading it once and my brain shut down. I ended up mumbling and walking in circles for an hour, trying to figure out what I had just read. That may be a slight exaggeration, but still. I tune in to Mr. Daniels explaining the Greek mythology behind the book, and even take a few notes.

At the end of class, I finally come up with a response to Vander's text—the next line to the song.

> **Me: Dontcha know I'm human... Not "too" because I'm not sure what you are. I've ruled out vampire though, you'll be happy to know.**

Suddenly, Vander's shoulders start to shake with laughter, and it draws the attention of Mr. Daniels, who calls on him to answer a question.

"Vander, what do you think the most beautiful creatures in Greek mythology are?"

I hope he falls flat on his face. I can almost see it now, Vander stumbling over his words and ending up only making grunting noises like the pig he is. I'd love to see him try to hypnotize a whole class to forget about that. His response is nothing like what I am hoping for.

"The Sirens, hands down. They are so beautiful, men would die just for a chance to get close to them."

Mr. Daniels nods his approval, and I bite my tongue. *Crap*. I can't believe he was actually paying attention enough to give an intelligent answer.

"Sure, let's talk about the Sirens. Who can tell me what a Siren is?"

Every female, other than myself of course, raises their hand for the opportunity to hear Mr. Daniels say their name. "Emily?"

Groans of disappointed teen girls fill the room before she even starts to speak.

"Um," she giggles. "Aren't they like the witches or something that sing to sailors to lure them to their island so they can kill them?"

Vander scoffs. "Not really," he mutters, loud enough for all of us to hear.

"What do you have to add to the discussion, Vander?" Mr. Daniels pretends to not like it when we blurt out comments, but he can't deny himself the pleasure of watching us have a lively discussion about his curriculum.

"The Sirens are beautiful women, cursed to live on an island for eternity by Demeter, goddess of the harvest, because they couldn't find her daughter when she went missing. Their mournful song calls to all who hear it and lures them to the island, which is located among many rocks and cliffs jutting out of the Mediterranean Sea. It's not their fault that inexperienced sailors crash their vessels on the way to get closer to the charming music."

"That's an interesting take on things, Vander." Mr. Daniels strokes his chin before continuing. "I've always understood them to be hideous creatures with the ability to use their *charming* music, as you say, to make people believe that they are beautiful."

Vander laughs out loud.

Mr. Daniels promptly ignores him. "Any ideas on how this particular myth came to be?" He pauses to gauge the hands waving in the air. "Siobahn?"

She doesn't waste time giggling. "I thought it was because some sailors were lost at sea and ran out of drinking water, and started drinking the salty sea water. It made them sick, and they would have crazy hallucinations. Combined with the reports of multiple shipwrecks in the area, this story was created to explain both issues."

"That's a good thought." Mr. Daniels ponders it for a moment. Vander has stopped paying attention altogether.

Vander: You think there is something wrong with me? Here I was thinking there is something wrong with you.
Me: Why? Because I don't like you and don't do what you say?
Vander: Ouch.

The bell rings, and I am on the way out the door when a thought occurs to me. I turn around and look for Kenzie-Grace. She's stuck behind Vander, but I decide it's worth it to wait for him to pass. I keep my eyes on her, making my intentions clear. Vander passes while looking down at his phone. I catch Kenzie-Grace by the elbow, and follow her along until we are in the busy hallway.

"Hey, Julia, what's up?"

Kenzie-Grace used to be blonde and dressed in a very preppy way. Her hair is now dyed black, and always twisted into braids. I won't say she wears the same color every day—black, naturally—though she used to. Literally. From head to toe. She even had black lipstick for when she dressed up. I'm not sure exactly when it started—sometime after the big breakup, over summer vacation, or the first day of school. I can't honestly say that I ever got used to it, though. Lately, she has been branching out, wearing reds and purples with some gray, while her hair still remains black.

"Hey, girl, I'm hoping you can tell me something."

"What's that?"

"When you were dating Vander, did you notice his ability to hypnotize people?"

"Hypnotize?" She laughs, but not in a way to convince me she thinks it's funny. It's a dry laugh, like she can't believe what she's hearing. "Yeah, something like that." She stops laughing then, looks around, and grabs my arm to pull me close so she can whisper in my ear. "*Never* drink around him. *Like. Not. Ever!*"

Kenzie-Grace is several rooms down the hall by the time I realize I've stopped in my tracks. *Why do people keep talking about drinking?* I have never touched alcohol, and I never will, I swear on my dad's grave. The tears are in my eyes before I realize how upset I am. Surprise grief attacks are the worst and this is an added insult to my ego, because it's been almost six months since my last one. I really thought I was over them.

I step into the ladies' room to clear my head. After a few minutes, I turn at the sound of the bathroom door opening. It's Lissy, with her arms open.

Wordlessly, I fall into them, and the tears fall down my face.

"Shhh. I know." She actually does know what happened when we lost my dad; she's one of the few who do. I let her hold me until the sobs subside. We're missing class by now, but I don't even care.

"I'm so glad you found me." I grab a paper towel and wet it to try and get rid of the streaks of mascara currently running down my face.

"Me too," she says while rubbing my back with the palm of her hand. "I'm so glad Vander sent me in here."

"Wait, *what*?"

"Yeah, he stopped me outside of our algebra class and told me that you needed me in here." I look at her like she has mushrooms growing out of her nose. "You didn't ask him to?"

I'm too dumbfounded to do anything but shake my head. That wasn't a very jerky jock thing to do at all. That was actually a really nice thing he did.

But now I can't stop wondering why.

CHAPTER EIGHT

Coach's whistle blows behind me, and it makes my head feel like it's splitting in two. It's been bothering me since my crying session during fourth period.

"Wright!"

"Yeah, Coach?" I reply, without even removing my hands from holding the sides of my head together.

"Can you please refill these water bottles? I'm going to be working the seniors extra hard today."

I take the basket of six water bottles and start on my way through the locker room to the training room. I open all of the water bottles and set their lids aside, then grab the scoop, putting ice in each bottle. An eerie sense of deja vu starts to creep into the back of my mind that I can't shake. I run the cold water so I can fill the bottles. When I turn the water off, the pipes squeal from the added pressure, and my head's painful reaction nearly brings me to my knees.

"I can help."

I'm not surprised; I knew he would be there, just like last time I was sent to fill these bottles. "No, I've got this, Vander. It doesn't take rocket science to put lids on bottles."

"I meant that I could help your headache go away."

I watch a drop of pool water roll from his hairline all the way down his face. When it hits the floor, I swear I can hear it plop.

"How did you even know I had one?"

I finish with the bottles and start toward the door. I try to brush past him, but he stops me by putting his wet hands on either side of my face. It seems like he's about to kiss me, like people do in the movies, and that thought makes my stomach lurch. *I think I would actually puke if he kissed me—or at least gag, maybe just want to spit—no, I would vomit. I'm sure. Really.*

I try to shove him off, but he starts to hum, and I feel a tingle of warmth through his fingers. Next thing I know, his hands are gone from my face. I feel them squeezing my hand between my thumb and index finger. When he stops humming and the pressure is gone, I realize the headache is retreating, too.

"How did you do that?"

"I guess you would say I *hypnotized* you."

He shrugs, turns, and walks out like he didn't just do something impossible, not to mention something he didn't have to do. I watch him walk out the door in disbelief. Now that's two nice things he's done for me in one day. Who is this guy? I'm going to have to get to the bottom of this change in his behavior, and how he can do what he can do, soon. I'm so confused.

After practice, I try to get up the nerve to talk to Vander, but it doesn't work. Instead, I decide to text him before I drive home.

Me: Thanks for your help.

The whole drive home, I keep wondering what is going on. Today is Tuesday. Saturday night, I hated Vander, and was pretty confident he hated me. Last night, he ran out of my house in the middle of dinner—actually, it was before dinner, if I want to get technical about it—without any explanation, and only after hypnotizing my mom to forgive his rudeness. Today, I'm texting him in class, and then thanking him for helping to relieve a headache he was probably the cause of anyway. This makes no sense. Maybe he figured out a way to hypnotize me, after all.

As soon as I pull up in front of my house, I will call the girls. I have to get them to understand what is going on so they can help me figure out what I'm doing. *Whew!* Just having a plan makes me feel better.

I breathe a sigh of relief ... a block too soon. When I pull onto my street, I see Vander is waiting there, outside of his car, in front of my house. *Strange.* Mom didn't say anything about a rain check on dinner tonight.

I grip my steering wheel tightly and for a moment consider turning around, though I don't. I pull into the driveway, since his car is in my usual spot, and pretend I don't see him as I get out of my car and head for the door. I can't believe he has the nerve to show up here. *What did I do to deserve having to put up with this nonsense, especially when I'm so conflicted?* I must have double dipped a chip at a party in a past life or something.

"Julia, we need to talk. I have some questions, and I'm sure you do, too." He isn't running, but his stride is so long, he reaches me before I can get to the door. I turn to face him, annoyance dripping from my features. He's serious, and something else is brewing behind those stormy blue-green eyes.

"No shit, Sherlock. Except that I'm the only one afraid of having her mind tampered with when we do." I put my hand on the door and turn to go in, but his response stops me.

"Please." His brows are furrowed, eyes begging; he means it. Holy shit, he *is* nervous.

It's so simple. He didn't use his creepy hissing voice, but he said it pleadingly.

Which is so far from his usual way of getting things done that it causes me to want to hear him out.

Or is he just using his tricks on me now?

"It's too confusing, Vander." I shake my head, but can't bring myself to look at him.

He grabs my hand, and I yank it away.

"Don't be afraid of me." He goes for my arm this time to turn me around. I jerk away again.

"Stop being scary then."

He immediately puts his hands up and takes a step back. "Please," he repeats.

I just can't handle this right now. *How am I supposed to know that he's not messing with my head?* I've seen him do it, several times now.

"Want to talk on the phone? Fine. Want to text? I'm okay with that, too. But please, talk to me." He seems desperate now. That makes me panic a bit more, but at this moment, I just want him off my porch.

"Text me."

He grabs his phone out of his pocket and turns to go.

I take a breath and open my door. My phone is buzzing before I even set my bag down. I drop my keys in the bowl and kick my shoes into the basket. When I walk over to the couch, I can see through the bay window that Vander is still sitting in his car in front of my house. Before I start in on this, I need to check in with the girls, so I open our group text window.

Me: I need to talk. Can you guys come over?

Before a response even comes through, I know what it will be. No matter how much silly girl-talking they do (which I'm used to), or the annoying games of twenty questions they try to play (which help me understand things better), or even the insane fangirl behaviors (which make me feel like the normal one for a change) they exhibit from time to time—ahem, all the time—I know they are always there for me when I need them. Truth be told, I wouldn't change them for the world.

Taylor: We'll be right there.

I know Taylor is speaking for both of them. They are the socialites in our trio, and are always together. I'm the only one who needs some time to myself every day. Knowing that my backup is on the way, I decide to go get something to eat. Leftover meatloaf and mashed potatoes sound delicious, especially since I didn't have the stomach to enjoy any last night ... thanks to the guy now sitting outside of my house, waiting for a text back from me. I can feel my anger and confusion returning.

Pouring a glass of milk, I wait for the microwave to beep. Just as I'm about to take a too-hot taste, the doorbell rings. My girls would *never* ring the bell.

Another sense of deja vu strikes, and I remember adjusting myself yesterday so Maddie's bra could be visible before answering the door. A smile sneaks onto my face as I pull the door open.

But it isn't my girls. And it's not Vander, either. In fact, his car is gone. It's Kenzie-Grace, and she's crying. I open the door without speaking, swallowing the lump in my throat and reminding myself this isn't about me. I don't know what to do so I just hold out my arms. She walks right into them, like I did with Lissy earlier today. I don't know what demons she's fighting, but I don't need to. It's girl code, and it's simple—we comfort one another, regardless of the circumstances.

Doing my best imitation of Lissy when she is comforting me, I hold Kenzie-Grace, brush the black hair out of her face, and rub her back soothingly. It takes quite a few deep breaths and false starts, but she is finally able to talk.

"Today, at school, when you asked me about Vander—well, I do know something. But everyone I have ever talked to about this seems to think I'm crazy, and then they forget that I ever mentioned it."

"That must be incredibly frustrating. But I promise you, I don't think you are crazy, and I was starting to think that *I* was, for the same reasons you just said. My friends don't believe me, and they don't remember it, either."

I guide her over to our couch and sit down beside her. When I look in her eyes, I see such a flood of relief. It's been six months since their relationship ended. I can't imagine going that long without being able to talk to someone about what I saw just a couple days ago.

"Well, it happened right before we broke—"

She's interrupted by the door crashing open, my two giggling friends bursting through.

"We're here!" they shout before they see the pair of us on the couch.

"No kidding. If it weren't for you telling me, I never would have known." I'm laying the sarcasm on pretty thick now.

"Yeah, sorry about that," Taylor adds as she straightens up, "We'll just go get a drink so you can carry on with whatever it is you were doing." They are halfway to the door when Kenzie-Grace stops them.

"No, it's okay. I want to tell you all what happened." Then, under her breath she adds to me, "It's not like they will remember, anyway." She sniffles and takes yet another deep breath in while the girls settle into the loveseat across from us.

"When I met Vander, he was so sweet and nice. As we started dating, he made me feel like a queen. It was the kind of relationship you always hope to have. He didn't pressure me physically, he listened when I had problems, and he always made me laugh when I needed it the most."

"We know. Your relationship was everyone's dream. So, what went wrong?" Taylor leans forward, so she doesn't miss a single syllable.

"Well, I convinced my older cousin to get me a bottle of champagne so I could give it to Vander for his birthday in April. I told him we could celebrate in style." She pauses to breathe, but none of us move or say anything. "I had two glasses before this woman appeared in his room. When I say appeared, I mean she just *appeared* out of nowhere. She didn't walk in through the door or fly in through the window. She wasn't there one second, and the next second, she was. She looked no older than my mom. She had long, blonde hair and she was wearing some kind of tiara, like she had recently won a beauty pageant. I was freaking out, but Vander looked like he had been expecting her.

"He called her his grandmother when he introduced us. She completely ignored me and spoke only to him. She warned him that things were going to be changing in the next year, and by the time he turned eighteen, he would be expected to return home and quit this foolishness. Then she told him to charm me and get rid of me before she took care of me herself."

"What does that even mean?" Lissy asked what all of us were wondering.

Kenzie-Grace simply held her hands up, as if to show she wasn't done yet.

"All I know is that after she left, he turned to me and lowered his head, so that he was looking at me out of the top of his eyes. He whispered like a snake, telling me to forget what that woman, *Demeter*, said. I didn't know if he was threatening me, or what. I took another drink of champagne instead of responding. I knew it was not the time to ask questions, so I didn't then, and I haven't since. He broke up with me the next day, saying he couldn't be with someone like me, someone who liked to drink. It was the first time I'd ever tried drinking, and it was champagne, for crying out loud, but it made me think he thought I was a drunk or something. He completely ignored me at school, as if he couldn't even see me, and he still does that to this day. We haven't spoken to each other since."

She's got tears running down her face, but she isn't sobbing like she was earlier. Her words make me realize the impact of my teasing him with her beauty earlier today, and my stomach twists in a knot.

"When you asked me today if I'd seen him hypnotize people, it brought back that awful night. I think when he was whispering, he was trying to charm me or whatever. Only, it didn't work for some reason, and he doesn't know it. For a while last year, I would follow him around. I was convinced that he had found someone new. I watched him charm his friend Wesley into skipping school with him one day. I asked Wesley the next day why he skipped school, and he said that he felt like going to the beach, and he persuaded Vander to go with him. Vander didn't just get him to go along—he got him to believe that it was his idea in the first place."

The girls on the loveseat are both speechless. I can't imagine what they are thinking as they listen to another person back up my claims about their precious Vander.

"Well, the hypnotizing or charming thing doesn't work on me, and he knows it. And these two *were* charmed or whatever, and have no clue what actually happened."

"Not this again." Lissy rolls her eyes. Taylor sighs.

"Yeah, they believe only what he creepily whispered them to, just like Wesley. He's done it to Coach, and to my mom—in front of me, too. And that probably explains why he's desperate to talk to me now."

"I don't know what Vander would think if I told him I remember. Or worse ... what that woman would do if she knew I didn't forget her."

"I understand that."

"Hold up! I'm pressing the bullshit button here." Lissy doesn't understand because she doesn't remember.

Lissy and Taylor jump feet-first into a series of questions and comments that neither Kenzie-Grace nor I could keep up with if we wanted to.

"Now he doesn't just hypnotize people, but he has a grandma who looks like a beauty queen?"

"Yeah, who can just materialize like a ghost and threaten people?"

"How long have you guys been planning this prank on us?"

I ignore them because I start to think of the other things I want to know. I grab Kenzie-Grace's arm and ask, "Did Vander ever sing to you?"

She pinches her brows together and looks away, as if trying to recall.

"He never sang along with the radio, or serenaded me, or anything like that. But the night before the ACT exam, I was so anxious that I couldn't sleep. I called him and asked him to tell me a story. He said he had a better idea. He made sure I was lying in bed and that my alarm was set. Then he started to sing *Beautiful Dreamer*, and that's the last thing I remember before my alarm went off in the morning."

"I *knew* it!" I'm on my feet to get my phone from the kitchen before I can even blink. The girls continue to bombard Kenzie-Grace with questions, most of which they don't give her time to answer. Others have nothing to do with what we are talking about. My patience is wearing thin.

My phone has six text messages on it already, and one missed call from Vander. *Seriously, boy?*

Vander: I think maybe you would be more willing to help me if you got to ask your questions and I answered them first.
Vander: My dad messaged me. I have to go home for dinner.
Vander: I'm ready whenever you're ready.
Vander: Or I could go first?
Vander: Which do you prefer?
Vander: I'm coming back to your house. We need to talk.

I look at the clock, and note that it has been exactly forty-two minutes since he left my house. That's one text message for every seven minutes. This is all too much as my friends' voices rise as they continue to pepper Kenzie-Grace with questions. I can't think straight and Vander is on his way back to my house. I'm officially irritated.

Me: No!
Vander: No, what? I thought you agreed to talk to me.
Me: No, don't come to my house.

"Hold on!" I wave my arms at my friends squeaking out question after question, most of which aren't making any sense anymore. They stop.

Taylor apologizes, "I'm sorry we have so many questions, this just doesn't make any sense."

Kenzie-Grace nods at them while digging through her bag. "I know how outrageous it seems. Until today, I wasn't sure anyone would ever believe me. It is so unreal. And now that I have it off my chest, I need to ask a favor. I'm ready to make some changes and put this part of my life behind me."

"Okay?" Taylor asks, intrigued.

"Will you help me with my hair?" She holds up a couple boxes of hair dye. "I'm ready for something new."

"Yes!" Lissy loves playing hairdresser, as evidenced by her blue-and-green-dyed locks. "Jules, can we do it here in your bathroom?"

"Of course. Use the towels under the sink though, not the good ones, okay?"

Determination is brewing deep in my soul to figure out who or what Vander is and why I can't be charmed by him. Maybe something really is wrong with me and now is the time to figure it out. Vander may hold the answers, so I can't ignore him any longer. Taking a deep breath, I mentally prepare myself for what I might learn about us both.

Vander: Are you ready to get started?

I watch the girls take off down the hall, take a seat on the couch, and start to tap away on my phone.

Me: You need to agree not to lie to me and to answer completely or this won't work.
Vander: I will answer honestly, as much as I can.

My dad hated it when people made excuses for future bad behavior. "Let your yes mean yes, always." That is one thing I learned rather quickly about being a good friend—promises mean nothing unless they are kept.

Me: Don't do that. Don't add "as much as I can." Just say you will be honest and be a man of your word or there is no point to this discussion at all.
Vander: I will answer honestly.
Me: Why did you send Lissy to me today?
Vander: I just told her I saw you crying and she took off.
Me: Why did you help with my headache?
Vander: So that you would agree to talk to me.

I've obviously been giving him too much credit. My headache relief was just a means to an end for him. Not to mention, his harsh words had contributed to the headache in the first place. I don't need to be nice to him. I owe him nothing.

Me: Why are you such an ass?
Vander: I just try to figure people out in whatever way I can. It will help me when I leave after graduation.
Me: Where are you going?
Vander: After I graduate, I have to go live with my mom.
Me: Won't you be 18?
Vander: Yes. But it doesn't matter in my family.
Me: Where is your family from?
Vander: All over. Literally.
Me: But where will you be going?
Vander: My mom lives near Greece.
Me: Why?

Vander: That is where she's always lived.
Me: No, I mean why do you have to go live with your mom?
Vander: I just have to, it's been decided. Any other questions? Or is it my turn?

My friends' laughter rings out from the bathroom. It reminds me of a few more questions I have about his abilities.

Me: What did you do to my friends, Coach, and my mom?
Vander: I charmed them.
Me: Why?
Vander: To get what I want.
Me: Do you always get what you want?
Vander: Not lately.

Yeah, not since he discovered I retain my own desires, despite his efforts.

Me: Why did you sing to me?
Vander: I panicked when I couldn't charm you. That's rare. So I wanted you to fall asleep.
Me: Rare? So then how did you know I would sleep?
Vander: Yes, rare. My charms usually work. My singing always does.
Me: So you're just a spoiled rotten, selfish ass.
Vander: Is there a question in there? Or is it my turn?
Me: You can ask, but I'm not promising to answer.
Vander: Who was your father?

The text hits me like a punch in the gut. A knot forms in my throat and I swear my eyes aren't filling with tears, Momma is just cutting an onion or I have allergies or something. Of all the questions I thought he would ask, this wasn't even on the list. *What could he possibly gain from asking about my dad?* Direct answers, short and to the point, are my only hope for surviving this line of questioning.

Me: Anthony Wright
Vander: Where did he come from?
Me: He is from Chicago. Met my mom in Waterloo, and lived here in Cedar Rapids his whole adult life.
Vander: Were you adopted?
Me: No, were you?
Vander: No, but it's still my turn. Why can't I charm you?

If he thinks I even remotely understand what the hell is going on, he's dumber than he looks. Although, the level of dumbness varies depending on who is asked. My stomach growls, reminding me that I still have food waiting.

Me: It's sick that you think you need to change my mind for me. Seriously, you should seek professional help.

I set my phone down to go check on the girls before I get my food. When I reach the open door of the bathroom, I find Kenzie-Grace with her head in the sink. Taylor is standing on one side of her, Lissy on the other. They are both wearing gloves and pouring what smells mildly like bleach on her hair.

"I'm having leftover meatloaf and mashed potatoes. Anybody want some?"

"Your mom's meatloaf? Yes, please." Lissy loves my mom's cooking.

"Count me in too, please." Taylor loves to eat, period.

"If you're sure you have enough, I'd love some. Thank you." I'm so glad Kenzie-Grace came here tonight—I know I feel less crazy now, and I hope she does, too. At least now I have a better idea of the kind of person I'm dealing with as far as Vander goes.

I retreat to the kitchen just as Mom rushes through the front door. "Is everything okay?"

"Yeah, the girls are doing hair in the bathroom, and I was about to reheat some food for everybody."

"Well, you never park in the driveway, so I was worried something was off."

"Oh yeah, sorry. I meant to move it after he left."

"He?" Momma gives me that look. The look parents give children who are caught doing something naughty. I want to kick myself for bringing him up at all, especially since my friends might have overheard. I can't handle fielding the questions that will come if they did.

"Nothing like that! Vander stopped by, but he didn't even come in the house. I would have offered him to join us if he had." I get four more plates down from the cabinet and start dividing up the leftovers among them.

"That's my girl." She kisses my temple and heads down the hall.

I decide it's probably best if I keep my conversation with Vander from any prying eyes or inquiring minds, so I go to pick my phone up. Only two texts are waiting for me this time.

Vander: Nobody can fix me.
Vander: Please don't try.

There are so many responses coming to mind at those messages, but he won't get any of them. I turn my phone off and put it in my bag, then head to my bedroom and see my overflowing laundry hamper, which gives me an idea.

I stick my head in the bathroom. "Kenzie-Grace, can I talk to you in my bedroom while you're letting the hair dye set, or whatever it is you have to do?"

CHAPTER NINE

We're fifteen minutes into class on Wednesday and Mr. Daniels is still giving notes about mythological creatures and gods. Kenzie-Grace is called on to share which god she would want to be if she could choose one. Nobody pays attention to her answer, because I can hear everyone murmuring about her now lime-green hair. I even hear one student say, "Plus, she's not wearing dark colors. Maybe she's finally snapping out of it."

I am particularly interested in Vander's reaction to that comment, because she is wearing blue jeans and a white peasant shirt with a scoop neck, and peeking out near the collar is the sight of a familiar red bra. She agreed to take a turn guarding it; there is no way Vander will try to take it off of her. He is clearly pretending not to notice, but when she passes his desk, I swear I see a dimple form on his cheek after his head does a double-take.

He catches me looking then and turns around, putting his thumb in his ear and his pinky by his lips. I understand that he wants me to look at my phone, and suddenly, I do not wish to look at it ever again. I stick my hands up to show they are empty, then put them down with a shrug—but not before I give him a view of the bird I have displayed on each hand.

He clenches his jaw and folds over his notebook with a passion I've never seen from him before. He starts scribbling across the page and then rips it out. Everyone in class looks at him because of the noise—except for me, and probably Kenzie-Grace. Vander ignores them and folds up the paper. He finally returns his attention to Mr. Daniels, and most of the girls in class—as well as Kevin, Grant's boyfriend—are more than happy to do the same.

"I'm going to assign the first ten pages of this packet for homework. I want to have a class discussion tomorrow, and I will know if you haven't read it." Mr. Daniels does seem to have a little something special going on today. Maybe he forgot to shave or something, but that five o'clock shadow is making me feel like I'm seeing something I shouldn't. It's like I'm looking at him in a whole new light all of a sudden.

He looks at me then, and stops talking. I shake my head to come out of my daze. The whole class is also staring at me now. This is one of those moments when I wish I could throw on an invisibility cape and walk away.

"I'm sorry, could you repeat that?" I ignore the giggles that break out around the room, because if I don't, I will blush redder than Maddie's bra.

"Sure, Julia. I asked what would be a drawback of being a god in Greek mythology."

"Oh." *Could he have asked a more loaded question?* "I suppose it would be rather difficult dealing with a complicated family, and handling such important responsibilities like controlling the seasons or elements. Not to mention the pressure of trying to remember who all of your enemies are at any given moment, because those gods are pretty willy-nilly with having arguments and making alliances."

"Very insightful, Julia. Have you read this before?" He's holding up his copy of *The Odyssey*.

"No, but I've read *Percy Jackson* by Rick Riordan, and the *Covenant* series by Jennifer L. Armentrout, both of which are set in that world."

“I will have to add them to my list. Thank you, Miss Wright.” He winks at me, and for the first time in my life, it doesn’t make me cringe. I let out the breath that I didn’t even realize I was holding.

Mr. Daniels moves the discussion along, and I relax in my seat. When I finally look up, Vander is making the phone gesture at me again. I shake my head and start to pack up my stuff. When the bell rings, I make a beeline out the door. I can’t handle any more drama today.

As I walk into the locker room after school, Coach is waiting for me. “I have an idea, and I need your help to see if it will work.”

“Okay, that sounds ominous. Should I be worried?” My eyebrows rise.

“Well, I would prefer if you were brave, courageous, and willing.”

Coach is not making a very good case for herself right now.

I so don’t like where I think this is headed. “What is it?”

“How fast do you think you can you swim two hundred free?” She looks so hopeful. I almost hate to have to disappoint her.

“Oh no, you can’t think it would be a good idea for me to swim with the men’s team!”

Coach laughs. She actually has the audacity to *laugh* at me.

“Not in meets, silly. I just thought we could stage a race in practice to get them training harder. You would swim the two hundred free, but they would have to do a medley. Think about it. Let me know what you decide. You are welcome to get suited up and swim some laps today and tomorrow to practice. If you want to try the race, we will do it Friday afternoon.”

I can see how the idea has merit. Vander, for one, would not want to lose to anybody, let alone a girl, and especially not *this* girl. That may just be reason enough for me to want to do it.

Coach leaves me alone to go out to the pool. I take a moment and pull my phone out of my bag. I turn it on and consider the pros and cons of this race while it starts up.

Pro—I think I could win.

Con—I don't want to do it.

Pro—it would really embarrass Vander to lose a race to me.

Con—I really don't want to do it.

Pro—it would be a good opportunity for me to "take one for the team."

Con—I still don't want to do it.

Vander has been busy texting me since I turned my phone off last night.

Vander: It's not that I think I have to be this way. It's just the way I'm used to getting out of trouble.
Vander: Honestly, I'm not proud of it. But it failing on you was my first taste of public embarrassment. I can't believe normal people have to deal with that so often.
Vander: Because he is deaf, I can't charm my dad.
Vander: Where did you go? I can't charm you, and I need to know why.
Vander: It's not normal. And it could be dangerous.
Vander: I slipped a note in the outside pocket of your bag after third period.

I open the zipper on my bag, and, sure enough, there's the paper he folded up during class. How he got it into my bag is beyond me. I open it up and read it.

I've got to figure out why I can't charm you. It's not safe for you to know what I can do. I had to push Kenzie-Grace away for the same reason. I don't want anyone here to get hurt because of me.

I respond with another text.

Me: For someone who acts like a horse's rectum most of the time you're around me, you're showing a lot of concern about my welfare. A girl could get whiplash keeping up with your mood swings. Are you an ass or aren't you?

He probably won't get that until after practice, but I still feel better having my response sent. I'm fired up now. Fired up enough to do just as Coach has suggested. I'm going to get into my swimsuit, warm up, and practice so that I can kick their butts on Friday.

The look on Wesley's face when I walk out of the locker room in my suit is priceless. He elbows his friend and points to me. "Hey, Van, do you know what's up with this?"

Coach nods her approval to me, and I join in on the stretches, ignoring all of the shocked looks and remarks. I keep my focus on the coach as she writes the day's workout on the board. When she finishes, she turns to me with a question on her face. I decide in that moment there are no longer any cons left on my list, so I smile and nod at her. She clears her throat.

"Listen up! This Friday, there will be a contest. Your team manager has agreed to race some of you, in the water. These are the specifics—Wright will swim a two hundred freestyle, while you guys will each swim an individual medley. First swimmer to touch the wall wins. Any questions?"

"Yeah." I knew Vander would have something to say. "What's the contest you were referring to?"

I shoot daggers at him, but he doesn't even notice. Just when I start to think he has some humanity in his body, he says crap like that.

"Quit being a smartass, Thelxinoe. You've just signed yourself up as the first challenger, and I'm not as sure as you seem to be that you'll win. Who else wants in?"

To their ever-loving credit, not a single team member says a word. None of them even raise their hands. In fact, most of them won't even make eye contact with the coach. We all know not to push any buttons when she starts cussing. I ignore them all and am the first one in the water. Coach points to me.

"That kind of go-getter attitude is how you win races, boys. Let's go! What are you waiting for?"

The guys all carefully hustle to hop in their lanes. It is only now that I realize which lane I've jumped into. To hide my embarrassment of picking Vander's, I take off for my first warm-up lap. This lap is just to get my blood pumping, and to remind my body what it's supposed to do when swimming. There is nothing competitive about a warm-up lap—at least not for me.

However, Vander takes it as a challenge evidently, because he passes me before I get to my first flip-turn. Coach will not like this. To be honest, I don't like it, either. When I get to the wall, I don't do a flip-turn. I don't even turn around. Instead, I climb out, move to the freshman lane, and jump back in. I'm not interested in playing games with him.

At the end of practice, Coach pulls me aside at the towel rack. "What's going on between you and Thelxinoe?"

"Nothing!" I stop myself from telling her that I think he is a major anal orifice, because he is the captain of the team and deserves some respect. Besides, she is probably already aware of his said attitude. I wrap a towel around my waist, shrugging. "Why? Did he say we had a problem?"

"I haven't talked to him about it, but I am about to, and I wanted to check with you first." Coach jots something on her clipboard, then looks up again. "Are you sure there is nothing you want to tell me?"

"Nothing relevant, Coach." I grab an extra towel for my dripping head and make my way into the locker room.

After I shower and get dressed, I take my phone out to text the girls. They still can't believe that their memories of what happened in this room a few nights ago have been altered. I am so tired of trying to convince them I am not playing a joke on them, but I need to know what they think of Kenzie-Grace's story, if they even remember it. Something about what she said has been bothering me, and I can't quite put my finger on it. I'm hoping Taylor and Lissy can help me out.

Before I send out my group text, a new one pops up on the top of my screen from Vander. I had asked before practice if he was or was not an ass.

Vander: Yes.

I groan in frustration, because what does that even mean? It's really something how quickly that one-word text set my blood to boil. *Boys are so annoying!*

I send a message to the girls about meeting for dinner and head out to my car. I'm out the gym door when I hear feet behind me. I turn to find Wesley jogging to catch up.

"Julia, wait up."

Out of pure curiosity, I do. I wonder what Vander has asked him to relay to me ... or *charmed* him to do, more likely.

"What do you want?"

"I just wanted to check with you if it would be okay if I raced on Friday. Vander doesn't seem to think it will be much of a challenge, but I've seen you swim, and you are fast. I'm sure it will be a close matchup with us swimming all of the strokes to your free. Anyway, I didn't like how Vander treated you today, and I wanted to make sure that it was okay if I got in on the race before I told Coach I want to do it."

My arms fall to my sides, my bag drops to the ground, and my posture straightens up. I've been blindsided by his kindness here, and I can't stop myself. I throw my arms around Wesley and give him a hug. It surprises even me.

After how frustrated I've been for most of the day, that was the sweetest thing for him to say and do. Even if he is doing this to mess with me, which is a possibility with Vander as his closest friend, I really need something good to come out of this day.

He wraps his arms around me and asks, "Is that a yes?"

"Yes, thank you, Wes. That was a real gentlemanly thing to do. You've earned an 'A' for the day, for sure."

I let him go and bend to pick up my bag. It's at that moment I look up and see Vander watching us. He does not look happy, but then again, when does he ever?

CHAPTER TEN

"No *way*!" Lissy squeals while hitting my arm, and starts shaking her hands in excitement. Everyone in *Panchero's* looks around to make sure the screaming girl isn't having a seizure or something.

"Just some fangirling going on over here, nothing to see," I'm quick to explain her behavior to the other customers.

"You have *got* to be kidding me! I have to see this!" Lissy is obviously very excited about the race on Friday. "Just to be clear, you're going to be in the water with the men's swim team?"

"Actually, I was in the water with them today to warm up and practice, since I'm racing them on Friday," I reply sheepishly. I don't mean to rub it in.

"Shut up!" She hits me on the arm again.

"I don't think Coach is planning to make Friday's race a spectator opportunity."

"That is *so* not fair. Those guys are going to have all of their teammates there to cheer them on. You deserve equal representation."

"I'm not half as confident as Coach seems to be that I can win, even if they are swimming the medley. In practice today, I was swimming with the freshmen, and they were faster than me at every turn. I guess I feel like the fewer witnesses to the event, the better."

"Nope! I'm not missing this for the world. I'm talking to Coach first thing tomorrow." *Well, that's as good as a done deal.* Nothing will stop her from following through on that.

"So anyway, Vander was a jackass to me before practice, but Wesley comes up to me after practice—"

"I can't even handle this! Practice today was like a hottie sandwich for you. I'm kind of wishing that I had gotten caught instead of you!" I roll my eyes, because I can't imagine being so wrapped up in everyone's appearance so much that the fact they are not my favorite people doesn't even matter. She takes a few deep breaths in through her nose and out through her mouth before motioning for me to continue.

"Anyway, he met up with me outside the gym on the way to my car and asked permission to sign up for the race. He said he didn't like the way that Vander had acted and wanted to make sure it was okay. It was such a nice thing for him to say that I put down my bag and gave him a hug."

"Oh, no." Lissy starts fanning herself. I roll my eyes again. *Seriously, give me a break!* I should probably be used to this crap by now, but does one ever get used to this level of insanity?

"When I let go and picked up my bag, I saw Vander standing there, glaring at Wesley."

"Okay, you need to stop! I'm about to have a 'fangirl down and out for the count' type of moment here. You are in some fantasy now, where two hot guys are fighting over you in, like, the most awesome love triangle ever! And it's not even a dream!" She continues to fan herself.

Taylor walks into *Panchero's* in the middle of this fangirl fit, and her eyes widen like she's about to hear the story of a lifetime.

"What did I miss?"

I hold up my burrito and show that I am going to eat it. Lissy takes it upon herself to fill Taylor in on what's going on. She uses a lot more adjectives and colorful terminology than I had when I told her, though. It's actually much more fascinating the way she tells it. She finishes with, "And then, Julia went and pushed her hooties up against Wesley's man-hooties. Vander watched their love scene live with his own eyes, and then he threatened to hit Wesley."

"Is that true?" Taylor asks, turning to me. She knows there is a difference between the truth and Lissy's fantastical version of things.

"More or less." I shrug, as there is no point in trying to tell the actual version of events. Taylor's fangirl filter automatically adds dramatic flair to what she hears anyway.

"Well, I'm coming, too! There's no way am I going to miss the race on Friday." Taylor seems to be as determined as Lissy is to be present at my race. Hopefully, Coach will make a good decision in regards to the size of the crowd she allows to witness my potential embarrassment.

"Okay, wait. Does it even matter, to either of you, that I don't want anyone there?" I look up from my burrito and make eye contact, first with Taylor and then with Lissy. They turn to look at each other and shrug.

"No, not really," Lissy answers for them both. Taylor nods her agreement. I throw my hands up in defeat. I would really rather suffer this experience without witnesses, but there is no way to change their minds ... and, unlike Vander, I wouldn't want to if I could.

"Fine," I say through gritted teeth to show my feelings on the topic. I know I won't win this battle, mainly because it has to do with boys, who will be wearing swimsuits, and getting wet—not to mention the fact that my friends are perverts when it comes to abdominal muscles. My best bet is to just change the subject and hope they forget about it.

"Have either of you guys read Homer's *Odyssey*?" I am supposed to read the first ten pages of the Greek Mythology packet today, but I'm scared it will be as hard to read as the first page of that book. I know Mr. Daniels wasn't kidding about being able to tell who had done the reading and who had not. I plan to read it before bed tonight.

"No, but I've read *Percy Jackson.* Does that count?" I like the way Taylor thinks.

"That's what I said to Mr. Daniels today." I practically sang his name, knowing that if anything would help them move on from the swim team topic, it would be the mention of the teacher voted most likely to have stalker pictures taken of him and posted on social media. And I was right—it totally worked.

"I'm still pissed that I took European Literature last year. If I had known the new teacher was going to be that hot, I would have taken another math class or something and saved myself for him." Lissy tells it how it is, but I know she will up the ante if Taylor takes my bait, too.

"I don't even care that I took it last year. I'm considering retaking it to *improve my grade*," which she put in air quotes before continuing, "and I got an 'A' in that class."

"Well, I named my car Daniel in his honor, and I walk slowly past his class during passing time just to catch a glimpse."

"Oh yeah? I make sure that I have to go to the bathroom in the middle of my creative writing class so I can stand and stare through the window every day."

"Well, I go to the bathroom every *hour* and stare at him."

They are starting to raise their voices, and are drawing the attention of all of the other patrons of the restaurant. This time I don't feel the need to explain what's going on. It's clear enough that these girls are having a one-upping match over a teacher who probably—quite literally—doesn't even know either one of them exists. I just sit back in my chair, sip on my lemonade, and enjoy the show.

All of a sudden, they both stop. Their faces turn red, their eyes are wide, and they are jerking their heads at me to let me know I should check out something going on behind me. When I look over my shoulder, I spit lemonade across the table in a huge fit of laughter.

Mr. Daniels in now in the building.

"Stop!" Lissy urges as she mops up the mess I've made with some napkins. I draw the short straw and am chosen to throw the sticky napkins away. I go to toss the mess, and that's when I realize Mr. Daniels is not alone. He must have held the door open for the older lady, followed in behind her, and is now seating her at a table before he goes to get their food.

The woman is adorable. She's wearing a dress, a pearl necklace, and her lipstick has been freshly applied. I think the first thing I noticed about her were the bright-pink tennis balls on the bottom of her walker. This woman has got spunk, and that makes me smile. Mr. Daniels catches me smiling at his companion and waves at me, then holds up a finger, signaling for me to wait. He says something to the woman before making his way over to me.

"Good evening, Julia. How are you?" His blue eyes are intensely locked on mine. I have no doubt he is listening to what I have to say. It's never felt this intense in class.

"Doing well, and you?" I offer cautiously. I can feel the girls staring intently at our interaction, even though my back is to them.

"Just fantastic, thanks. I volunteer at Heritage Manor once a week and today is Viola's birthday. After dinner, we are going to the library to celebrate." His gaze is starting to make me feel like I'm being studied.

"Burritos and books? Sounds like a perfect date night to me." I throw a slow, animated wink over his shoulder at the elderly woman, which causes them both to laugh. Honestly, I just need a good reason to break eye contact before things get any more awkward.

"Yeah, that's what I thought when she suggested it. Anyway, I'm glad I bumped into you because I can't remember the name of the Greek-inspired series you mentioned in class. I am hoping the library has it."

"The *Covenant* series by Jennifer L. Armentrout? I know the library downtown has it, because that is how I found out about it."

"I will look for it. Thank you. Have a good night." He walks away, and I return to my friends, where the table now needs another cleanup due to the drool pouring out of their gaping mouths.

Lissy is the first one to find her voice. "You are officially the luckiest girl at Eisenhower High School today. Don't even talk to me, I just can't even."

"Yeah, what she said," Taylor adds poetically.

I guess neither of them *can even* right now, but I don't know what it is that they "can't even" do. *Fangirls are so strange!*

"Okay, so now we have something important to discuss."

That gets their attention. It's about time they learned about this underwear capturing game, and how we are going to play it.

CHAPTER ELEVEN

I only get one text from Vander before bedtime, and it's actually a group message for the whole team.

Vander: Anyone else that wants to swim in the race on Friday against our team manager needs to let coach know before practice tomorrow.

I'm kind of relieved that he doesn't try to talk to me, and also grateful I now have access to the whole team at once. *This text group might come in handy sometime.* I turn my phone on airplane mode and open my book.

I fall asleep after finishing the whole packet, and end up dreaming that I am a Siren like Mr. Daniels described. Once I shake the eerie feeling of luring sailors to their deaths, I realize how lonely it would be to be trapped on an island forever. An eternity like that is definitely cruel and unusual punishment.

❍ ❍ ❍

Mr. Daniels waves the book *Half-Blood* by Jennifer L. Armentrout at me when I walk in the room.

"Looks like you had a successful date night." I smile at him as I move toward my seat.

"Sure did." He's so good at ignoring the adoring stares and jealous remarks made by my fellow students.

It's only after the bell rings when I hear someone ask, "Who does Julia think she is talking to him like that?"

Really? I don't have a right to talk to my own teacher because someone thinks they have some claim to him, exclusively? *I will say it again—fangirls are weird!*

"Put away your books and take out a pen or pencil." Mr. Daniels is holding a stack of papers. We all know what this means—*it's time for a pop quiz.*

I'm so grateful I did the reading last night. I only hear two people groaning about being tested, and I roll my eyes at them because we are seniors, not preschoolers.

"I warned you that I would know who had done their reading and who had not. There is an opportunity for extra credit if you read beyond the assigned pages." He hands out the papers, while most of the girls—*and Kevin*—are watching his every move as he goes up and down the aisles, tapping on cell phones and instructing students to put them away before he hands them a quiz.

I find the quiz to be extremely easy. I'm not the first to finish, but am confident that I aced it, and got the extra credit portion correct as well. Even though I did well, I hear Mr. Daniels' AP class actually has to read the *Odyssey* in full, and I am so grateful that I didn't sign up for that. This is turning out to be a great day.

❍ ❍ ❍

"I need to talk to you."

Coach stops me in the hall outside of the cafeteria after fourth period. I rarely see her outside of the locker room, pool, or gymnasium.

"Yeah, Coach?"

"Would you have a problem with sharing your managerial duties with another manager, starting today?"

"I don't think that would be a bad thing. But is that even up to me?" I wonder who she has in mind…

Oh, wait. I know exactly who would sign up for that job.

"Not really, but I thought I would run it by you first. Lissy Edmonds was adamant that she has a deep desire to start being an asset to the team." I knew it. I'm not surprised she's offered to "help out," but I do hope she's prepared to do some actual work. I will not be covering for her just so she can sit back and watch.

"Yeah, it will be good to have another person to share the duties with. Can you tell me what your thoughts are about having spectators for tomorrow's race?"

"Absolutely *nobody* outside of school staff and team members will be allowed into our closed practice, which is what I told Edmonds this morning right before she volunteered to be a manager. We can really use an extra person for timing splits during meets, so I allowed it."

Ha! Well, that makes perfect sense. She did say she would be there on Friday no matter what it would take, and now she will be.

"Good. Thanks, Coach. See you later."

I can't wait to hear Lissy's version of events. I'm sure it won't include how she tried to weasel her way into a closed practice before begging to be a manager. Knowing her, it will probably be full of colorful words and exaggerated hand gestures. She may even throw in a flip of her hair to emphasize a point.

I look over the students in the cafeteria, and my eyes land on Maddie. I start toward her, and suddenly Vander is standing in front of me, blocking my path. I really wasn't expecting to have to deal with him again until after school

"What the hell are you doing, Vander?"

"I need to talk to you, since you stopped texting me." At those words, some girls at a nearby table stop talking to glare at me.

Vander leans down and creepily whispers to them, "Forget you've witnessed this conversation, and mind your own business."

"Was that one hundred percent necessary? You have to stop doing that! Do you even know if there are side effects associated with that?" I try to walk away, but he steps into my path again.

"It was necessary, unless you want to start receiving a lot of shade from those members of my fan club."

"Give me a flipping break, you overinflated buffoon. I can't wait for our race tomorrow, so I can pop that bubble of delusion you are currently living in." I turn around in place to head in the other direction, and he grabs my arm. Anger fills me to the brim and spills over. I do the only thing I believe will get him to let go—I scream.

"Aaaaahhhhh! That hurts, Vander Thelxinoe! Please let go of me!"

The cafeteria goes silent. I watch two security guards making their way over, and even Principal Ralphman has given us his full attention.

"Good luck charming the entire cafeteria in order to save yourself the embarrassment of this moment," I tell him under my breath, while I yank my arm from his grasp. I hope he receives the message that I am not at his beck and call. Just because he wants to talk to me doesn't mean I have to listen.

I continue to walk out of the cafeteria, ignoring the stares. I can handle it. I glance back once to find Vander red-faced, with his lips together in a hard line and his hands clenched tight in fists. Maybe he won't even try to charm his way out of this one, but I don't care what he does. He's made this mess; he can wallow around in it like the pig he chooses to be.

I don't get the chance to talk to Maddie. After the disaster in the cafeteria, I didn't want to take the chance of bumping into Vander again, so I head to the women's locker room for some quiet. I decide to text Maddie instead, and get out my phone. When I turn it off airplane mode, I watch it buzz and flash, displaying missed message after missed message. I ignore them all to text Maddie.

Me: Can you call a team meeting in the locker room after school? I have a way I think we can win the challenge if we all work together.
Maddie: OMG, Julia! Are you okay? I can't believe Vander grabbed
you like that!!
Me: Yes, I'm fine, thanks for asking. So, can you send the team text?
Maddie: MANDATORY TEAM MEETING! After school today in the
locker room! BE THERE!

I guess that is a *yes*. After a few more texts pop up, inquiring about my welfare in regards to the scene in the cafeteria, I turn my phone back on airplane mode and try to survive the rest of the day.

Sure enough, the entire team (plus Kenzie-Grace, whom I've personally asked to be here) has gathered in the locker room after school. I stand up on a bench and call the meeting to order.

"How many of you know about the contest going on between Maddie and Vander, as representatives of the teams?"

Only a few hands go up: Maddie's, Taylor's, Kenzie-Grace's, Lissy's, and mine. I give a pointed look to Maddie, who shrugs. I understand her desire not to tell anyone, though, because maybe then they wouldn't know it was *her* bra up the flagpole if she lost.

"Next question, how many of you own red bras?" After some guffaws at my audacity and a few giggles, about half the team raises their hands.

"Perfect! The game is like capture the flag: Vander's goal is to capture Maddie's red bra, and Maddie's is to capture his red, white, and blue-striped boxers. The first to capture the flag has to run it up the flagpole. The rules are that Vander cannot take his boxers out of the school building, and Maddie cannot take her bra out of school. They have to be in the building at the end of every day.

"At first, Maddie was just leaving her red bra in her own swim locker. However, on Saturday night, Vander and Wesley almost got away with it. We used a loophole in the rules, and I ended up wearing her bra home Monday night and Tuesday to school. I gave it to Kenzie-Grace Tuesday night, and she wore it yesterday and today. The thing is, I made sure Vander knew I was wearing it, and he saw that Kenzie-Grace was wearing it, too. He knows Maddie is no longer alone in this." A few questions come out of the crowd at me, but I silence them with my hand.

"Wait until I'm finished. I have a plan, but it will only work if we all work together, and if we are all capable of not falling for Vander's *charms*." I say that last word knowing only a few of us realize what I'm actually saying. "All of us that have red bras need to wear them to school tomorrow. It is vital to our plan to make sure that it can be seen. We are trying to keep him guessing as to who actually has *Maddie's* red bra on. Before I start to explain phase two of the plan, are there any questions?"

Maddie looks around nervously and raises her hand, saying, "It is my responsibility to inform you at this point, if you do not want to take part in this game, you are free to leave now. No questions asked, and no hard feelings between us."

She holds her breath and makes a show of closing and covering her eyes—as if she wouldn't be able to figure out which members of the team weren't present after she opened them. After a few seconds, she lets out her breath and looks around. Not a single girl has left the room. *I love my team.*

"All right, so those of you that don't have a red bra are on the recovery team with Taylor. Your job will be to locate and retrieve Vander's boxer shorts. I know for a fact that he won't be wearing them during practice tomorrow, and according to the rules, they have to be in the school. We need to check his swim locker, his school locker, and probably Wesley's lockers, as well. If they aren't there, then they could be hidden in one of his classrooms. I would check Mr. Brandt's room in the science wing first, because Wesley may have asked his dad to store them."

"Any questions?" A few hands pop up.

"Sara?" I ask.

"How are we going to get in Mr. Brandt's classroom, or any other classroom, for that matter?"

"Someone on the team has access to a set of school keys, and they will be available for your use tomorrow. Any other questions?" I hear Amy remind Sara that Lissy's brother was the captain of the football team this year. I try not to smile at how many people are aware of the captain's keys tradition. There is no way school officials are in the dark about it, either.

"I have one," Maddie states. "Who will be wearing my actual bra?"

I smile at her. "The person he would least likely suspect, of course. Any other questions?"

Smiles are breaking out around the room, along with murmurs of excitement. I think we can really pull this off.

"One last thing." Everyone quiets down again. "It is imperative, and I mean *absolutely necessary*, that nobody looks Vander in the eyes tomorrow. We want him to see that we are all unified in our efforts and he is all alone."

I make eye contact with as many members of our team as I can to drive that point home. Then I yell, "We are going to win tomorrow! Right, team?"

They all start hooting and hollering like a pack of wolves, howling for our upcoming victory.

Coach heads into the locker room after a few minutes to investigate the commotion.

"What are all of you doing in here? Edmonds, Wright—on deck, now! The rest of you, your season is over. Go home!" She blows her whistle to motivate movement, and it works. Everyone starts to clear out. I give a pointed look to Kenzie-Grace. She nods to let me know she understands what she needs to do.

"Sure thing, Coach!" I shout, and pull Lissy along with me out to the pool.

When we step out of the locker room, the smell of chlorine and the sound of stretches being counted off greet us. I walk over to participate in the stretches. I plan to swim a few laps today to prepare for the race.

Coach hands the water bottle basket to Lissy, and tells her to go get ice water in them. It shocks Lissy out of the apparent daydream she is having about all these boys. She looks at me, as if asking if this is the kind of stuff I've been forced to do. I bite my tongue and nod. *Did she think I just sat around and stared?*

That's probably exactly what she thought.

When the team gets in the water for warm-ups, I let the sound of the guys splashing around cover our conversation.

"I honestly didn't think you were doing anything as the team manager. I'm starting to regret signing up for a whole season of this." Lissy's words don't match the awed look on her face as she studies the bodies gliding through the water.

"Too bad—you're all in now. I have to go get my suit on so I can swim a few laps. You're all on your own today."

"Thanks a lot, Jules!"

As I walk through the locker room door, I hear Coach calling out to her. I silently thank Coach for putting her through her paces today.

I grab my suit from my locker and decide to take it with me to the bathroom. The locker room is empty, but I still feel like Vander might walk through at any moment. He has an annoying habit of following me any time I leave the pool, and I wouldn't be able to keep from strangling him if he caught me while I was undressed.

When I make it back out to the pool, though, he's still there, in his lane, where he should stay. I make sure Coach sees me hopping into the freshman lane. If she has any tips for tomorrow's race, I want her to know where to find me. She just salutes me and goes back to telling Lissy what's expected of her as the team manager.

The water feels warm today. I hope none of the freshman have peed in here. Boys are so gross, I wouldn't put it past them. I decide not to dwell on that thought and lose myself in the stroke instead.

I make sure that my hand is entering the water in the proper way to ensure the least resistance as I go forward. When it comes out of the water, I check that my hand is propelling the most water it can out of the way. With every breath, I make sure to only allow my lips above the water. Lifting my whole head out wastes a lot of energy and time. I push hard off of the wall with every flip turn. My kicks are strong and sure, and the rhythm of the swim takes over.

Before I know it, I have worked up a lot of heat. I'm definitely sweating, and the water is starting to feel like bathwater on my skin. I stand up in the shallow end and walk to the side to keep out of the way of the other swimmers in the lane.

"Lissy!" Shouting, I motion for her to bring me a bottle of water. I'm barely able to pull myself out of the pool. It feels like the time Vander started singing to me. Rolling onto my back, I focus on my breathing. *I will not pass out, I will not pass out, I will not ... pass ... out.*

"I will not pass out." Mumbling, I become aware of the crowd gathered around me now.

"Well, it's too late for that, Wright. You've been out for a few minutes now." Coach is shooing the others away from me and hands me some water to drink. Lissy has my head in her lap.

"Are you serious?" *Why do I keep passing out? Wait!* "Did Vander sing or something?"

Coach just laughs at me. "Yeah, she's going to be fine. Her sense of humor is back already," she announces to the retreating team, then turns to me. "Is it true that you skipped lunch today, and then got in the water and pushed yourself harder than I've ever seen you do before?"

Oh, yeah, I guess I did forget to eat after that scene in the cafeteria. "I kind of forgot to eat, and I didn't mean to push myself so hard—it just felt so on today. But then the water started to feel hot on my skin instead of refreshing, and that's when I climbed out."

Coach gives me a strange look and walks to the middle lane. She pulls on the rope that the water thermometer dangles on and looks at it. Then she puts her hand in the water and shakes her head. She blows her whistle long and hard.

"Everybody out!" I wouldn't go so far as to say that the team panicked, but they sure did hustle getting out of the water.

"What's up, Coach?" Of course, Vander is the first to ask.

"Wright here noticed that the water is warmer today. The thermometer says that the temperature is normal, but when I put my hand in, it definitely felt warm. Something fishy is going on here, and I don't mean swimming." That's one of her favorite jokes. "We're done for the day, gentlemen. Hit the showers!"

When Vander walks by, he again puts his pretend phone up to his ear. I put my own pretend bird up to his face. Lissy cages it, and helps me to my feet.

"I can't believe you antagonize him so much," Lissy admonishes.

"*I* antagonize *him*? Are you kidding me right now?" I grab a towel, wrap it around my body, and take an extra one for my hair. It's not a very effective way to storm off, but I am done with her hero-worship of this selfish, demanding butt-munch with a habit of charming people—and not in a fairytale type of way, either.

The last thing I hear before I turn the shower on is Coach telling Lissy, "Make sure she is okay and then make sure the towels get picked up."

It gives me a little joy to think of her doing towel duty on her own, and I silently thank Coach for the second time today.

When I get home, all I can think about is sleep. I curl up on the couch to take a nap, so my mom won't let me sleep too long. Except she doesn't wake me—the doorbell does an hour later. I look out the window and groan.

Stomping to the door, I throw it open and march outside. "What the hell do you want from me? In case I haven't been clear enough, I don't like you. You are a sad excuse for a human being, and I don't want to talk to you. So, why don't you just get back in your slime-mobile and slither off like the snake you are?"

"Well, now, that's just plain rude. First, you think I'm a vampire, and now a snake? Let me assure you, I do not speak parseltongue."

"Gross. I'd rather not talk about your tongue, if you don't mind!"

"Well, which of my body parts would you like to talk about?" He crosses his arms, grinning at me. *Did he really just ask that?*

"How about your ass?" I suggest and he raises his eyebrows, but before he can respond, I add, "Getting into your car, and leaving!"

"Good comeback, Julia. Truly inspired. You should be proud of that one."

"Seriously, what can I do to get you to leave?" I hadn't stopped to put shoes on before I marched out here, and the cold pavement is starting to seep through my socks.

"I'm not leaving until we talk."

"Well, talk then, and let's get this over with."

"Okay. Why can't I charm you?"

"I don't know. Good talk, Mr. One-Track-Mind. See ya at school tomorrow." I turn for the door, but his words stop me this time, instead of his hand.

"I'm in trouble, and I need your help," he says, while I freeze in place. "Please, help me. I'll do anything."

"The great and powerful Vander Thelxinoe needs little ole Julia's help?" I ask.

"The scared and threatened Vander Thelxinoe is begging you for your help, actually." His voice is quiet and unsure when he speaks this time. I turn around to search his face. I'm not going to get pulled into another round of I-know-you-are-but-what-am-I type of word games with him. I let out the breath I didn't even know I was holding and take another one.

"Full disclosure, I still don't like you. But the fact is, I've helped wounded birds who've fallen from nests, and I'm still willing to help the likes of you. That should tell you the kind of person I am. Here is my question, though. What kind of person are you?"

"I'm the kind of person who loves birds, and I repay debts sevenfold. I will most definitely be in your debt."

"What do you need from me? I'm not giving you my liver or anything like that."

"I need to figure out how you are different from others. Not because I need or even want to charm you. But because I can't, and that is dangerous for me."

"Tell me more about why you're so scared, and tell me who is threatening you, or this deal is off."

Vander bites his lip and looks over his shoulder. "Can I come in?"

"Not until you answer my questions."

He groans in frustration, and the sound reminds me of the time he saw Kenzie-Grace wearing Maddie's bra.

"Fine." He spits it out between his clenched teeth, then takes a slow breath. On its release, he rushes to tell me what he has to say before he loses his courage. "I'm in danger of being kidnapped by my mother's family. Can I come in now?"

My jaw drops to the pavement we are both standing on. Unknowingly, my arm lifts up as an invitation for him to enter my home, and I numbly follow him in. I can't imagine what he's said is true.

"Like I said before, I need your help." Vander is sitting on my couch, but he doesn't look like he's comfortable. He's perched on the edge, like he may have to take flight at any moment.

"Am I going to be in danger for helping you?" I tuck my feet beneath me on the loveseat across from him.

"Technically, yes. However, no more or less than you already are, due to the fact that I can't charm you."

"I'm going to need a little more information than that." My mother would be upset if she came home and I had a boy in the house, but she may forgive me if she knows I'm helping him. She would absolutely be unhappy to learn I had a guest who I wasn't treating well. That thought drives my next question. "Can I get you anything? Some water, or a cookie?"

"I'm sorry. Did you just offer me a cookie?" He looks surprised at my question. He runs his hands through his dark hair, and it falls right back to where it was before.

My eyes roll involuntarily. I may not like him, but Momma has taught me to be polite.

"Yes, I did. You are the wounded bird that I've brought in from the cold, and I am trying to nourish you. Now, do you want something or not?" I stand up to show how willing I am to go retrieve refreshments, should he want some.

"Actually, I'd really like some water, please."

He stands to accompany me and I let him, resisting the urge to drop a snarky comment so that we can continue our conversation.

"What happened to your parents?" I take two glasses down from the cupboard.

"What do you mean?"

Before I clarify my question, I fill both glasses with ice.

"I mean, why do you live alone with your dad?" I have heard several stories in the halls at school, but I don't know which one is true, or if any of them are.

"My dad took me away from my mother as soon as I was born. My mother's life is complicated. My dad loves her, but he didn't want me around her for my own safety. It wasn't worth the risk, he thought. They said taking me away was the best course of action." He is scary good at maintaining eye contact when he talks. Probably a side effect of needing to charm someone on a moment's notice, but I don't have to worry about that, so I hold his gaze.

"Take you away from where?" I turn the tap on to fill the glasses without looking away from him.

"From where my mother lives, near Greece." I hand him his glass, but neither of us move.

"And she's never come to visit you?" It's an honest question.

"She can't visit me." He takes a sip of water, and I catch my gaze following the glass to his lips.

"Because your father won't let her?" I snap my eyes back to his.

"No, because she physically can't make the trip."

"Is she ill?"

"Something like that," he says with a shrug as he looks down and away from me.

That pisses me off in a hurry. I thought we were not going to be playing games anymore. I slam my glass down, spilling some water on the counter, pissing me off even more because now I will have to wipe it up.

"I thought you needed my help." I grab his thick bicep and start to shove him toward the door.

"I do." After one step, he stands still, no matter how hard I press.

"Then stop being vague and mysterious. I don't find it endearing, and it's making me not want to help you at all." I put my hands on my hips and glare at his blue-green eyes, hoping he can figure out that I mean business.

"Are you this impatient with baby birds?" He tries to laugh it off, but I won't be shut down so easily.

"Tell me why your mother can't make the trip. Now." My foot begins tapping for effect. The look I am going for is vicious and fierce like a lion, but I fear I may appear more like an upset kitten. Regardless, I stand firm.

He stares at me, and I stare back. This is a showdown, a test of whose will is stronger: his to keep information from me, or mine to insist on having it.

I will win, and he knows it.

"Promise me you'll have an open mind. If this doesn't go well, I can't take anything back." He looks more scared now than he did in the cafeteria, or when he was begging for my help on my porch. I stop the foot tapping and lower my hands to my side.

Not trusting my voice, I simply nod to show my agreement.

"She can't leave the island she lives on, because she was cursed to live there forever." For the second time since he arrived, my jaw drops open.

"Did you say *cursed*? And are you serious?"

"Yes, and yes."

"Cursed how, and by whom?" *I'm about to lose my shit.* This doesn't make any sense.

"Demeter cursed her to stay on the island as punishment for not locating her daughter, Persephone, in a timely manner."

"Your mother is—" No. She can't be.

Holy shit! I can't even believe he's trying to tell me something so far beyond the bounds of reality. The guy obviously needs to be medicated.

"Yes, she is. My mother is a Siren."

As. If!

"Vander, I think it's time for you to go." Pressing my hand against his chest, I back him toward the door.

"I'm telling you the truth," he says as he steps out onto the porch.

"Yeah, well, I can't handle the truth." I slam the door in his face.

CHAPTER TWELVE

My mom is shaking my bed down near my feet, and I blink my eyes open slowly. *Holy crap!* I'm going to be late for school. The memory of what Vander told me last night floods back as I blink myself awake, and I am just as pissed off by it now as I was then. I remember grabbing his arm and forcing him out of my house after his major revelation. I had no other ideas for how to stop the violent feelings welling up inside of me from becoming a full-blown attack. *Sirens aren't real. Demeter and Persephone are names from our Mythology packet.* I wonder how long he has been working on this one. I take a deep, calming breath and sit up.

"Did you forget to set your alarm last night?" Momma has moved closer now. She must be pretty confident that I won't lash out and hit her for waking me, like I sometimes do when I'm not quite awake enough to stop myself. She's rubbing my back gently in an effort to help my blood start pumping so I can get up.

"Yeah, I must have." Truth is, waking up was the farthest thing from my mind when I crawled in bed last night, trying not to scream in frustration. My annoyance at Vander rears its ugly head again, and now I can't wait to see the look on his face when he sees his boxers flapping in the wind above our school.

I reach in my drawer and pull out my own red bra, a light-gray V-neck sweater, and some black yoga pants. I race to the bathroom to brush my teeth. It's going to have to be a bun day for my dark, curly hair. I slather on some fresh deodorant and mascara before I pull on my boots and grab my keys from the bowl. Mom tosses me a granola bar and a banana before I reach the door. I drop them both because my hands are shaking. *Argh!*

"Thanks, Momma!" I say over my shoulder as I pick them up.

I didn't have dinner last night, either. *I have to stop forgetting to eat.* It's been twenty-four hours since I last had a meal. Also, I took an hour nap after swim practice and went to bed for the whole night, probably less than an hour later. *Maybe I have mono.*

I laugh that idea off as I slide my book bag into my car. I don't kiss anybody, and I don't share drinks. Probably the stress of thinking I'm crazy. There's a note on my windshield, which I grab before taking my seat and buckling up.

Julia, I know you are confused, but please don't share what I told you with anyone else. I've never told anyone before that could remember, so I'm trusting you. I will be happy to talk more any time you want. Just please, keep this between us. Vander

I toss the note into my bag and take off for school. He's really playing this prank all the way through. When I look at the clock, my foot eases up off the gas pedal. I'm actually leaving my neighborhood about five minutes earlier than I normally do. *What a whirlwind of a morning.* On the bright side, I should be fully rested for my race this afternoon. Winning will add insult to injury as far as sticking it to Vander goes, and I am all for that.

My first class whizzes by, and before I know it, I'm in the computer lab working on a piece for my creative writing class. I have to complete several searches for common words and write a story using their alternative meanings. Whenever I get bored, I open Google Images to search for myself and see what pictures show up. Today, there is a new picture of me in my swimsuit, lying unconscious by the side of the pool, my head in Lissy's lap.

Someone is going to regret posting that! A part of me hopes it was Vander. If so, he has just added unnecessary fuel to the fire that I'm going to use to burn him.

That thought has me putting his name in the search box. I want to see what kind of dirt I can dig up on him. I try *Vander Thelxinoe*, and it's basically a replay of his social media pages. Then I try putting in just his last name to see if I can find something out there that I can use against him.

What I do find has me shocked. It's not scandalous, but it is enlightening. There is a moon of Jupiter that shares his name, but more interesting is the second hit. Thelxinoe is the name of one of the Sirens of the *Odyssey*, and what hits me right in the stomach is what that name means in English: mind-charmer.

Before I get too carried away with believing him at his word, I consider the fact that he has probably performed this search too, and that's where he got the idea for this joke in the first place. But I've also seen him hypnotize and charm people with my own eyes—more than once. *Oh. My. Word.* I am going to get dizzy from all of the wheels turning in my brain. *What if he really is who and what he says he is? Could he be the son of a Siren? And what does that even mean?*

When third period arrives, I'm so anxious that it's ridiculous. Vander begged for my help, and made me feel guilty for thinking of denying him, and then he spit out such a ridiculous claim that I kicked him out of my house!

But what if it's true?

What if his name actually tells a story about who he is and what he can do? Can this actually be happening? Myths are supposed to stay myths, damn it! Not up and decide to come true and start irritating you at school and in your own home!

I sit on the edge of my seat, my feet bouncing up and down under my desk. My hands are shaking, and for once, it's not because I've forgotten to eat. I'm not nervous about class, either. Since I read the whole packet the first night, I'm ready for another quiz or a class discussion about any of it. I just hope I can stay in my seat after Vander walks in the room. I have so many questions for him, I'm afraid I might spit one out at an inappropriate time.

The warning bell chimes, and Vander hasn't come into the classroom yet. Mr. Daniels is sitting at his desk, looking comfortable. Maybe he will give us a reading day. Thirty seconds left until class starts, and I'm staring at the clock. I'm not sure I can handle sitting in the same room as Vander and not talk to him about this. *I can't.*

I can't.

I definitely can't.

I'm up out of my seat, slinging my backpack over my shoulder, and headed to the door when Mr. Daniels speaks up.

"Julia, are you feeling okay?"

"Not really, Mr. Daniels. I'm sorry." And I'm out the door.

Standing outside the classroom is Vander Thelxinoe, with an expression on his face I don't remember seeing before, which makes it hard to place.

"I thought I was going to have to go in there and give you this pass so we could talk." He holds out a hall pass with both of our names on it, signed by Principal Ralphman.

"Does he know he signed that?" I can't believe, of all the questions running amok unsupervised in my head, *this* is the one to come out of my mouth.

"Is that really the question you want to start with?" He crosses his arms and leans against the lockers.

Are we really going to stand and talk right here in the hallway?

"No, it isn't. Do you want to go talk somewhere else?" I look up and down the hall, but there is nobody else in it.

"Not really. Nobody will bother us out here, and if they do, we have a pass. What are you thinking?" His head falls a bit to the side, like he's trying to figure me out.

"Is it true?"

Vander sighs. He takes another deep breath and lets it out slowly.

"Yes, it's true. My father took my mother's name, since there was no way for them to get married. He showed his commitment to her in that way."

Mentioning his dad brings this to a whole other level. His dad would have to know what was going on. *I can't even imagine how Vander came to be!*

"How were you made? I mean, I thought all sailors were lured to their deaths by Sirens. Is your dad a sailor, or is that a myth, too?"

He laughs at me. I think about taking a swing at him, but remind myself that I am at school. And that violence isn't the answer.

"I think this would be better if you let me start at the beginning. Is that okay?"

Now it's my turn to cross my arms and lean against the lockers. I watch his eyes change. Not the color, but what's going on behind them. They remind me of a summer storm brewing in the sky. If it's true that he's never told anyone about this before, then it must be difficult for him to let go and open up to me.

"My mother was an ordinary Greek teenager who had a small group of friends. One of them was Persephone, daughter of Demeter. One day, the four of them were running through some fields together, playing some musical version of Marco Polo, when Persephone went missing. None of them knew at the time that there was a bounty on her, made by the king of the Underworld. He wanted her as his own.

"My mother and her two remaining friends were given wings and special abilities by Demeter so that they might search for Persephone with greater speed. When they failed to find her, their wings were painfully removed, and they were cursed to stay on an island that rises out of the water among rocky bluffs. They can communicate just like we can, but when they sing, their voices carry over the rocks and water for several miles." He has a far-off look in his eyes, like it's a memory for him. But, that can't be...

Or can it? I don't even know what to believe anymore.

"So, that part of Greek Mythology is true?"

"There is no Greek Mythology." He says this so sharply that immediately after he says it, he apologizes. "Sorry, I just get tired of all the pretending. What I mean is there is only a partial truth in what we know of it."

His stony expression reinforces his words. He is adamant, so adamant that I begin to understand. He's desperate for someone to share the load of his burden. The cracks in his usual armor are starting to expand, and I'm beginning to see the real Vander emerge underneath. He bites his lower lip as if he is exposed and waiting for me to laugh.

I won't do that. He's truly a scared little boy with a confusing history, and nobody around him actually knows his struggles, except for his dad. This makes Kenzie-Grace's story come to the front of my mind.

"Your mother's *family* that is threatening you isn't really her family, is it?"

"It's the only group of people she has now, besides my dad. If they hadn't visited her, nobody would have. Demeter likes to visit the island in the Northern Winter when Persephone is in the Underworld, just to hear them sing. Persephone visits in the Northern Summer and brings them gifts for their entertainment. My dad tries to go at least once every year, which is easier now that I can take care of myself while he is gone."

"But how can he go there? Don't people die because of Sirens?"

"That's where it gets tricky." He presses his back against the locker and slides down to a sitting position on the floor. "People die because they focus so much on the songs and getting closer to the sound that they forget to pilot their boats and ships through the rocky waters. They end up damaging their vessels, and they can't return home. My dad used to be a sea captain of his own boat. He was recruited about twenty years ago to plot the area surrounding my mother's island. He used his sharp eyesight and increased sense of balance to safely pilot around dangerous waters. He's never been affected by the sound of the Sirens, because he can't hear it."

"That makes sense!" The wheels are still continuing to turn in my head, but at least they are connected now, working together to create a useful gear. I'm pacing back and forth to use up some of my nervous energy generating from learning all of this information. Vander's eyes follow me, while his hand is on his necklace, running the stone back and forth as I go. "Okay, so how did they communicate?"

"They wrote to one another. A lot, evidently. Until he was able to teach her to sign. My dad is her first love, and she is his. My mother is beautiful and compassionate. She used to try to save the sailors who made it to the island in bad shape. But the three Sirens would fight over the men's attentions and use their abilities on them, driving them insane—to the point that they would jump off the cliff onto the rocks below. It was too painful, so she learned to just lull the injured ones to sleep to ease their suffering."

That makes me sad. *How many deaths over the years has she had to witness?*

"Wait! Your dad is a talented sailor, and yet you live in *Iowa*? Why?"

"My mom told my dad that it is vital that I choose where I live, and they both agreed I would be safest away from the sea. Water enhances the abilities that my mother passed down to me. They will continue to evolve until my next birthday. At least, that is what Demeter seems to believe. There isn't really a precedent for the son of a cursed mythological creature. I'm not a demi-god like Percy Jackson. I'm not exactly a Siren either. I'm just Vander, son of Thelxinoe, cursed handmaiden to Persephone, daughter of Demeter and Zeus."

"Well, that is a mouthful." I laugh to try to lighten the mood. The corners of his mouth turn up, but only for a few seconds. "But, you aren't human, you can do things humans can't do. Do you want to tell me how I can help? Or maybe fill me in on what threat you have hanging over your head?"

He's quiet for a moment, and I decide that my pacing could be making this harder for him. I sit down next to him in the hall. He drops his head to his arms resting across his knees. We wait in silence as one of the security guards walks by, then nods at the pass Vander holds up without saying a thing to either of us. After he passes, Vander lifts his head back up and turns to me.

"Demeter has told me that I will need to survive a month on the island without any interference from her or my mother. In order to do so, I will need to fully understand my powers and be able to use them without hesitation. I need to learn as much about my abilities as I can, because my mother can't guarantee that the other two Sirens are going to cooperate. That means that I may throw myself off of a cliff if things don't go well."

"Has that ever happened when you've visited your mom before?"

"I've never visited my mom before; her sister Sirens could kill me with their song. There is a fair amount of jealousy about the fact my mom has a man to love and a son while the only visitor they ever get is Persephone. I have not been anywhere near their island since the day I was born." There is sadness in his tone, like he is embarrassed to admit that. "It's not like I can just call her whenever I want, either. My dad goes to visit a couple times a year and my only other real connection to her is Demeter."

My heart drops into my stomach. I know what it's like to miss a parent. I think I'm starting to understand this guy a bit more.

"So that's why you practice using your abilities so much, so you can survive meeting your mom. Is that why you need to know why you can't charm me? There's a loophole somewhere, and I am standing in it." Things are starting to click into place in my mind.

"Exactly." His eyes are pleading with me now, like his voice has already done twice before. "So far, anyone who can resist my charms fit into three categories and I need to know if you fit into one of those, or if there is a fourth category I need to figure out."

"How can I know, without a doubt, that you are not playing an elaborate joke on me, with the help of my friends, Coach, and my mom?"

I've pulled a lock of hair out of my bun, and I'm twisting the hell out of it.

He grabs my hand, and then holds it in a handshake sort of way while looking directly into my eyes.

"I solemnly swear, I have shared the truth with you. The whole truth, and nothing but the truth about how I came to be, who I am, and what is going to happen to me." He didn't even blink, or make a hint of looking away. I lift our hands to shake them without looking away, either. He uses his free hand to wipe a tear from his face. My heart breaks a little bit, and now I know for sure that I have to help him with all I've got. Maybe helping him will help me figure out what's different about me, too. But, for now, I need to lighten the mood again.

"I will do everything within my *human* power to help you with your—"

"Quest?" he offers.

"Yes, your quest. But I need your help with something as well."

"You do?" He scoffs, then clears his throat. "I mean, how can I help you?"

"Someone on the team posted a picture of me passed out in Lissy's lap yesterday at the pool. I want it taken down."

Anger rolls off of him in waves; his fists are clenched and his teeth are grinding together. "Someone is going to pay for that. Consider it done. Anything else?"

"Not that I can think of at the moment, but you can owe me. And while I'm thinking of it, I will not help you with the other thing. So don't ask."

He puts his head to the side. "What thing are you talking about?"

"The replacing the school flag, silly. You are *so* going down." I adjust the collar of my sweater to make sure he can see the color of the strap beside it. He groans in what I choose to believe is frustration, but quickly follows it up with a laugh. "Also, I won't be helping you win the race today, no matter how much you beg."

We laugh out loud together for a few seconds, and it is only then I realize he is still holding my other hand. When I look down at it, my stomach does some weird flip-thing.

"We'll have to see about that." He stands and helps pull me to my feet. Before he lets go, he poses a serious question. "Friends?"

"Friends," I reply. "Though I can't promise not to verbally spar with you every once in a while for the sake of my own mental health."

He chuckles and then gets a serious look back on his face. "Can you start helping me by keeping your phone on and answering my messages?"

"Oh shit! I haven't turned my phone on since yesterday!" I pull my hand from his to dig frantically through my bag. I find my phone, and turn airplane mode off. While I wait for the messages to stop popping up, I check the time. Class is almost over. But I don't mind. I've learned more during this hour than I've learned in my entire high school career.

CHAPTER THIRTEEN

My nerves have returned in anticipation of today's race. The excess energy I might have had from getting a good night's sleep must have been spent talking with Vander instead. I had a good lunch today, to help fuel my body, and then I had a chocolate bar from the German club's fundraiser, but I came down from that sugar rush with a crash. Splashing cold water on my face seems to be helping, but I feel worse than I do on a regular meet day. I don't know what's wrong with me.

Suddenly, one of the texts from Vander that showed up on my phone from yesterday comes to mind.

Vander: The hot water thing may have been my fault. Sorry about that.

I pull my phone from my pocket to text him back.

Me: That hot water thing was your fault? Please tell me what

you mean and whether I can expect the same to happen today?
Vander: It's kind of hard to explain because it has to do with projecting my powers. I didn't even know I was doing it, but I will try not to do it again today. I think you will be okay anyway because you won't be in the water with me as long as you were yesterday.
Me: You'd better do more than try.
Vander: I won't do it. You will be fine.

I hope he's right about that. Before I can respond, another message comes through.

Vander: I took care of the photo thing. That won't happen again.
Me: Thank you.

I smile, knowing that awful picture is gone. I put my phone away as I proceed to get ready for the race.

Lissy walks into the locker room whistling just as I finish putting my suit on. I watch as she opens several of the team lockers and dangles a loop of red satin ribbon from each of them. It looks very suspect, as if any of these lockers could hold the treasure.

"That's actually genius. Where did you come up with that idea, Lissy?"

"Well, this beautiful thing on top of my shoulders is not just a hat rack, my friend." *I love her so much.* "We are going to win both competitions today. Julia, you've got this! Swim hard, girl."

That pep talk is exactly what I need to get over this funk. My phone vibrates in my open locker with another text from Vander.

Vander: Good luck, friend.

The message brings a warm smile to my face. At that, Lissy looks over my shoulder, but I don't care. I have nothing to hide.

Me: Good luck to you, too, friend.

"What the hell, Julia? Are you making a move on Vander now? I thought you had better things to do than worry about relationships," she attempts to mimic my voice when she says that, "and then *bam*! You set your sights on the hottest guy at our school? Oh man, I so have to tell Taylor right now!" She already has her phone in her hands.

"Whoa! Hold your horses and all the pretty little ponies, too. I am not making a move on anyone. We've agreed to a truce to work on a school project together. That's all. Don't get too carried away in your fangirl brain, making this into something it's not."

"'That's all,' my ass! I saw that smile on your face. I haven't seen that look since our end-of-summer bonfire when I suggested that we make s'mores with double fudge brownies instead of chocolate and graham crackers."

I can't help the big smile that lights up my face at the memory of that delicious mess.

"*See*? There it is again. You *like* Vander, and it has nothing to do with some mysterious project. You should know by now, you can't lie to me. Who do you think you're fooling?" She resumes tapping out a message to Taylor, and for some reason, I don't stop her.

She can't be right, can she?

No.

No?

No. Absolutely not.

"I don't have the time, not to mention the desire, to be interested in anyone.

We are friends, and we will complete this mythological project and then go about our lives again. Our *separate* lives."

She scoffs at me. "Whatever you say, Juliet. Whatever you say." She doesn't even bother sounding the least bit convinced.

"Wait! Did you just call me *Juliet*? What the hell?"

"If ever there were star-crossed lovers at this school, you and Romeo Thelxinoe are definitely it." She laughs as she makes her way out to the pool, leaving me behind.

"Traitor!" I shout at her, but the door closes, so I don't hear her response. I have always thought she understood me better than this.

My phone goes back in my locker. When I close the locker, I make sure that my actual red bra strap is hanging out like the dummy straps Lissy arranged. It's time to get my head in the game. *I have a race to win.*

I walk out to the pool in my warm-ups, carrying my meet towel with "Wright" on it, my goggles, and my swim cap. The stretches are already in progress. I join in, making sure I avoid eye contact with my new friend, lest Lissy accuse me of making bedroom eyes at him or something.

After stretching, we all get in the pool for some warm-up laps. I don't push myself too hard, because there is no last-minute benefit that will help just before a race. The water feels good and refreshing today. I hope Vander keeps his power projection under control for the next fifteen minutes or so.

After ten minutes, Coach chirps her whistle a couple short times and lists off the names of those who are participating in the race today. Other than Vander, Wesley, and me, there are three other guys who've asked to swim. Two of them are freshman who probably just want to get their first high school racing experience behind them. Then, there is Miles Udell, whom I like a lot, largely because he dislikes Vander as much as I do…

Did?

Oh, crap.

Coach gives us all lane numbers and tells us to get ready. I put my swim cap on and grab my towel, but I don't bother using it to dry off. I will be getting back in the water soon enough. Wesley comes alongside me and nudges me on the way to the starting blocks. It's friendly and I don't mind it at all, somehow.

"Good luck. I think you'll do great."

"Thanks, Wesley. Good luck to you, too."

I turn to see if Lissy caught that interaction and is now going to accuse me of going after Wesley, too. We *hugged* earlier this week for crying out loud, and she didn't make this big of a deal out of it. But she's watching someone else. I check to see who, and end up looking into those familiar blue-green eyes. He gives me a double thumbs-up, and I return the gesture.

"'Oh Romeo, Romeo, wherefore art thou, Romeo?'" I hear Lissy tease behind me. I give her a glare, but it's totally ineffective on her. One of the reasons I love her is because she doesn't play into what other people think—she goes her own way.

Without missing a beat, Wesley chimes in, "'But soft, what light through yonder window breaks? It is the east, and Juliet the sun.'"

As soon as he's finished, a sophomore named Dan yells, "Gnomeo! Oh, Gnomeo!"

Before anyone else can add his own line or two of Shakespeare references into the mix, Coach chirps her whistle and reminds us to get focused. She has a point.

I get to my starting block and lay my towel across it so that my name hangs over the edge of the pool. I do a few last-minute stretches to make sure my arms and legs are loose. Then, I bounce around a little bit to get amped up and to get my blood pumping.

Lissy comes to my lane, telling Wesley on the way, "Good luck, but you'd better not beat my best friend."

She stands behind me and gives my shoulders a quick squeeze. "You've got this! Just swim your own race."

"That's the plan." I crack my neck to the left and right to make sure I'm able to breathe in both directions when I get in. Then I pull my arms straight across my chest one at a time.

Lissy turns to the swimmer on the other side of me and winks. Then she blows several kisses while shimmying her chest at him. Instead of making me angry, it makes me want to laugh, but I don't dare piss Coach Winter off. Vander must not have been looking, because Lissy is bold, but not all that forthcoming. I'm pulling my leg up behind me to stretch my quads when it evidently reminds Lissy of something else she wanted to say.

"Oh, and kick some ass!" She grins at me devilishly.

Coach blows her whistle for real, not a chirp this time, and uses a megaphone to ask, "Swimmers, are you ready?"

That's our signal to step up onto our blocks. Coach reminds the guys they are to swim an individual medley, and I am to swim all four laps freestyle.

Her booming megaphone voice says, "Swimmers, take your mark."

Then she sounds the horn. We all tuck our heads between our arms and push off. Well, I assume we are *all* doing that, but I only know for sure that I am in the water. Currently, I'm still underwater, using my dolphin kick to propel myself while maintaining a streamline position below the surface.

When I take my first breath in another few seconds, I will glance over to the lane on my right to see where Wesley is in the water, too. The splash of his butterfly stroke should be plain to see if he is anywhere near me. On my second breath, I will try to see where I am in relation to Vander on my other side.

Just as I kick my way to the surface and start in with a flutter kick and windmill strokes, it dawns on me that *Operation Underwear* is also happening right now!

I take my breath and see splashing, which means I'm not alone in the water and I'm also not falling too far behind. The girls should be making their way into the men's locker room right about now. Maddie and Taylor were in charge of making sure there is no interference from any male coaches or other school staff. Kenzie-Grace is the one leading the small team of seekers. She knows

Vander's personality best and would be able to think through any mousetraps he may have set for us.

It's time for my second breath, and there are splashes on my right as well. I'm grateful that I can see them. The butterfly stroke is pretty fast, especially a male's versus a female's freestyle. But any ground I lose here, I should be able to make up during their backstroke and breaststroke laps.

My first flip turn is perfect—I'm definitely feeling the same smoothness I felt yesterday. Additionally, the water temperature is cool and refreshing, unlike during the last practice. This is going to be a great race for me, regardless if I touch out the guys or not.

Kenzie-Grace wore our team prize home last night, washed it, and, according to the rules, had to wear it back to school. But then she met up with Maddie and gave it to her.

Right before my second flip turn, I see splashes coming off the wall in the lane next to me. Vander must have beaten me in that first leg, and he's now on his backstroke. I have two laps to catch up before we race head to head for the last fifty yards, both swimming freestyle.

Personally, I don't like doing the individual medley. The butterfly wears me out so much that the other strokes suffer because of it. But it's Vander's best event, and it makes sense that he's a good swimmer, now that I know where he comes from. He mentioned something about seawater potentially affecting his powers. *Maybe chlorinated water positively enhances his strength?*

I like to think things through while I swim as a way to ignore the ache building in my muscles. Some people have songs in their head, some people have a checklist for their body or stroke, and others swim in relative silence with nothing but the rush of water in their ears. I've found that thinking helps me the most, especially if I have a puzzle to work on.

Vander is nothing if not puzzling.

I see an arm sticking out of the water slightly behind me on a breath, and deduce that Wesley must have the same problem I have with losing steam a bit after fifty yards of the butterfly. I won't count him out, though—he's a co-captain for a reason. That reason being he never gives up, and he knows how to rally.

I can't see Vander when I breathe on the other side, and I decide it's time to put my head fully in the game. I make sure my hand is slicing through the water like a hot blade through butter as it cuts the surface. Pulling all of my upper body with each stroke and kicking just a little bit harder has me propelling down the lane at a pretty good clip. I feel good—a lot like I felt yesterday, before the water got hot and I passed out.

I keep hoping Vander has control of whatever it is that was causing the water to heat up. When I complete my fourth flip turn to start my third freestyle lap, I realize that this lap is my last chance to catch up to Vander and pass him. Because when we get to that final lap, he will be able to finish strong and win. I do not want to give him the satisfaction—friends or not.

My first breath has me pulling even with Vander's breaststroke frog kick. I decide to take my next breath on the same side so I can see my progress. Wanting there to be a lot, I push harder. By the time I breathe, I'm even with his hands. I could be mistaken, but I could swear he was turned toward me to see how well he was doing, just like I am. After this flip turn, I am going to stop looking—Coach preaches how bad this habit is, but a lot of us do it anyway. We can't help ourselves. At this point, I just have to do my best and hope it is enough.

I really hope the girls are successfully completing their mission. This race will only last for about two minutes, though it feels like a lifetime when I'm the one in the water. It's only been about thirty minutes since I left the locker room, giving Vander's cohorts (whomever they may be) the same amount of time to capture his "flag" and run it up the pole. I think they will find it somewhat difficult to locate.

When I start my final lap, I'm in the zone. I feel like I'm flying through the water. As my head pulls to the side to suck in oxygen, I close my eyes so I am not even tempted to gauge my position in relation to the other swimmers.

My final flip turn is the best one I've done today, and I'm like a missile launching off the wall. My arms feel like a windmill in a tornado, they are slicing so quickly into the water and back around through the air. When I have the wall in my sights, I pull the last ounce of special reserve energy from every single muscle in my body to ensure I hit the wall as hard and as fast as I can. It feels like I am attached to a bungee cord by the way my body recoils. I immediately turn, only to find Vander turning to me, as if he is my mirror image.

Coach is positioned between my starting block and Vander's when I finally have the energy to look up that far. There are no times on the board, but she has her stopwatch in her hand and she looks pleased—which is rare. If the purpose of this event was to motivate the team, I think we can count that as a success, if the cheers and applause coming from all of them are any indication.

When I look over to Vander, he is nearly breathless and amazed at the reaction of everyone. Wesley looks the same. I honestly don't know who finished first, because I have had to work so hard to catch my breath. She keeps clicking splits every time another guy touches the wall.

"If this were a swim meet, we would have two new pool records. Thelxinoe, that was the fastest I.M., and Wright, that was the fastest two hundred free for the women! I'm so proud of you both!" *No wonder she looks pleased.* The smile on my face would be broader if I could breathe, and also if I didn't think Vander's special abilities were somehow responsible.

"As for who touched the wall first—Julia, you had him by mere tenths of a second. Nice swimming, Wright! Maybe you can beat her next time, Thelxinoe." *Wait!* Who said there would be a next time?

Vander reaches over the lane line to congratulate me. Wesley does the same from the other side. And then Lissy is hovering above, telling me how fast I looked in my final twenty-five yards.

I'm still wheezing a bit when Vander gets out of the pool. Lissy puts her hand down to help me out, and I take it. When I'm finally upright, I look around and see Vander entering the men's locker room with Wesley. *Uh-oh, I hope the girls are done in there.* I see the same look of concern on Lissy's face that I am sure is on my own.

Just before we make our way to the women's locker room to get an update, we hear the squeak of the spectator door to the bleachers above the pool. Coach hears it, too, no doubt, but when we look up to see who it is, all we see is a carefully manicured hand giving us a thumbs-up.

"This is a closed practice!" Coach shouts, and then adds to herself, "I could have sworn I locked those doors."

It's no mystery to us how the door was opened—Grant let us borrow his keys again for this worthy cause. I'm sure seeing Vander Thelxinoe's undershorts flying around in the breeze for all to see had something to do with his eagerness to help us out. I give Lissy a high five and add this success to the list of reasons why I'm going to eat a pan of double fudge brownies tonight.

CHAPTER FOURTEEN

Lissy and I walk as quickly as possible to the locker room without drawing attention to ourselves. I think the team managers can take a short break to find out what the thumbs up was all about. After all, it was my fast pace that got Vander to give his best-ever effort in the pool tonight.

I slap my hand over my mouth as I enter, because the locker room is a chaotic mess. My red bra is in the middle of the floor, and all of Lissy's red ribbons are scattered there as well. It's obvious someone was looking everywhere. Vander must have some allies outside of the swim team helping him out with only a picture of Maddie's bra to go on. Several lockers have been left open, and others have been emptied out, but slammed shut. I step into the bathroom and find that one of the stalls is occupied with someone who is crying.

"Lissy, get in here!" I'm not very good at being around crying girls, but Lissy seems to speak their language fluently.

"What is it? I'm trying to clean up in here."

I point at Maddie's moccasins under the stall door, and Lissy nods in understanding. I'm good with putting up with her hysterics, and she's good at helping me with my tears. When I see someone else cry, it reminds me of the weeks I spent flooded by my own tears when we lost my dad. I can't handle that right now and back away. I know Lissy is the best person for the task of comforting someone who needs it.

I start cleaning up the ribbons and tossing them in the trash. My hand is halfway in my locker, putting my bra back with my clothes, when I remember the reason we came in here in the first place. My phone is lit up with messages, and, for once, I'm anxious to read them instead of ignore them. Taylor must have been assigned the task of sending the updates.

Taylor: We are in the locker room but something is not right. There is a sign in here that says, 2 can play this game!
Taylor: We got all of the lockers open, but every single one has a pair of patriotic boxers in them. They are all different flag boxers and Maddie can't decide which ones are Vander's!
Taylor: We are taking them all!
Taylor: Heading to Mr. Brandt's room just to make sure there aren't more in there.
Taylor: Glad we checked, there was a grocery bag full of patriotic boxers in here too.
Taylor: Checking school lockers just in case.
Taylor: Yep! 2 more pairs in Vander's locker.
Taylor: We have about 30 pairs of boxers now. Maddie has it narrowed down to 5 pairs. We have a plan. Heading to Home Ec.
Taylor: Just sayin' Kenzie-Grace is a wizard with a sewing machine.
Taylor: DONE! YOU WON'T BELIEVE HOW AWESOME THIS LOOKS!!!
Taylor: A pic won't do it justice, but we took some anyway

with Kenzie-Grace holding her phone up showing the date and time just to prove we did it first.

As I'm heading back into the bathroom to share the news with Lissy and Maddie, the locker room door bursts open. Vander and Wesley storm inside, followed closely by Taylor. The former two have a look of disgust on their faces, and the latter has a look of smug victory.

Vander is the first to speak. "Where is Maddie?"

"What's up, Vander? Are you going to be a sore loser, or are you going to concede gracefully?" Taylor demands.

"She shouldn't have been able to win this game!" Vander says to all of us, but with a pointed look at me. It takes me a second, but then I put it together—I asked Maddie to keep music playing in her ears to protect herself against Vander's charm if she saw him today. *It must have worked.*

"It's not what you think, Vander. But evidently, it's exactly like how *I* thought it would be. You never had any intention of losing this game." I grab his arm to keep him from going into the bathroom and confronting Maddie while she is still a puddle of tears.

"Of course not! Why would I play I game I didn't think I could win?" The look he gives me doesn't match what comes out of his mouth; I can tell his concern is about what she was able to do.

"Okay, look. I may not know why you can't charm me, but I can tell you exactly why you lost twice today." I smile at those words. Then a glance at Wesley tells me he knows exactly what we are talking about. *How come I get sworn to secrecy about who he is and what he can do, but Wesley gets a front-row seat?* Not to mention, Taylor is now hearing all of this, too. "But later, when it's appropriate. I want you to trust me on this."

My nod to Taylor and then back to where Lissy and Maddie are seems to click in his brain.

"Right, well—congratulations. I will deliver the prize on Monday morning."

He turns around and leaves the room. Wesley hangs back.

"Oh, hey, Julia?"

"Yeah, Wesley?"

"Great swim today!" Wesley smiles before Vander bodily yanks him back out through the door.

I shout, "Thanks! You too!" to a closing locker room door.

The next thing I hear is Coach's bellowing.

"What in the world is taking you so long? Are you shaving your legs for a hot date or something?" But when she steps past the shower room to where I'm standing amongst all the lockers, she looks down her nose at me. "Is there a reason you aren't getting dressed right now?"

"I, um—I couldn't find my bra."

Taylor adds, "And I was helping her look for it."

Coach looks from me, to Taylor, to my open locker, and then back to me.

"Do you mean the bright-red one sitting right on top of your clothes pile in there?"

"Oh, wow! Yeah, thanks for the help!" One look at her is all it takes to let me know Coach is not buying what I'm selling.

Lissy, who makes a spectacle of herself on a regular basis, walks out of the bathroom, fanning her behind with both hands. "Whoo-whee! Do *not* go in there!"

Taylor and I stifle our laughs, but Coach gives up on trying to figure us out. She turns and walks back out to the pool, shouting, "Lissy, bring an ice pack stat!" over her shoulder.

We all bust out laughing when the pool door closes. I may never get the image of a mermaid-haired Lissy fanning her ass to get rid of Coach by pretending she had just dropped a rotten deuce.

"Okay, but seriously, don't go in there. Maddie just needs some time to herself." Lissy is such a good protector. Whatever is going on with Maddie, I'm sure Lissy helped her through it better than I could have. That's what she has always done for me.

"Thanks, Lissy, for everything. You're the best." I stand up and put an arm around her. She doesn't even mind my wet swimsuit getting on her. She just huffs some air on her fingernails and polishes them on her shirt.

"That's what friends are for. Now, get dressed!" She playfully pushes me away and chuckles. "I have to get some ice, stat!"

The sound of Lissy mocking Coach makes me laugh again as she walks out to go across the hall.

"I can't wait for you to see what we did to their boxer shorts!" Taylor says as she holds up her phone to me and I zero in on the photo.

Kenzie-Grace has sewn them together, hip to hip and leg to leg. Four rows of seven pairs of teen boy underwear created a giant, quilted pattern of Old Glory. There is something so very *glorious* indeed about the fact that we won in such a massive way. It honestly has to be the coolest-looking flag they've ever had flying above Eisenhower High School, by far.

Waiting until practice is over to go and see it with my own eyes is going to be hard. The satisfaction I feel about winning both the race and this ridiculous underwear challenge is off the charts.

Coach doesn't really ask much of Lissy or me today. We end up timing some laps, and then putting the kickboards away. After Lissy got the ice for Wesley's shoulder, there was no other need for us to leave the pool. Maybe that is what Coach was aiming for, come to think of it.

As soon as we are released for the day, we get giddy and practically gallop out of the locker room on our way to the flagpole. We aren't even out the door when we catch our first glimpse through the window in the door, and are capturing it on our iPhones. *It's humongous!* It's easily twice the size of the flag that normally waves there, possibly even three times as big.

Wesley and Vander walk out of the gym doors a few minutes into our cell phone photo shoot. Vander joins us, just shaking his head. The four of us are standing there, looking in the same direction, and it reminds me of one of those nursery scenes in the movies. I nudge Vander's shoulder from beside him and ask, "So, proud papa, which one is yours?"

Lissy laughs out loud, and even Wesley can't maintain a straight face. I notice Vander biting his lip, too, trying to keep his laughter in. He loses the battle. Suddenly, the absolute insanity of what we are looking at just takes over. I don't realize how hard I'm laughing until I end up on my knees, and Vander is asking if I am okay.

"She always does that when she laughs too hard," Lissy manages to form words before I am able to get my own mouth to cooperate.

"She does that a lot?" Wesley asks Lissy. She nods, because I'm still not fully functioning. In fact, it may take another minute before I'm able to make it to my feet.

"My theory is that because she sleeps so much, her body will find any excuse to take a nap. Whenever she's laughing like that or crying hard, she loses control of her muscles. I keep warning her that if she doesn't get a grip, she will be one of those ladies who pee their pants every time they laugh, sneeze, or cough."

Vander's head tweaks to the side, like what she said reminded him of something. It has a strangely sobering effect on me. *I don't want anyone thinking about me peeing my pants*. I make my way to my feet and turn to face him completely.

"What's that look for?"

He doesn't answer, and at first I think it's because he didn't hear me, but then I see the way he looks to Lissy and Wesley before making eye contact with me.

"Do you guys want to go out to eat with us?" Wesley breaks the silence.

Lissy nearly squeals, but somehow manages to play it cool. "I think we would love to. Wouldn't we, Julia?"

I can't read the look in Vander's eyes because it didn't change when Wesley or Lissy spoke—he doesn't even seem to be blinking.

"I think that would be nice?" I answer, unsure. I want to know if Vander is interested in eating with us before I agree whole-heartedly. "But we have plans with Taylor tonight, so either count her in, or count us out."

"The more the merrier. Is Mexican okay with you guys?" Wesley offers.

"I sure do love free chips and salsa! We'll meet you there," Lissy replies.

On the way to my car, I send Taylor a text.

Me: We are all going to Carlos O'Kelly's with Vander and Wesley.

Me: We're on the way to pick you up. Be ready!

Taylor's response looks like she just sat on her phone for a minute. I show it to Lissy, who translates it from fangirl to English.

Taylor: SDFJKL:JADSFOIYDUFIOWAEJFLKAJSDF!!!!!!

"She's excited."

Of course she is. I can't help but consider the fact that last weekend, Lissy and Taylor were stalking Vander and Wesley's Instagram accounts, and now this weekend, we are going out to eat with them. I've always heard that high school offers a unique and strange experience. I'm beginning to understand what people mean by that.

CHAPTER FIFTEEN

Carlos's is extremely busy, but when Vander tells the host we are a party of five, we get led to a booth right away. It makes me wonder how many hostesses he has charmed in Cedar Rapids so he wouldn't have to wait. *They probably remember him, and have an innate urge to do what he wants.* That thought of so many people having their minds messed with disgusts me. I slide into the left side of the booth and find it curious when Vander slides in next to me.

Taylor and Lissy are on the other side, with Wesley. I start looking through the menu and I don't even know why, because I always get the same thing, every time we come here.

"I highly recommend the chicken chimichanga," Vander says without even picking up his menu.

"What a coincidence. That's what I usually get, too." I put my menu down as Lissy rolls her eyes at me. She hates that I'm so predictable when it comes to food. I guess I get that from my mom. I just find comfort in knowing what to expect.

Our chips and salsa arrive after a few minutes. Vander immediately pulls one of the two salsa bowls to our side of the table. Then he does something I wouldn't have thought I'd enjoy in a million years—he puts his arm on the back of the booth behind me. It feels intimate, and I don't hate it.

Something must be very wrong with me. A shiver runs down my spine, and I choose to ignore it and eat some chips.

My first bite goes down the wrong tube, and I start coughing all over the place. Vander hits me on the back. Every pat makes my head jut forward, but the chip isn't moving from where it has taken up residence in my throat.

"We need some water over here, *stat*!" Lissy yells at no one person in particular, and Wesley hops up to go find some.

"Relax your shoulders!" Vander shouts at me.

It's the dumbest thing I've ever heard, which might be why it works. I do what he says, and when my shoulders go down, I feel my throat let go of the chip and it goes down, as well. It's like all of my tension was holding that chip in place. Wesley returns with some water, and I gratefully gulp it. It feels soothing all the way down.

Vander takes the cup from me to set it back on the table while he rubs my back with his other hand. He leans in so close that the hair next to my face moves with the force of his breathing. He pours a few drops of my water out on the table and dips his fingers in it while humming softly. Then he puts those fingers on my throat, and I immediately feel a soothing warmth radiating from there. My eyes meet his, and he smiles reassuringly as he puts both of his hands back in his own lap.

"Are you all right?" Taylor asks. The look in her eyes is part awe and part jealousy. She is shoved in against the wall, watching me and Vander interact, while Lissy at least has Wesley on her other side.

I nod in response to her question, just as our waiter arrives with five glasses of water. After setting them down, he takes out a notepad and pen. "Are you ready to order?"

He looks first to Vander, who turns to me as if asking for permission. I nod. "We will both have the chicken chimichanga."

I don't think anyone has ever ordered for me before. It's kind of nice. Telling the waiter what I want to eat isn't that big of a deal, but it *feels* like more than that somehow. It feels like Vander is taking an opportunity to tell the group that he knows what I want, and he is going to get it for me. *Why the hell do I care about that?*

I wish I didn't—but I do. *Ugh!*

I start to grab another chip, but change my mind.

"Um, I have to go to the bathroom," I announce to the whole table in an awkward way, and then not-so-subtly motion for the girls to follow me if they know what's good for them.

"Excuse us, please."

"Just promise us you aren't going to skip out and leave us with the bill," Wesley jokes, but Vander looks at me nervously, showing a bit of fear that we might actually be doing that.

"I promise," I say solemnly as I walk away, trying to comprehend the look of relief on his face at my words. That thought makes me walk a little faster to the place where my girls can hopefully provide some answers for me.

"All right, biotches, I have a problem. There is something wrong with me, making me act weird and feel—*things*."

Taylor's mouth drops open and her eyes widen. It is the exact reaction I'm expecting.

"First of all, we know there is something wrong with you, but we love you anyway." Lissy never makes me feel like being different is bad. "Second of all, you are going to need to be more specific."

"I don't know what to say." I'm totally out of breath. "How do you guys handle this? I mean, how do you ... you know? I can't even..." My brain doesn't have an ending for that sentence.

Taylor and Lissy exchange startled looks with each other before turning to me. Then, Taylor exclaims, "Did you just 'can't even' us right now?"

I put my hands on the counter to steady my suddenly dizzy self. My vision is narrowing.

"Whoa, Julia, just breathe. No need to hyperventilate. Let's just stick to the facts, here. What is it you're feeling?" Breathing does help. The dizziness recedes. *I love Lissy so much at times like these.*

"Well, when Vander put his arm around me, I liked it. And we all know *that's* not normal for me. Then, when he put his fingers on my throat after I choked—which was also weird—I wanted him to leave them there, and even missed his touch when he took it away." I haven't been able to look them in the eye since I started talking, instead making myself busy fixing my hair in the mirror. *Wait*—my hair that I don't give a shit about is suddenly my top priority? *WTF?*

The silence in the bathroom forces me to look at them. They are standing right behind me, one on either side, and they are looking at each other like they are in shock.

"*What*? It's not like I just won the lottery or something. Why are you so silent? What's going on here? Do you know what's wrong with me?"

"Honey, I don't know how to tell you this, but you have a major crush on Vander Thelxinoe," Taylor puts it to me simply.

"What? No! That's crazy. I—" don't like him at all, I want to say, but can't find my voice. He makes me so crazy and he's not even normal.

"You want to date Vander Thelxinoe, and kiss him, and marry him, and make babies with him!" Taylor adds.

Okay, ew. No, that can't be what's happening. Can it? I watch my own eyes widen in the mirror.

The two of them start jumping up and down, holding hands, and I vaguely comprehend that they are singing some ridiculous song about my milkshake bringing boys to the yard. Meanwhile, my life as I know it is over when I realize they are right. This is the feeling I have somehow avoided my whole life—*liking a boy as more than a friend.*

Now I know there is definitely something wrong with me. My first crush ever, and it's on someone like Vander Thelxinoe? *The guy who changes people's minds, literally?* Somewhere inside of me is a minion laughing his ass off for his part in giving me a crush on Vander Thelxinoe, of all people. My cheeks are turning red at the realization and my heart is racing. I can't believe this is my real life.

The girls stop their celebrating long enough to bring down my anxiety. It involves a cold, wet paper towel and lots of breathing. Taylor also takes the opportunity to remind me that, "It could be worse."

"How? How could it possibly be *worse*? My body has somehow decided to become attracted to the rudest, jerkiest, most self-obsessed, penis-packing person at Eisenhower High School—against my will, I might add. So please, for the love of all things holy and unholy under the sun, tell me *how* could this be any worse?"

Lissy shrugs and offers a simple answer, "Well, it would be worse if he didn't like you back."

"*What?*"

"He sat next to you, and he put his arm around you. He ordered for you, panicked when you choked, and looked sad when he thought you were going to leave. Those are just the signs from the last ten minutes. Need I say more?"

I don't know how those things mean that he likes me, but I will have to defer to my friends, who know more about these things than I do. *Oh my word, Vander Thelxinoe likes me.*

The thought of that used to make me want to hurl, but now I find I'm smiling. Taylor looks in my eyes, like she's seeing me for the first time. I look away from her into the mirror and realize I'm crying at the same time.

"Honestly, Julia, you are acting like it's a bad thing, or unnatural somehow. Being a teenage girl that doesn't care about relationships is the unusual thing. This—" Taylor's struggling to find the appropriate word for what's going on here, and I can't say that I blame her. None of the words I'm coming up with would be appropriate in a PG-13 movie. "—*potential* start to a relationship between you and Vander is actually the most normal thing I've ever seen you do when it comes to boys."

"Taylor, do you understand how I feel about him? Because I don't. I don't know what's happening here. It's like a battle raging in my head between what I should feel and how I do feel."

"Yeah, I know what you've said about him in the past, but what does that matter? The real question here, the most important question, the question you need to search real deep and find the answer to is—what are you going to do about it?"

My heart sinks to my stomach. I can feel it pulsing beneath the front pocket of my sweatshirt. She's right. I know what I'm feeling. It's all foreign to me, and it may as well be Greek—like my alleged new love interest. So, what *do* I do about it? *Gah!* Why doesn't liking a boy come with an instruction manual?

"You could do a lot worse, you know?" Lissy asks as she hands me a dry paper towel. I use the corner of it to dry my eyes.

"I guess I could fall in love with Mr. Daniels, like you two suck-ups. That would be worse." I nudge Lissy's elbow and manage to put a real smile on my face. "What am I *supposed* to do now?"

Lissy starts to answer, but Taylor interrupts. "You haven't needed our help so far. Why don't you just keep doing what you've been doing, and you'll be fine."

"Yeah, what she said." Lissy links arms with me and leads me out of the bathroom. "You can't hide in here forever."

Back at the table, Vander and Wesley are on their phones. As soon as they see us, they stand up to let us back into the booth and put their phones away. I immediately grab my water and drink every last drop. The ice in the cup splashes forward and wets my whole face.

My nervous giggle is covered up by everyone else's laughter, and for once

I'm actually grateful to be laughed at by my friends.

Lissy engages Wesley in a conversation about the merits of corn versus flour tortilla chips that Taylor seems completely enraptured with, if her leaning in is any indication. It leaves Vander and me to talk amongst ourselves on our side of the table. It also gives me the perfect opportunity to explain why his charm failed on Maddie today.

"Maddie wore earbuds in her ears all day today. They were connected to her MP3 player in her pocket. She was instructed to play it on full blast if she saw you coming, and to keep the music in her ears until you were well out of earshot. When you tried talking to her before school today, she was just nodding along to her music. She didn't hear you."

The look on his face goes from surprised, to irritated, and then lands on concerned as I finish the story.

"How did she know to do that? Did you tell her what I can do?" he whispers to me, no doubt trying to keep our conversation even more private.

"No, but what would you have done if I had? Sued me?"

He shakes his head.

"Kenzie-Grace told me about your birthday last year."

His eyes widen at that revelation, and the vein on the side of his neck engorges. His cheeks turn red, and his eyes are searching mine. He hangs his head after a moment, and I can't help but wonder if he's concerned about what I think of him or if he's planning how to fix it.

"I had to let her go. We weren't supposed to be together. My grandmother made sure I ended it. She has the power to make people fall very ill or even disappear and her moods change as often as Iowa weather, so there's no way I'm going to test her patience."

"Why did you cut Kenzie-Grace out of your life completely? It took a long time for her to get over it." Our whispers are forcing our heads really close together. Lissy and Taylor are keeping Wesley entertained, no doubt to give me time to explore my new feelings.

"I know. Every time you ask me if I am an ass, I think of that. The single most frustrating thing I ever did comes to mind, and I want to shout, 'Yes, I am an asshole!' But I had to push her far away from me. I had to find a way for her to stay away from me, to protect her from my grandmother. It worked out the way it was supposed to, didn't it?" I can feel the bitterness in his tone.

"But why?" I still don't understand.

"Because I care about her, and I wanted to keep her safe. And safe is a long way away from my side."

He straightens, and I can't summon a response to that. His plan is to keep everyone away, and I'm not sure why that doesn't include me. That's been the source of my frustration for years; I couldn't shake him. Is his grandmother going to threaten me?

The arrival of our food ends the hot topic of chip superiority across the table. We all dig in to our meals, accompanied by the sound of conversations at other tables as our background music.

"What are you guys doing tonight?" Vander asks.

Without missing a beat, Lissy replies, totally deadpan, "We're going to the cheap theater to watch our favorite new release one more time. *Death Match: My Little Pony vs. the Care Bears.* What are you guys doing?"

I try to focus on my plate in an effort not to laugh. Taylor laughs before I do, and I glance up to find the most confused looks on Vander and Wesley's faces. It makes me laugh harder. They all join in, and the tension is successfully broken.

"We haven't really decided what we are going to be doing tonight." Wesley looks to Vander and bites his lip. *Is Wesley nervous? Could he be falling for one of my friends?*

"We don't have any definite plans, either. We'll probably end up watching a movie and playing on our phones while we stuff our faces," Lissy explains.

"I have movies," Vander speaks without looking up from his plate. Grinning, he adds, "My dad doesn't even complain if it gets loud. Would you like to come over?"

When he does look up, it's at me. There is hesitation there, but also hope—it's the strangest thing. It's clear that he doesn't know what the right thing to do or say is, and he's obviously not used to that feeling. Using his ability to charm people has probably always saved him from facing rejection.

I don't know what to say, so I don't say anything. Taylor comes to my rescue.

"I think that would be fun, Vander. Doesn't that sound like fun, Julia?" She raises her brows and turns her head up at me to force me to reply.

"Yeah, that would be fun. We'll stop and get some snacks on the way." I look down at my hands.

"Just so you guys know, my brother, Andrew, is going to meet us there. He's on his way home from UNI for the weekend," Wesley responds.

My head snaps up to Taylor, and she blushes. She's frozen, and Lissy has to nudge her to get her to blink. The idea of watching a movie with her crush tonight seems to be overwhelming her.

Wesley leans across Lissy to see what's going on with Taylor. "Is there something I should know? Do you have a problem with Andrew, or something?"

"Um, no. No problem whatsoever. Uh—what movie should we watch?" The pitch of her voice had raised at least two octaves by the time she finished talking. Now it's obvious to everyone what's really going on.

Wesley chuckles to himself, and Vander shakes his head.

The waiter stops at our table to offer us dessert. When we decline, he leaves our checks on the table. He put my dinner on Vander's bill, probably because he ordered for me. I reach in my pocket for some cash, but Vander won't take it from me.

"I've got this." But before I can get too excited, thinking this is a date or something, he adds, "I'll let you get it next time."

Wait, did he just basically promise that we'll be going out to eat together? Again? Soon?

Crap! I hate the way that having a crush is making my brain work. I feel so lame and helpless, waiting for him to make decisions about how *I* will feel. *I need to get over this shit, and fast!*

"If that's how you think it works, then you are mistaken. How would you like it if I paid for you, and left you in debt to me?"

He holds the check out to me in his hand. "Go right ahead, and we'll find out together."

"Um, did you just trick me into buying your dinner?" I don't think that was the response I was anticipating.

"Are you two done?" The others already left the table, and Taylor had to come back to get us. I didn't even realize they had gotten up, let alone walked away far enough for Taylor to have to come back to us.

I am in so much trouble.

"Yeah, I think we're done." Vander smirks. He actually smirks, and I suddenly have the urge to kick him in the shins. I don't.

"Do you guys know where I live?" he asks as he puts several bills on top of our check.

"Yep," Taylor and Lissy say together. *Oh brother, they have probably spent a few nights driving slowly by, hoping to catch a glimpse of Vander in a window or something.*

"Okay. Well, we will see you in a little bit?" It's definitely a question in Vander's voice and not a statement of fact. His eyes are locked on mine, waiting for a reply. Nodding in affirmation, I make my way to my car.

I start the car and wait for Taylor to get in the backseat. Lissy is already in the front, turned around to talk to Taylor. I am one hundred percent sure there is about to be a fangirl freak-out in my car.

They don't let me down.

Taylor starts. "Andrew. Hottie. Brandt? I'm going to watch a movie tonight with Andrew Brandt! I can't even." Oh, but she can, and she will. I know her better than that.

Lissy takes over. "Guys, I actually think Wesley likes me. Like, *likes me* likes me. He kept scootching closer to me in the booth, and his smile lights up my life. I would *die* if he likes me."

Back to Taylor. "I think he likes you too, Lissy. And Vander is way into you, Julia. I can totally tell—it's so obvious. I thought for sure he was going to make out with your ear when you two were whispering back and forth."

Speaking of back and forth, the two of them freaking out like this is a lot like watching a tennis match. Only, I'm not watching—just listening, as I drive us to the drug store for snacks.

Lissy's turn again. "When Wesley said his brother was coming, I thought you had slipped into a coma. Are you sure you can handle this?"

"*No*! I can't even!"

"I can't even, either!"

I can't take it anymore. "Dear God, please give my friends the ability to *even* tonight. It will be majorly awkward if I am the only one able to *even*. Amen."

"Do you think you're funny?" Lissy asks through her laughter.

"Yes, as a matter of fact I do, but you had us all rolling with that movie title tonight. It was hilarious. Where do you come up with this stuff?"

Vander lets us in with a wary eye at all of the bags we are carrying. I really, really want to eat brownies while they are still hot from the oven. I bought a couple of mixes to make a big pan of them, but I wasn't sure if he would have the oil and eggs, let alone the necessary quantities of milk one must consume when enjoying freshly baked brownies. So, I bought it all. And then the girls each bought their own movie-watching necessities as well. It really is quite the haul, but at least nobody will go hungry.

Inside the door of his house, there is an archway into a formal living room that looks like it hasn't been sat in for years. I stand looking around, while my friends wander off with their goodies. There is a piano along one wall, and a fancy couch on another. Above the couch is a beautiful painting of a rolling sea at sunset, with just a hint of land far off in the distance. It makes me feel like I am leaving the place I love most, and like I am heading to the place I love most at the same time. The dueling thoughts are mesmerizing, and I feel enchanted.

"The kitchen is this way." Vander grabs my elbow to direct me away from that room and down the narrow hall straight ahead. We pass a tiny bathroom on the way. The only other option would be to go up the stairs, no doubt to where the bedrooms are located. The idea of checking out Vander's bedroom makes me shiver in a bad way … I think. Shaking my head to chase away the feelings isn't working. I don't care what my body thinks, or that my dark heart must have some pink in it after all. I'm not sure if I am ready to pursue a relationship with Vander Thelxinoe, or if I have any say in it.

Though I'm not sure I do.

I set the bag on his breakfast bar and start unloading it as I listen to the distant sound of Lissy and Taylor arguing with Wesley about what kind of movie we are going to watch tonight drifting up from downstairs. Vander puts the milk in his refrigerator, next to two other full gallons, but he doesn't say a word. When I put the brownie mixes on the counter next to the eggs and oil, I watch a smile break out on his face.

"Brownies are my absolute favorite! Are you planning to share, or will I have to charm your friends into giving me their pieces?"

"I *was* planning to share, until you threatened to mess with my friends' brains again." I give him a stern look. He needs to understand that I am not playing around about that. If he wants my help like he says he does, there needs to be some ground rules. "I'm serious, Vander. If I ever see, or hear, or even have an inkling of an idea that you have charmed my friends again, I will stop trying to help you."

"I know." He sounds resigned, if not defeated. "Don't worry, I get it."

"Good. Then we shouldn't have any problems."

We busy ourselves with the making of the brownies. He gets out a mixing bowl, measuring cups, and starts digging in a lower cabinet for a pan. I get a great view of the back of his jeans, and I'm glad I don't have my phone in my hands, because I wouldn't be able to keep myself from capturing this moment for later viewing.

He stands up with the pan in his hands, and I notice that his blue stone necklace has fallen outside of his shirt. I guess I'm too embarrassed from checking out his fine booty to make actual eye contact now. I walk from the breakfast bar, past the sink, to the stove to busy myself with figuring out how to preheat the oven. When I turn around to make the mix, he is standing right in front of me.

"There's something you should know." He says this like it's extremely important, and it stops me in my tracks. He takes a deep breath and lets it out slowly, like talking is such an effort for him.

"Geez, just tell me. I can't handle all the suspense."

I cross my arms to put a barrier between us and try to laugh it off, but he doesn't let me. He puts his hands on my shoulders and looks right into my eyes. *Why do we always end up touching when we are in kitchens together?* That's it—I'm never going into a kitchen alone with Vander again. That will fix this problem. *What the heck is my mind doing right now?*

"I think there is probably something abnormal going on with your brain."

"Are you kidding me right now? That is harsh!" I try to push him away, but he won't be moved.

"I'm serious. I think it would explain why you can't be charmed."

"What are you talking about?"

"I think you might have a brain disorder."

"Are you seriously standing there, telling me that you think I'm brain damaged? Who the hell do you think you are? Why don't you go ahead and add this moment to your reasons-I'm-an-ass list right now, buddy!"

"Please listen to me, I didn't say damaged. I'm trying to tell you that I think your brain works differently than others' brains do. You're unique—*special*—

see? My uncle and Miles Udell have sleep disorders, and my regular charms don't work on them, either. But when I sang to you, it worked the same as when I sing to them. Instantly! Most others get drowsy, and then they have a dizzy feeling, and then finally fall asleep, but it takes a couple minutes. And my dad said he had a hard time waking my uncle up in high school, and he napped all the time. Also, my uncle sits down when he laughs, or he would fall to his knees too. Doesn't that sound like you?"

My mind is reeling, and I can't keep hold of any one thought. The fact is, it *does* sound like me. He's got my attention now, and my anger is gone. Instead, I'm just worried about what he will say next.

"The thing is, my charms don't work on people who have been drinking. Nor do they work on people who can't hear, for whatever reason, as you know and proved with Maddie today. And they also don't work on people who have a damaged or an otherwise affected hypothalamus."

"I'm a pretty smart gal, but I don't know what a hypothalamus does or what's wrong with mine. Can you be more specific, and get to the point, here?"

"Julia, I will do that. But remember, I am not a doctor, and I'm telling you this so that you can get tested for it and maybe stop getting those headaches you have every morning. I think you could have a sleep disorder called narcolepsy."

"How did you know that I have headaches every morning?" *Honestly, Julia, after all that you've just been told, that's the question that comes to mind?* I'm starting to believe there definitely *is* something wrong with my brain!

"I didn't." He looks me in the eye, and I understand why he wanted to keep his hands on me. I feel like running away, but that wouldn't make anything he said less true. "Not until just now. But my uncle always did before he discovered a way to live with narcolepsy instead of ignoring it."

"Do your charms work on him now?"

He shakes his head. "No. He was my first Achilles' heel, and that helped me figure out why it doesn't work on Miles Udell, whose sleep disorder is insomnia, but you are somehow different and I can't figure it out."

My flight or fight response is back with a vengeance. I shove him off me and rush past the breakfast bar, back down the hallway, toward the front door. I slip into the tiny bathroom, closing and locking the door behind me. I bend over, putting my head between my knees, and try to catch my breath. I'm in panic mode, and the last thing I want to do is hyperventilate.

I always knew I slept more than others, but I thought it was a normal teenage thing to do. Maybe Momma wouldn't notice, because I am her only child. Maybe Dad would have known, but he's not around anymore.

Now I feel like a freak. Everything he's said makes sense. It could be true. There might actually be something wrong with me. My brain is deformed, and I'm going to start falling asleep with my head in my dinner plate and wake up with sauce all over my face and up my nose.

"Julia, open the door so I can make sure you're okay." *For such an evil person, he is awfully nice sometimes.* He must have a pinkish heart in there somewhere, too.

See? Those are the kind of crap thoughts that must be coming from my broken brain. My hand betrays me by opening the door. Honestly, I don't even put up much of a fight.

"I'm a freak." My lips formed the words without my traitor brain's permission, and I start to cry.

Vander shocks me even more when he pulls me into a hug.

"Shhh, that's nonsense. You are no different than you were before I told you what I think is going on. You're definitely not a freak."

"You called me your Achilles' heel. Was that a compliment?" I don't want him to see my slobbery face, so I pull him tight with both arms.

"*I* think so. It means you have the ability to hurt me in a way that nobody else can."

"Why is that a good thing?" I sniffle. The motion creates an opportunity to get closer, and I take it.

"Because you are forcing me to feel things for you in a way I have never allowed myself to feel before." He reaches up and pats my hair down away from my face.

"Feeling things? Like what?"

He tries to pull away from me, and I can tell he wants to look at my face. I'm sure it's covered in tears and snot. Therefore, I don't want him to see it, and I put my head flat against his shoulder instead.

I open my eyes and find his searching mine in the mirror. This damn bathroom is ruining my ability to hide my face. He doesn't look grossed out. Actually, he doesn't even seem to want to let go of me. His eyes are obviously trying to tell me something.

"I can't stop thinking about you."

What?

He's stunned me into silence. The sniffles stop, and the tears dry up.

"Literature class is torture because you sit behind me, so I can't see you, but I know you're there. Texting you is also horrible, because you don't check them, and you never reply anymore. I write you notes, and you don't even mention them." His hands are pressing firmly against my back; he's not letting go. It's such a comforting feeling.

"Maddie asked me out on a date in exchange for giving me her bra so that I could win. I bet that's why she came up with this contest to begin with."

"It was her idea?" I would have bet money this had his name written all over it.

"Yes. Anyway, I had to tell her there is someone else as I anticipated watching my boxers fly around in the breeze."

"When was this?" I ask, my voice hoarse as I try to piece together what he's saying, to make it line up with his erratic behavior these last few days.

"This afternoon right before swim practice … Maddie was going to let me have her bra, but I said no. I couldn't go out with her. Not when I feel like this for someone else."

My mind is swirling with all these new feelings stirring. But wait, that means Maddie must have changed her mind about trying to win the contest at the last minute. *That explains her tears this afternoon.* No wonder she was crying—she must have felt so extremely embarrassed.

"I spend moments like this wanting to hold you close and tell you all of these things. At the same time, my conscience is telling me to let go and push you away so that you don't get hurt. I'm such an ass, and the worst part is, you know it."

"You *are* an ass!" I push him away only far enough that I can look in his eyes without the aid of a mirror. The unease in them from having just laid his heart on the line tugs at my own heartstrings, and I am left with no choice.

I lean into him. My hands are shaking, and my eyes close as I inch closer. I'm still fighting a battle inside about whether I actually want to do this or not. I'm losing the battle, because I *do* want this. We are so close now, I can feel his breath on my lips.

Ding dong.

"Shit!" we say it together, and loud. Then we break apart, straightening out our shirts and hair. He gives me an *I'm sorry* look as he steps out into the hall to answer the door. I'm still breathing heavily when he opens it. I bend over to splash some cold water on my face, hoping to get rid of the tearstains.

"Andrew." I hear Vander greeting him with one of those manly handshake/back slap things at the door. "Good to see you, man. Julia and I are making brownies, everyone else is downstairs."

"Good to see you too, bro." Andrew walks past the bathroom on his way downstairs. I don't look up, but I hear him go. The other set of feet pauses at the door of the bathroom, and then proceeds into the kitchen.

Did I really just almost kiss a boy? And not just any boy, but Vander Thelxinoe? And did he say that he likes me, but he's not going to do anything about it? Or that he likes me, and he is going to do something about it? Because he didn't try to kiss me—it was definitely the other way around. *Relationships with boys are so complicated, it's ridiculous.* I can't imagine why girls seem to look forward to spending their time trying to figure out these mind games.

"Maybe I should go?" I ask Vander as I slowly reenter into the kitchen.

He sets down the box of brownie mix he was reading and looks up.

"Listen, I really, really don't want you to do that. Please stay." It's the second "really" that tells me he doesn't regret telling me what he did. It's him coming around the breakfast bar to take my hands that tells me he wants to pick up from where we left off before the doorbell. But I need a minute. I drop his hands and pick up the same box he just set down, and take a breath.

"Well, if I'm staying, then we'd better get these bad boys in the oven."

I focus all of my attention on mixing up the batter. Vander assists from a relative distance, cracking open the eggs and pouring the oil while I stir. He's not risking making another move that could get stopped before it starts. I relax a little after we put the pan in the oven, and sit down on one of the stools at the breakfast bar. Vander sets a timer, and then stands on the other side.

"How does your uncle manage his narcolepsy?"

"I texted him about that while you girls were in the bathroom during dinner. He said that he used a website called wakeupdiet.com to learn about how narcolepsy affects him and what things he should avoid to help control his circadian rhythm, since that is what the hypothalamus is supposed to do for you."

"What is a circadian rhythm?"

He smiles warmly at my question.

"I had to look that up, too. It's basically your natural sleep and wake cycle. When you have to wake up early or take a nap, you are affecting your body's clock, which tells you to sleep these eight hours and stay awake for the rest. Teenagers usually mess ours up by sleeping in on the weekends, making Mondays suck that much more."

We both laugh nervously at his attempt at a joke. He touches the blue eye pendant around his neck to tuck it back inside of his shirt.

"I know this is a lot to take in and it may not even be what's happening to you, but it can be managed. Let me just read you this message from my uncle: some changes in what you eat, when you eat, and how and when you exercise can put your circadian rhythm back on track. Since your hypothalamus isn't telling your body what to do and when to do it, you have to self-regulate it. When you do get back on track, you should find your knees giving out less with strong emotions, and excessive naps will become a thing of the past."

"But I love to sleep." *This is an awful lot of information to try to process on a Friday night.*

"You're a teenager, of course you do. I love to sleep, too. But if you do have a sleep disorder, wouldn't it be nice to know for sure so you can have control over when and how often you sleep?"

"It's still kind of scary to think that there might be something wrong with me."

"There is absolutely nothing wrong with you from where I'm standing."

He doesn't meet my gaze, choosing instead to turn and check on the timer. I study his profile. It's really not that hard to believe that he is part Greek god from this angle. His chiseled jaw and dark, floppy hair are like something out of a magazine advertisement. His eyes, too—they aren't dark to match his hair, like mine—they are parts of green and blue, much like the painting of the sea in the other room.

"Who painted that piece above the couch in there?"

He shrugs, not answering me in any concrete way. Then he shifts his weight from one foot to the other and his awkwardness makes it clear to me.

"You did it, didn't you? You're a painter."

He shrugs again. I hop down from my stool to go take another look at the painting. The artist must have signed it, and I will get my answer that way.

I go down the hall, past the bathroom, the stairs, and the front door until I'm standing in the parlor, looking at Vander, who is blocking the painting from my view. He must have gone through the dining room next to the kitchen to end up in here before me. He's staring at me and chewing on his lip while flexing and balling his hands. He's more nervous than I have ever seen him—not before a swim meet, not in class when he didn't know an answer, not when he told me how he felt in the bathroom a little bit ago. This is where his heart lies, in this painting of what must be his mother's island home.

I try to look around him, and he leans over.

"Don't." He is stern, but gentle. He clears his throat. "Please don't touch it. You will want to, but don't."

He's right. I do want to touch it; I want to climb inside of it. I'm seeing it, and somehow it's seeing me, and it's making me feel pulled apart. I want to dive into the waters, to swim to that far-off land, and I also want to turn the boat around and sail as far and as quickly as I can in the opposite direction. Meanwhile, the light from the sun is dimming, laughing at me for thinking I can have any control here.

I want in!

Vander grabs both of my arms, which are currently outstretched toward the painting. My knees are on the seat of the couch, and I don't even remember moving forward. His voice startles me. "You can't."

I blink hard and turn to look him fully in the face. "I can't *what*?"

"You can't go there, and you can't go away from there. It's just a painting." *Was I talking out loud, or can he read my mind? How does he know what I was thinking?* I let him lead me through the dining room, back into the kitchen, where the timer is going off. I shake my head to let loose the feelings that painting stirred in me.

"It's more than that, and you know it. How?" I don't even have to finish the sentence. He knows exactly what I'm asking.

"I mixed some of my mother's tears in with the paint. Her Siren song is not only something you can hear, it's also something you can use all of your senses to connect with—you can touch it, smell it, taste it, and see it."

Holy crap, this is the Twilight Zone. I have just a small understanding of why so many sailors have thrown themselves off of a cliff after experiencing the call of the Sirens, and it's more than enough.

"What would happen if I touched it?" I want to find out for myself, and I don't *ever* want to find out at the same time.

"Everyone else who has touched it has passed out, that's why it's above the couch." He takes out some hot pads and removes the brownie pan from the oven. His kitchen suddenly smells like heaven, which reminds me...

"Why does the sea look like your eyes?" As he turns to close the oven door, I hover over the brownies and waft the chocolatey scent up toward my nose.

He turns around so slowly that it makes me wonder if I am somehow seeing things in slow motion. He rushes to the small desk next to the fridge and gets out some paper and a pen.

"Draw it. Draw what you see when you look at my painting."

I stare at Mr. Bossypants like he has two heads before I respond. "I'm no artist—I can't draw. Besides, why would I do that when you could just walk in there and see it for yourself?"

"You said you saw a sea that matches my eyes?"

"Uh, yeah." I cross my arms in annoyance. This ranks pretty close to my top ten list of pointless, dumb conversations.

"What else?" He grabs his phone and starts jabbing at it with both thumbs. I guess I might as well play along.

"It's a seascape under a sunset, with a tiny little speck of land off in the distance. What's going on here?"

"You can see it as it is!" His thumbs race across his phone. "You can actually see my painting."

"Uh, yeah, I'm not blind. Care to fill me in on what in the hell you are going on about?"

"Have you ever been there?" His phone buzzes in his hand and he types more into it.

"Been where?"

"To Greece or Italy, or anywhere remotely Mediterranean?" His phone buzzes again.

"Um, no. Mom and I went on a cruise to the Bahamas a couple years ago. Does that count?"

"No, it doesn't. Julia," he puts his phone down and looks me square in the eye, "I have to do this right now."

He kisses me. Full on the mouth. His hand is holding my face still, so I can't break away. My whole body tenses up at first, and then after a few seconds, it reacts. Violently thrusting my hands into his glorious hair, I let loose a soft moan. He replies with a groan of his own, and it ignites a fire, blazing its way through my body from head to toe. He backs me into the sink and I don't mind a bit. This is the kind of thing my friends should have told me about. I would have boarded the "yay boys" train long ago if I had known about something like this.

"You're the one she told me about. You're *mine*." He pulls away long enough and barely far enough apart to say that, and then his mouth is firmly planted on mine again. He tilts his head, and I feel his tongue on my lips. I open them in surprise, and he sweeps it into my mouth in such a sweet way, I have a thought that I may never need brownies again, if I could have a lifetime supply of Vander's kisses.

Wait, did he just say I'm his?

"Stop." I pull back for a second, and my stern word makes him let go. "I'm yours?"

"You are meant to be. There is a reason I've been drawn to you and couldn't leave you alone, no matter how hard I tried. You can see me clearly. You are part of my destiny."

"Whoa, slow down. Destiny?" I repeat, shaking my head.

Suddenly, he seems so sad, and I don't know how to take it. An actual tear is forming in each of his eyes, making it clear. He thinks I'm rejecting him, and he's breaking apart right in front of me. My own heart is breaking at the realization.

"Can you explain that more?" I ask, but I don't let him. Instead, I pull him in and kiss him just as hard as he's been kissing me. My hands are pulling and my tongue is pushing. It feels like the painting has come to life inside of me. He groans again, and his hands are moving all over my back. I don't want this kiss to *ever* end.

This is completely unbelievable ... and amazing.

CHAPTER SIXTEEN

At the sound of applause coming from the other side of the breakfast bar we pull back, but don't let go. I *can't* let go. My body is not listening to me at all.

"We smelled the brownies," Taylor offers, with eyes as big as the headlights on my VW Beetle. "But I'm glad we didn't miss the show."

Lissy gives her a high five and adds, "I'm kind of pissed off it wasn't rated R, to be honest."

Vander throws a hot pad at her.

Wesley yells, "Hey, watch out!" but not fast enough. I giggle when it hits her in the head.

Vander leans in a bit, and it doesn't take much, because he is right there as he whispers a question, "I could make them all leave and forget what they saw, if you'd like?"

"Nope, can't let you do that. There are worse things in the world than getting caught smooching your crush." Heat floods my cheeks. I can't believe I said that.

Vander's eyes narrow. "You have a crush on me? I thought you said I was an ass."

"You are an ass, but for some reason, I like you anyway."

"That's good."

"It's good you're an ass?"

"No, it's good you like me anyway, because you are my destiny." He speaks so softly, but that word "destiny" is ringing in my ears.

"Excuse us, love doves, but can we get the brownies now, or what?" Lissy is really getting on my last nerve. I don't even try not to laugh when Vander's other hot pad hits her on the shoulder.

"Keep it up, Vander, and you will have to answer to me," Wesley threatens, then he puts his arm protectively around her. Wesley must really like Lissy. I smile at her, and she smiles back.

"You and what army, pipsqueak?" Andrew puts him in a headlock and rubs his head from behind. "Are we getting some of these brownies, or what?"

I reach into the utensil drawer where Vander got out the whisk and find a knife to cut them with. I slice them into six even pieces. Vander gets down some plates and takes out the forks. We serve them up together, while Wesley and Lissy take charge of getting some glasses out of the cupboard and pouring the milk.

Vander is never more than a couple inches away from me as we enjoy our hot snack and cool drink. His left hand keeps landing on my back, as if he can't stand not to be touching me at all times. Less than one week ago, I was all set to enjoy my senior year without any boys stealing my sanity the way Lissy and Taylor have lost theirs. At this moment, I can't imagine why I ever felt that way. My disinterest in boys and frustration at feeling so different than my friends seems so foreign to me now.

It doesn't take long for us to finish our brownies and milk. The rest of the group has made the final decision on movie viewing for the night, and I am pleased to learn they have chosen *The Breakfast Club*. Ever since I fell in love with *Pitch Perfect*, I've wanted to see it.

Vander settles down into a loveseat, taking my hand to sit next to him. When I do, he doesn't let go. Instead, he twines his fingers in between mine. It strikes me as completely odd that I have had my tongue in his mouth, but have never held his hand like this. It feels more intimate, in a way, and sends a shiver down my spine.

Vander looks at me with concern in his eyes. "Are you okay?"

"Yeah, I'm just a bit cold, I guess."

"We can't have that." He lets go of my hand and reaches around the side of the loveseat to grab a blanket from a basket on the floor. It's super soft, like my mom's bathrobe. I grab it and eagerly pull it up around my neck. Vander wraps it around him, too, and puts his arm around me. That maneuver forces me to snuggle into his shoulder, where I can breathe in his scent. My hand that is not stuck between us comes to rest on his abs. At least, I'm pretty sure the rock-hard formation under his shirt is muscle, or else he has a cookie sheet tucked away up there.

I'm a little bit intimidated by all of this closeness after so actively pushing him away for so long. My mind keeps racing through all the questions I have. I would much rather get to the bottom of what's going on with us and with his quest than sit here in silence for a couple hours.

He uses his free hand to hold mine close to his stomach. Suddenly, I'm too hot for the blanket, but I don't even care. My decision is to focus on this moment, and deal with the rest of it later.

I look over to the couch, and find that Wesley has his arm on the back of the couch behind Lissy. I can imagine by the end of the movie it will be around her, like Vander is holding me. Taylor is sitting next to Lissy, leaving no room for Andrew on the couch. He sits in the comfortable-looking armchair, but Taylor seems content to be able to steal glances whenever she wants as she opens the noisy plastic to enjoy her Smarties. It's nice to see my friends so happy.

CHAPTER SEVENTEEN

Vander is unreachable all weekend. He warned me when he kissed me goodnight on Friday that his dad was taking him hunting as part of his survival training for when he goes to visit his mom. Even if he could get good reception, he wouldn't have his phone turned on, because it would scare the animals he was trying to hunt.

Thinking about that now causes me to wonder if his charms work on animals. I'll have to ask him about that tonight when he calls to say goodnight, like he promised me he would. I'm trying to pay attention to my homework, but it's not easy. I spent most of yesterday reading about narcolepsy and self-diagnosing. Momma says she will set up an appointment with our doctor to discuss having a sleep study done. In the meantime, the wakeup diet website gives lots of tips and plans on how to stay awake and alert during the day, and how to have better sleep quality at night. I will try to implement some of those things into my life and see if they help. My brain feels like it's on a hamster wheel, though. No matter what I do, my mind keeps drifting to the feel of Vander's arms around me, or the crush of his lips on mine, and his hands in my hair.

Momma asked why I was so distracted. I decided to tell her about kissing Vander. It was awkward to talk about that with my mom, but she was understanding, even saying, "Honestly, I thought I would have to worry about you being in relationships a long time before now. You are a mature young lady, almost eighteen, and I trust your judgement." If her faith in me doesn't cause me to make good choices, then I don't know what would. It's almost as if she likes the idea of us dating.

A small part of me worries what Kenzie-Grace will think of our relationship. It was only a few days ago that she was crying on my couch because she was worried I would think she was crazy when she told me what she remembers from Vander's birthday. We aren't close friends. In fact, before Monday, she had never even been to my house. But I can't help thinking I'm an awful person for listening to her warnings about him, and then diving in with both feet anyway.

When I shared that with Lissy, she said, "It's been six months. She's gotta be over it and moving on by now."

I hope so.

The thing with Lissy and Taylor not believing anything about Vander's charms is frustrating. But other than having him demonstrate them on someone else, which I have repeatedly asked him not to do, there is no way I can convince them he's not a normal guy. They already believe he's part god because of his abs, so who am I to convince them that those are not his most magical asset? *Sweet Mama Llama, it's not even close.*

I try once again to focus on my homework, but my phone buzzes, and the distraction is a relief.

Vander: I turned my phone on just because I had to let you know I can't stop thinking about you.

Before I can reply, another message comes through.

Vander: These deer have some amazing racks, but they are nothing compared to yours.

Oh, wow. *That is awful.*

Me: I can't wait to talk to you tonight, but you are an ass.

I don't know why I thought he would be less of an ass just because I know he likes me now. I'm not fully convinced that he meant it when he said, "You're mine." *Who even talks like that? Am I a piece of property to him, or was he claiming me like a werewolf claims a lifelong mate? Is he my boyfriend now? Ugh!*

Boy stuff is *hard.*

Vander: Did you expect anything different? Powering down.

I throw my homework packet back in my bag, since I'm not getting anywhere. I text the girls to let them know I am on my way to get them.

We sit down at *Perkins* for a hot chocolate date and take in the view of the giant flag waving in the wind outside. It makes me think of the flag currently flying outside of our school, unless the staff has taken it down.

"Hey, do you guys know what the prize is that Vander has to bring to school tomorrow?"

"No, shouldn't we be asking *you*?" Lissy waggles her eyebrows at me.

"I haven't had much time to talk to him. But I have lots of questions burning inside me, waiting for answers."

"Is he your *boyfriend* now?" Taylor leans on the table to get closer to me, making googly eyes.

"That's one of them."

"Can I just say it's awesome that you have finally joined hashtag TeamBoysAreGood?" Leave it to Lissy to use a Twitter hashtag in a real-life conversation. I roll my eyes at her because she expects me to—I'm such a good friend.

"Can you tell me once again what happened?" They were both confused when I told them what actually went down at Vander's house. I changed a few details, and evidently, Taylor still doesn't get it.

"I noticed the painting in Vander's fancy living room, and when I discovered that he painted it himself, I complimented him. He said nobody else could see his painting the way he does, and it made him feel connected to me. Also, he has had a little crush on me for a while, and he discovered my feelings about him, so we kissed. And then you guys walked in, and you know the rest."

"Are you talking about the painting over the couch of the beautiful galloping horse running along a stream, with the farm in the background?"

Taylor must be confused.

"I thought the painting over the couch showed a majestic eagle in flight over fields of grain, with a river flowing in the background. Very patriotic," Lissy mentions.

"No, I'm talking about the painting over the couch in the formal living room with the piano."

"Yeah, that's the one I'm talking about." Taylor looks to Lissy, definitely confused.

"Me too." Lissy adds her confused look to the mix.

"Maybe I'm thinking of the one over the piano?" I offer, *but I know I'm not.* I know what I saw. Vander's response to me when I said that the sea matched his eyes is starting to make sense. His mother's tears must make the painting look different to every person who looks at it. Except—*somehow*—I saw the image he actually painted.

"Well, I guess you have another question to add to your list." Lissy shrugs it off. There is no way either one of them could predict why we all saw different things hanging over the couch.

"I suppose so." I shake off the uneasy feeling that the painting continues to stir in me. "What about you guys? Have you heard from Wesley?"

"On Friday night, I kept leaning into him on the couch, but he never put his arm around my shoulder or held my hand. Though, he didn't move away from me, so I had the privilege of smelling like him when I got home."

"Have you guys texted or anything?" Taylor is grasping for something to celebrate. Things didn't progress for her and Andrew on Friday night, either.

"No. How about them Cubs?" Lissy has a way of changing the subject by talking about out-of-season sports teams she doesn't even follow when they are in season.

"Okay. How are you liking being a team manager?" I take a sip of my cocoa and get whipped cream under my nose. As I lick it off, my mind drifts to feeling Vander's tongue in that vicinity, but I shake those thoughts right out of my head.

"It's a lot of work, which doesn't leave much time for gawking. But I don't regret signing up for it—even if Wesley never talks to me again. I get to enjoy the view at every practice. Also, I broke the same rule you broke, so I feel less guilty about that situation now."

"About that—" Taylor lowers her eyes to her cup before continuing, "I tried to talk Coach Winter into letting me be a manager, too. She said all positions were currently filled."

"Oh, Taylor, it's fine. I don't regret covering for you guys. It's what friends are supposed to do. It means a lot that you tried, but please don't worry about it." The corners of her mouth turn up a bit at my words, and she lifts her eyes to make sure I mean what I said. I do.

"Exactly, Taylor. No worries," Lissy agrees.

It's almost ten when my phone finally rings, and I can't answer it fast enough. I had been hoping he would get home from hunting early enough tonight to come see me, and the list of questions I have is growing longer and longer as I anticipate getting some answers.

"Hello?"

"Hi, Julia. What are your plans for Thanksgiving this week?" The sound of his voice soothes me instantly.

"Um—usually it's just my mom and I, and a very unfortunate rotisserie chicken from the grocery store. Why?"

"Well, my dad wants me to invite you and your mom to our house for a traditional Thanksgiving dinner."

"That's so nice, I can ask her about it." *How did this conversation get hijacked so quickly?* I'm the one who is supposed to get some questions answered here.

"Go ahead, I'll wait."

"You want me to go talk to her right now? Even though I have been waiting two days to talk to you?"

"Well, my dad is going to continue to pace until he gets an answer from you guys, so yeah, now would be good."

"What makes you think I'm anxious to try another meal with you?" I ask.

"Are you serious? Have you changed your mind about us?" He sounds panicked, so I rush my reply.

"Relax. I haven't had much time to even make up my mind, let alone change it. Like I said, I've got some questions that have been stewing for forty-eight hours. Longer even, if you count the questions I had before Friday night happened."

"Well, ask! I'm not willing to waste any of our time going backward!" The tone of his voice makes it seem like this discussion is the most important thing in the world.

"Vander, please just take a breath and relax your shoulders." I pause to wait for him to exhale or maybe even laugh at my using his line on him, but it falls flat. "Now, I never said I was interested in going backward, but there are some things I need to know before I commit to going *forward*."

"I thought we covered this Friday night." He still sounds all worked up.

"When?"

"When you saw my art, and I told you about my destiny."

"All I remember is you saying I was yours and meant to be, but I still don't know what that even means. Not to mention how terrifying it is to be told that my life has already been determined for me!" My voice is getting louder the longer we argue, and neither of us is getting any real answers.

"Well, I couldn't answer you Friday night, because right after you asked me to explain, you kissed me!" His volume is now rising to match mine.

"Well, it's not my fault you are such an unbelievable kisser!" I'm practically screaming now.

I don't hear anything for a minute, and when I do, I wish I couldn't.

He's laughing.

He's *laughing* at me.

"Are you seriously laughing at me right now?" *I swear on all things holy, this guy has a mountain of nerve.*

"Yes." It sounds weird to me when he says it. I can't tell if he's still laughing, or has moved farther away from his phone, or what.

I feel a tap on my shoulder. *Crap!* My mom must have heard me in my room yelling at him. I take a second to affix a smile on my face. When I slowly turn around, I find Vander standing in front of me, shoving his phone back into his pocket. My eyes widen and my jaw drops open.

"I couldn't wait any longer to see you," he explains simply. Then, seeing my shocked expression, he adds, "Your mom sent me in here while she goes over some work stuff with my dad." He mimics my mom, "As long as you keep the door open and your clothes on. I'm not ready to be a grandma."

I want to hit him for mocking my mom, but that does sound exactly like something she would say. I can't stop myself from throwing my arms around him. Dang it, he smells so good right now.

"Let me tell you how this works," He pulls back farther to take my hands in his. "You are meant to be mine—not in a 'completing me' way. More like a matched set. The reason you can see my painting is because you have been preapproved, for lack of a better word, by the gods to be with someone with powers. Someone like *me*. My dad can see the painting as it is, because he's been approved to be with my mom. I can see the painting as it is, obviously, because I painted it, and also because I am preapproved to be with someone with powers. Everyone else in my life sees what he or she wants to see. But you—"

He uses his right hand to tuck a wayward strand of hair behind my left ear. The slight touch sends a shiver down my spine. He pulls me back into a hug and rubs my back to warm me up. *He must think I'm cold again.* The truth is, things are definitely heating up for me here. "You can see the scene I actually put on the canvas, and uncovered the Easter egg I put in it just to be sure. I painted the sea the color of my eyes because my dad told me they look just like my mother's."

"Why let it hang there where so many people will see it?" I ask.

"I was thirteen when I started painting. For my sixteenth birthday, my mother sent me some of her tears with instructions on how to use them. She told my dad about how to mix them with the paint, and the importance of keeping track of what people saw. Since that time, nobody from school has seen it as it is, until you." He squeezes me to show how pleased he is about that. He's lost in thought, and I'm happy to listen to him explain. "Demeter thought it was foolish. When she saw it, she told me most mortals would be confused by it, and I would have to spend the rest of my life charming people's memories of the changing painting. It's not a very effective way of searching for your soul mate, but I knew I had to try to find someone I could love the way my dad loves my mom."

"But you were with Kenzie-Grace for a long time."

I don't understand how she fits in, if he was looking for someone he could love forever. My question causes him to shake his head and pull back from me; he leans on the corner of my small desk. I take a seat on my bed, giving him the space he needs to get this off his chest.

"What she saw in my painting was a lake house full of comfortable chairs and books. But I liked her anyway. I felt like a normal boy, in a normal relationship, at a normal school. I had real feelings for her, and I thought we could be together despite her lack of the gods' approval. But on my birthday last year, Demeter stopped by for an unexpected visit, and when she saw Kenzie-Grace, she told me, in no uncertain terms, to eliminate her from my life or she would take care of it herself. I charmed Kenzie-Grace, so that she would know it had to end."

"She told me about that," I remind him. I'm not willing to keep anything from him now, especially since he's being completely open with me. His eyes lock on mine, silently asking me to continue. "She said your young, hot grandma appeared, and said things would be changing in the next year, and that Kenzie-Grace had to go."

"She remembers seeing my grandmother? Shit! I tried to erase that. She had been drinking some champagne, but I was pretty sure I timed it right."

"You need to talk to her about that. ASAP. She felt threatened."

"I will. I wish I would have known before now. I wonder how many people she has tried to tell who went on to forget she ever mentioned it."

"What do you mean?"

"Haven't you noticed how Lissy and Taylor are confused when you try to talk to them about what I can do and then they forget about it like it's no big deal? That's part of what happens when people have been charmed."

"That explains a lot actually. I thought I was losing my mind. Which makes it that much worse for her."

"I know. I never intended to hurt her. I will make it right. Did she mention anything about my quest?"

"No, she didn't say anything about that to me, but she remembers being charmed. She said she heard you whisper in that snake voice." I can practically see a weight lift off of his shoulders.

"I wanted her to stay away from me, and it worked. I never meant for her to feel threatened. You've got to believe me." He takes a deep breath and lets it out slowly. "I want to thank you for what you did for her this week. It was good for her to participate in embarrassing me with the rest of your team and I think I have you to thank."

I nod. Nothing else seems appropriate. "I was just there for her. She came to me, really. Lissy and Taylor are the ones who helped with her hair."

"But you are the one who brought her in on the contest, am I right? You are the one who gave her an opportunity to beat me?"

I nod again. I hadn't thought of it like that at all.

He takes a few steps toward me and lifts my chin with his finger. "Thank you."

I nod yet again, and before I start to feel like a bobble-head doll, I stand up and grab his hand to lead him out of the room. Having Vander in my bedroom is making it hard for me to concentrate on anything, like getting my most pressing question answered—*do I have a boyfriend or nah?*

"What are you to me now?" I barely whisper the question, but he hears me.

"I'm yours, Julia." I can hear the smile in his voice, but a small groan escapes my mouth.

"I don't know things about boys like most girls do, and until recently, I didn't care about any of them in any real way. So I don't know what that means. Can you simplify it for me?" I'm sure I'm blushing, and I am grateful the hallway light is off.

He uses my hand in his to stop our forward progress. We are standing in the hall beneath a family picture from several years back. He takes both of my hands in his and makes sure my focus is on him. "From this moment on, I am anything you need me to be. You can call me your protector, because nobody will hurt you on my watch. You can call me your escort, because there is nowhere you will go that I won't be at your side. You can call me your date, your boyfriend, your man, your *anything*, because I promise to be all of those, and more. There is no way I can turn my back on you—I'm not allowed a second match with destiny. Is that simple enough for you?"

I smile so wide, my face starts to hurt. I can't breathe. "Yeah," I say dumbly, "I understand now."

"Good." We seal that deal with a kiss of epic proportions. As soon as his lips touch mine, my toes curl and I see stars behind my eyelids. It feels like I'm floating away on a warm cloud of happiness. It ends when I hear my mother opening a drawer in the kitchen. After taking a moment to collect myself, I take his hand and lead him to the kitchen, deciding there is no time like the present to ask my momma about Thanksgiving dinner.

CHAPTER EIGHTEEN

I actually wake up early for school. I want to take my time straightening my otherwise kinky, curly hair. I don't want to just pull it back in a ponytail like I usually do during swim season. I want to look extra good for my boyfriend today. It still feels weird to call Vander Thelxinoe that, though I like the sound of it.

I put on gray fleece-lined leggings and my long, black sweater with two gray stripes around the cuffs of the sleeves. Lissy once told me the blue notes in the gray outfit set off the dark tones of my skin in a flattering way. I've never forgotten that. I even use some blue eyeliner to help them stand out. I look like I'm going on a date, instead of just going to school, and I kind of am—today will be the first time I have lunch with my boyfriend.

Taylor and Lissy were squealing like dolphins—forever, it seemed—last night, when I called them after Vander kissed me goodnight. Maybe it should bother me that they have spent so much time looking at my boyfriend's abs and comparing his body to others' bodies. It doesn't.

If anything, I appreciate the education they've provided me through osmosis, because I certainly wasn't paying attention to them intentionally.

In all of the excitement over having a boyfriend, I forgot about today's prize being delivered to the women's swim team from the captains of the men's team. Maddie is waiting in the main foyer with an actual camera hanging around her neck. I don't see those much anymore, as most people are content to use the cameras in their phones.

"What's up, Maddie?"

"Vander and Wesley should be here any minute with our donuts."

"Ah, donuts? That's the big prize?"

She shakes her head. "Only part of it," she says before she starts to laugh and click with her camera. I follow the lens to see what she's capturing, only to find my boyfriend and his best friend wearing their meet Speedos—the kind that covers only what a bikini bottom covers on a lady, and not much more.

The boys are wearing their backpacks on their shoulders, and they are carrying boxes of donuts in their hands, but they don't have clothes on, or warm-ups, or jackets, and it's near-freezing outside. I can't help but laugh at how ridiculous they look. Vander looks at me appreciatively.

"Are you going to come get a donut and help me warm up?" For someone who is not accustomed to being embarrassed, Vander is handling this situation like a champ. Before I can catch my breath and move to him, Maddie has stepped right in front of him as if he was talking to her. I don't hear what he says to her, but I hear the snakelike way he says it. All of the humor of this scenario evacuates the foyer.

Maddie turns around empty-handed, eyes downcast, and heads down the hall with her dark hair flowing free behind her.

"You can't do that, Vander." I point to Maddie's retreating back to make sure he knows what I'm talking about.

"I didn't have a choice," he replies.

"You always have a choice. You just made the wrong one, you gigantic ass."

I turn and walk to my first class, pretending I don't hear him calling my name. He has a prize to deliver in the foyer, so I can have some time to myself to figure out a way to convince him not to use his charms on people. I have a major problem with anyone or anything that messes with someone's mind and alters their ability to think for themselves in a normal way.

After I toss my bag on the floor next to my desk and take a seat, I get out my phone to text Lissy. If this is what guys are like—talking all about protecting and watching over me, but then completely disregarding my wishes the next day—then maybe I was right not to have anything to do with them in the first place.

Me: Boys are frustrating and complicated. I'm not sure anything is worth putting up with this jackassery.
Lissy: What R U talking about? Just last night you said everything was right in the world.
Me: Vander.

And that's all I can say, because she doesn't believe or even remember that his powers exist. What does this boil down to if I take his charm out of the equation? I have to go talk to Maddie and hear what she has to say. I'm halfway out the door when Vander storms in. I stop where I'm standing and cross my arms, fighting the smirk that wants to make an appearance on my lips when I take in the sight of him wearing a tiny speedo and sneakers. When I see the worry written all over his face, a part of me is glad. He seems to be getting the message.

"I'm sorry. I'm not used to this," he murmurs as he searches for a way to connect with me. My posture is definitely closed off. There is no hand for him to grab, and a hug would be awkward. He puts his hands back down to his sides. "Please tell me what I should have done differently."

Well now, that's not what I was expecting at all. His words totally take the wind out of my sails. I put my arms down, too. "Vander, there is something you need to know about me."

"There are a lot of things I've yet to learn about you." He puts his hand behind my elbow to pull me closer. Touching him makes everything seem less awful, and my anger starts to evaporate. We hear a throat being cleared in the corner, where my teacher sits at his desk. Neither of us looks over, but we've received the message that we are not alone. We walk out into the busy hall to take advantage of the relative privacy allotted to those trying to converse in a crowd.

It proves impossible though, because of all the people stopping to gawk at Vander. The number of phones aimed at him from all angles and the sound of laughter erupting all around us extinguish any hope for an actual conversation here. A nervous smile brightens my face when I realize I'm in all of these pictures of him. I try to back away, but Vander isn't having that. His grip on my elbow tightens, and he pulls me closer, using my body to shield his.

"You wouldn't abandon me in my time of need, would you?" He laughs.

"Maybe I would; our team has earned this," I suggest, flashing an authentic smile up at him. Quickly, I spin out of his arms and walk backward to the door of my class. The bell ending the early bird classes rings, and Vander has to get back to the foyer as part of the deal. *Maybe he's worth a little more trouble than I thought.*

"Some girlfriend you're turning out to be!" he playfully shouts to me with a wink. The hallway goes silent for a minute, and then someone cat whistles. By the time I take a seat at my desk, my phone is blowing up. There are several notifications of mentions on Instagram, Twitter, and Facebook, and the texts are rolling in, too.

I decide to turn the distracting thing off and survey the damage over lunch. Also, I decide that a donut would taste delicious right about now. I get out of my seat for the second time this morning to go collect one from the foyer. When I step around the corner, I see Vander and Wesley posing for pictures while flexing their muscles. My eyes probably bulge out of their heads at the sight of my boyfriend's stomach. There is a defined six pack there—the one Lissy and Taylor have been squawking about—but also, there is a wedge shape that starts below his ribs and ends somewhere underneath the Speedo.

How have I never noticed this until now? The guy must spend an absurd amount of time in the gym. I slowly make my way to the boxes of donuts while I enjoy the view, and eventually help myself to a fresh-baked glazed one. Vander catches my attention and smiles at me. He's trying hard to be the kind of boyfriend he said he would be, my protector and all that. I need to cut him some slack, at least until we have time to resolve this issue. I raise my donut to show my appreciation. Several of my teammates are enjoying their sugary, deep-fried rings as well.

I smile back at him until I see a member of the school's security team over his shoulder, making her way to where all the commotion seems to be focused. I give Vander a pointed look and hope he receives the message. There are consequences for normal people displaying abnormal behavior. This is his chance to reap what he has sown. Even though the stupid contest was Maddie's idea, he didn't have to agree to it. For a second, I consider the fact that Wesley had to wear *his* Speedo, so maybe he had a say in the contest or not. And then I shudder, thinking about what Maddie would have had to do if she had lost. As I finish my donut, I can't help but to shake my head. Every single one of those who agreed to this competition and the resulting prizes are nut jobs—*the lot of them!*

Evidently, security agrees with me. The other two guards have arrived. One of them is taking Vander and Wesley into the office, and the other two are trying to get the gathered crowd to disperse. I hope this doesn't affect their eligibility for the swim team.

The one-minute warning bell sounds, and I head back to class. What a strange way to start this two-day, pre-holiday week.

Before our lit class, Vander walks in, fully clothed. He informs me that he has not been suspended, but he was required to dress appropriately for the rest of the day, and will serve a detention after Thanksgiving break. It could definitely have gone worse for him.

By the time I find Vander at lunch, my palms are starting to sweat, and not just from all of the attention we've received. It's time for me to open up to Vander, so he can understand why the mind-charming bothers me so much. It's not easy for me to talk about how my dad lost his life so I ask if we can go sit in my car for some privacy. Once we are seated, I use a bold approach by taking a deep breath and just letting it all out at once.

"I was in seventh grade, and it was Black Friday. My dad and I were sitting on the floor of my bedroom, starting to work on the border of a one thousand-piece puzzle of the Christmas trees in Rockefeller Center. He got up to go to the bathroom, teasing me about not placing the last piece until he got back. Then I heard him shout in our hallway, 'Man, I'm not letting you in there, if it's the last thing I do. Have you been drinking? Get out of here, you're drunk!' Then, I heard a grunt, and felt the floor shake before my door opened. I saw a bright light and heard a loud heartbeat sounding in my ears, and then everything went dark. I regained consciousness to the sound of my mother wailing over my dad's body, begging him to wake up. My heart broke when the paramedics used the paddles on him for the third time, with no response. I knew he was gone."

I take a deep breath to steel my nerves. It doesn't work. The tears I've been expecting start to well up in my eyes.

"There was no evidence of a break-in, and the autopsy showed that my dad died of a heart attack. Nobody can explain why he was yelling, and I never saw anyone. We don't know why I passed out, either. But I know that the last thing my dad ever said was 'you're drunk,' and so I never want that to be true for me."

Vander puts his arm around my shoulders, and uses the other one to still my shaking hands between us. He's hanging on every word.

"Now, every year for the rest of my life, I have to watch everyone around me observe the anniversary of my father's death by trying to get the best deal on the latest gadgets." I wipe away the tears that have fallen onto my cheeks and take another breath. "The thing that I want you to understand from all of this is that anything that alters someone's ability to make a logical and safe choice for themselves is not okay with me. It's just not."

"I'm sorry, Julia," he says and kisses my temple. "This week is a hard one for you, and it was an insult when I asked if you'd been drinking last Saturday night. Also, if there is something wrong with your brain, then you're scared it will affect your ability to think clearly."

"Right, but I hadn't even thought of it all like that." I let him hold me for a minute to gather my strength to address the other thing on my mind. When I feel in control again, I forge on. "Okay, second subject, what happened with Maddie this morning?"

"I was talking to you this morning, not her, when I asked to be warmed up. She thought it was an invitation to come and touch me. It made me mad, thinking about you seeing someone else touch me, so I told her I wasn't the one for her and she needed to walk away."

"She *did* touch you? Where?"

"Well—" I can tell he doesn't want to say. "Let's just say she now has a good idea of what the backside of my speedo feels like."

"Oh? *Oh*! So you told her to walk away and that's all?"

"That's all. I didn't even realize I was charming her until you reacted. I was just shocked, and that's the voice that came out. I promise, I will try harder to control my impulses. But I am going to make mistakes, because I'm not perfect. Even though I am extra-human. Also, try to remember that I need to know exactly how to use my charm and other powers when I start my quest, so I have to practice somehow."

"I want to help you, Vander. There is just a mental block there for me. We'll have to figure something out. Last thing, for now—why don't my friends believe you are capable of charming minds? They sat and listened to Kenzie-Grace's story, just like I did. But they don't seem to remember it."

"Unless I tell people about it myself, or they fit into an exception category, once they have been charmed they receive an automatic 'do not store this in your memory bank' kind of message, along with the reason for the charm. An after effect is discussion about charms is confusing and eventually pushed out of people's minds." He sounds so sure of himself, like this is natural, but I can't believe humans were intended to have their memories tampered with in this way.

"See, that's messing with their minds, Vander. Who knows what else could be getting deleted from their memory when you do that." I lean into him as I say this as softly as I can. I don't want him to think I'm getting worked up and angry with him again.

"I understand what you are asking, Julia. I want to ease your mind about that, but the only way I know how to ease minds is not an option for you. I get what you're saying, I do. Just give me some time to process all of this. It's not easy for me—there isn't some website I can go to in order to learn about what's happening, or what effects result from it. I have to figure this all out on my own." His eyes are focused on me, and he sets his jaw. He looks determined.

"Well, you're not alone anymore." I squeeze his hand. There has to be a way to for him to practice surviving the island quest without messing around with human brains anymore.

CHAPTER NINETEEN

Coach Winter starts practice with a short speech about what being part of a team means. My favorite moment is when she says, "When one idiot, or two buffoons for instance, make big, red baboon bottoms out of themselves, it makes the whole team look like sore, overly wiped rear ends."

I wish the whole team was laughing with us, but sadly, it is just Lissy and me, which causes us to fake coughing fits to cover it up. We motion toward our throats, and Lissy grabs the basket of water bottles to fill with ice water, since we are headed that way for the drink we obviously need.

We cough-laugh the whole way through the locker room into the shower area, but the giggles subside when we see that Maddie is waiting for us, and the look on her face means business.

"What's wrong?" Lissy asks. Maddie ignores her, puts her hands on her hips, and speaks directly to me.

"Are you seriously dating Vander?" Her question and attitude make me defensive. I put my own hands on my hips before I reply.

"Yeah, I am. Is that a problem?"

Lissy steps up next to me and puts her one free hand on her hip as a show of solidarity. *Was it really only three days ago when Lissy was calming Maddie down in this very room?* I flinch as I remember why she was so upset.

"Maddie, do you even remember what happened this morning with Vander?" If I were her, I wouldn't want to admit it.

"Well, I didn't know you were dating then, but I do now, so just drop it." She turns with a huff and walks out of the locker room. *When did we become enemies?* We can't be friendly anymore because she wants Vander for herself, and she can't be with him because I already am? That is so crazy. *I'm glad I stayed out of this world for so long!*

Coach has finished her rant by the time we get back with the water bottles. The guys are almost done with their stretches, and about to get in the pool. Vander comes to me for a drink before hopping in his lane, and it reminds me of another question.

"What happens with you and water? Why did you make the water hot last week, and why did it soothe my throat at the restaurant?"

He just winks and then gets in the water.

Coach hands me a stopwatch and tells me to have them swim in thirty-second-long rotations. Lissy is instructed to get the leg buoys and kickboards ready for each lane. While she fetches those and the ice water for swimmers who need it, I spend the rest of practice shouting, "*Go*!"

When Coach finally ends practice for the night—I think she made them stay extra-long tonight as punishment for Vander and Wesley's antics this morning—I have hardly any voice left.

"Did you know your mom invited Dad and I over for take two on the meatloaf dinner tonight?" Vander smiles at me.

I shake my head, but I'm not surprised. Knowing my mom, being invited to Thanksgiving dinner last night would equal a return invitation as soon as possible.

"I think—"

The state of my voice has me croaking like a frog, and I grasp my throat, wishing I knew sign language. I give up trying to explain my mom's affinity for manners and just shrug as I make my way to the locker room. It would be easier to text, at this point.

"Wait up!" Vander calls from behind me. As he makes his way to me, he's checking to see if anyone is watching us. While I wait, I tuck a stubborn piece of hair behind my ear. The pool is nearly empty when he turns me to face him and guides my hands down to my side. Then he runs a hand through his hair before he gently strokes my neck from chin to clavicle a few times, all while humming. I close my eyes and lean into his touch.

The musical lull of his voice relaxes me. It reminds me of when he made my headache better, and it gives me the feeling I get after a refreshing nap. When he's finished, he smiles at me and asks, "Now, what were you trying to tell me?"

Hesitantly, I try again. "I think—" *Whoa!* My throat feels totally back to normal. I clear my throat just to be sure. "Thank you!"

"You're welcome." He grabs that wayward hair and tucks it back behind my ear again. I love it when he does that. I try to keep my eyes on his face, despite his wet body calling for me to check it out. I'm blushing, for sure.

"Anyway, I think my mom feels like she owes you guys a meal in a preemptive strike before Thursday. We are both really grateful for the invitation, by the way."

"Well, I am really looking forward to eating both of those meals with you, and many more in the future."

"I—I guess I will see you in a little b-bit." I want to walk away into the locker room, but my legs aren't cooperating with me here. I'm pretty sure he can tell from my blush and my stuttering that he is having an effect on me.

"Yeah, you will. I'm just gonna walk away real slowly now so you have time to check me out, okay?"

I roll my eyes at him. "Thirsty for a compliment much, Vander?"

He laughs, but I sure do stand there and watch him walk away. I don't even notice that Lissy has made her way over to my side. I pat my throat one more time, finding it hard to believe it's been healed so thoroughly from Vander's touch.

"So not fair." She blows a low whistle as my retreating boyfriend makes his way into the men's locker room, and I lightly smack her arm.

"One two three, eyes on me, shorty!" Okay, so maybe it *does* bother me a little bit that she and Taylor fangirl over his physique. I give her a squinty-eyed look and almost walk into the door she's opening in the process. We sure do seem to have a good team manager partnership going on.

As we get our coats on and collect our bags, Lissy turns to me, suddenly excited to tell me something.

"Hey, did you hear about the Homecoming proposal that happened at Teen Karaoke night a few weeks ago?"

I nod. That was a huge deal all over Twitter and Instagram when it happened. The couple involved goes to Mt. Springs, a small country school not too far from here, but everyone ended up hearing about it. The guy didn't actually do karaoke; he played a keyboard live while he sang their song to his boyfriend. I guess it was totally epic—the guy has pipes.

"Well, Grant says he knows the guy, and he's going to be at Karaoke tomorrow night. Taylor and I really, really want to go, and you have to go with us. Do you think Vander would want to come? And maybe Wesley and Andrew, too?"

I smile at the last part of that. Of course she wants me to go and bring Vander and his friends. *My girls haven't given up on making their own love connections yet.*

"I want to go see that guy, absolutely. Let me check with Vander tonight, and I will let you know."

She rubs her hands together like it's already a done deal.

"Hold your horses—I said I would *ask*."

"I know. I'm just anticipating great results. Maybe when you ask, you can shimmy your chest or something to distract him, so that he will agree to anything you say."

"Get serious, psycho."

CHAPTER TWENTY

It seems we now have assigned seats at our dinner table when Vander and his dad come over. I smile and wave at Mr. Thelxinoe as I sit in the chair next to Vander. He smiles back and returns my wave, then he smiles at Vander in some approving way and makes a fanning gesture over his face. Vander nods in agreement and shakes his hand up and down.

Things are all very different from one week ago, sitting at this same table with the same food on it. I'm used to the routine and structure that my mom provides, especially since I wasn't aware it was unusual until I was too old to care much. Looking at Vander and his dad makes me realize that they don't care, either. They seem perfectly content to have meatloaf served to them again.

"Hey, Vander, before I forget, do you want to go to Teen Karaoke at the bowling alley tomorrow night with the girls and I?" I busy myself with dishing food onto my plate. If I look at him, I will laugh at the idea of shimmying for him in my head. Vander continues to translate for his dad.

"I can't sing."

Mr. Thelxinoe grins and signs something to him. Then Vander shakes his head, chuckling.

"You aren't required to sing just because you show up, Vander. Also, that guy who asked his boyfriend out to Homecoming there last month is supposed to be performing. I think that will be seriously entertaining, don't you?"

"I would like to see that, but just remember, I *can't* sing."

"Oh yeah, right." I can't imagine what would happen if a room full of people started acting drunk and falling asleep all over the place.

"You don't like to sing, Vander?" my mom asks.

"I like to sing just fine, ma'am. But I've never received a compliment on my voice, if you know what I mean," he replies. "Would it be all right if I brought Wesley?"

"Of course it would. Andrew too, if he's still around."

"I'll ask them if they want to go, but count me in for sure."

"I already have."

We spend the rest of the meal in relative silence. Vander sets down his fork any time someone talks to keep his dad in the loop. It doesn't slow his pace though; I think Vander has a third helping of mashed potatoes before I reach for seconds. Our parents continue to type back and forth on the laptop between them while they eat.

When it's time to clear the table, Vander stands to help me. It doesn't take half the time it seems it should with two of us working on it, but it is done quicker than usual. We leave our parents at the table and make our way to the couch in the living room. We both sit with one knee on the couch, facing one another.

"Have I mentioned how beautiful you look today?" Vander puts his right arm on the back of the couch so that it's resting next to the left side of my head.

"I'm not sure, but thank you. I hoped you would like it."

He toys with the edge of my sleeve. "You did this for me?"

"I usually start to straighten my hair when swim season is over, but I don't usually put makeup on as well."

"Well, I appreciate it, but it's totally unnecessary. You are such a beautiful girl naturally. I love your dark complexion and your curly hair and the way you scrunch your nose when you laugh."

My face is heating up at his attention. "I just wanted to put my best foot forward for our first day at school as a couple."

"I don't think you realize how much I've been drawn to you. Sometimes the only way I could get your attention was to tease you or flirt with your friends."

Chuckling, I say, "Believe me, I noticed."

"I'm just so glad I have your attention now." He bites his lip.

"You don't *just* have my attention. I've never felt anything for any other guy, or girl for that matter. So much has changed for me in the last week."

"Has it really only been a week?" He glides his hand through my hair, lightly touching my neck.

"I want you to explain the water thing, and what you did to my throat today."

He gets a far-off look in his eye before he acquiesces. "The thing is, I've had to learn these things as I go, because there is no one else like me. Demeter is the one who suggested that I try to find an element that could amplify my powers. Can I try something?"

"Um, that depends. You're not trying to get to third base or anything like that, are you?" I joke.

He laughs. "No—I wish—but no, nothing like that. Just trust me."

Now it's my turn to laugh, but nervously. Did he just say he wishes he could get to third base? There are butterflies having one hell of a party in my belly right now.

He lets go of my hand and places both of his gently on my face. He starts to hum lightly and closes his eyes, which makes me feel like I should close mine, but I can't. I'm still not used to having someone so close to me, touching me, and doing who knows what else to me. Then I feel something. It feels like the heat of the warmed water, but less hot and more powerfully intense.

"Whoa." I take a short breath. It doesn't hurt, but it's the most unusual sensation I've ever felt. It's like when I know a headache is coming on, but faster, and in reverse. I can't comprehend what he's doing, but it feels amazing.

He stops humming, lowers his hands, and opens his eyes. A smile plays across his face when he sees the look on mine. I'm fascinated.

"That was awesome! What did you do?"

"I shared some of my energy. It takes a lot of focus and concentration, unless I do it with a water conductor. It's how I helped your throat both times now, and how I heated the pool," though he says "heated the pool" with air quotes.

"Why did you do that?" I demonstrate the air quotes.

"Well, let's just say that the energy I exert naturally when swimming doesn't affect other males. You felt the heat, and Coach Winter felt the heat, but the thermometer didn't sense it, and neither did any of my teammates. Didn't you notice that?"

"Are you saying it's some perverted hormonal energy that you just shoved in my face?"

"Yeah, exactly. It's a mating call." But he laughs when he says it, and I don't believe a word he's saying now.

"No, really. Tell me how you do it." I cross my arms when he reaches to hold my hand again.

"I honestly don't know why, but it doesn't work on males. I've tried sharing energy with my dad and Wesley when they've been hurt, but it never works. Not even when I use water. I found out about it on accident, last winter. I was out for a run with my headphones on, humming along, when I saw a neighbor-lady who was born with spina bifida fall down in the snow. When I went to help her up, I felt my energy leave me, and she said I must have a fever from how hot my hands were. Only, they weren't hot—they were cold, if anything, from being ungloved on my run. The next thing she said was that her hip didn't hurt anymore and her headache was gone."

"You healed her?" I exclaim. "That's amazing."

"Well, she still had spina bifida, but I watched as her cracked, chapped lips healed before my eyes. I let go of her and realized releasing my energy in that way actually created more."

"What does it feel like to have your energy leave you? And do you ever run out?"

"It feels like I'm letting go of a frustration, and actually, it makes me feel calm. It makes things easier for me to share, but only if someone else is receiving it. And no, I've never run out. I'm sharing it, but I'm not giving it all away. What happened in the pool was that I was sharing it and you were taking it. But I think I gave you too much, and then you got out of the pool before I did. There was so much extra energy waiting in the water that Coach got all of it in her hand when she reached in for the thermometer."

"Wait, are you saying that the water wasn't hot for everyone?"

"The water wasn't hot at all. Your body was overheating from the energy in the water. The water was not affected at all, and none of the guys in the water were able to absorb my energy."

Suddenly, a light blazes out from the kitchen, brightening the living room for a few seconds, and I hear a dish crash into the sink. I'm on my feet and flying through the house in no time flat. Mr. Thelxinoe is a statue at our table with the computer in front of him. I find my mother standing in front of the sink with her mouth agape and eyes wide. I follow her gaze and find a beautiful woman with a long, flowing dress that's almost shining with its own light, and on her head is a crown. She is so otherworldly that her feet don't even seem to be touching the ground. My mom looks frozen in place, like if I touch her, she might shatter. I step in front of her unblinking form to guard her from whatever this strange woman is capable of. I think I know just who she is.

"To what do I owe this pleasure, Grandmother?" Vander steps in front of me as he speaks. His words are kind, but his posture, tone, and the vein popping out on his neck show that anger is brewing just below the surface. I fully understand why Kenzie-Grace was so frightened and felt threatened by this woman. She hasn't even said anything yet, and I already feel that my life is at risk.

"Son of Thelxinoe, I see you have found your betrothed despite our efforts to keep you apart." *What in the heck does* that *mean?* "You've shared water immersion, so my hands are tied. She must accompany you on your pre-quest."

"What are you talking about?" His hands have clenched into fists and his teeth are pressed tightly together, so he's not even moving his lips as he talks. I don't think I've ever seen anyone so upset, so quickly, in my entire life.

"We've tried to remove her desire for male companionship, and gave her the ability to resist your charms. She sees you as you are, and no amount of charming will change that. Not everything she's witnessed has been flattering and yet, she chose to immerse herself in water with you, and now you can never be apart."

"Never?" I interrupt. "What the hell are you talking about?"

She turns her body to face me.

"Who do you think you are to speak to me in this manner?" Her eyes are mesmerizing. I make a vow not to look at them again. I focus instead on her beautifully formed lips. She's truly breathtaking, in addition to terrifying.

"Well evidently, *I'm* the one who you messed with, to make me different from every other teenage girl I know, and then messed with my brain in order to keep us apart. And *I'm* the one who lives in this house that you have so rudely entered without an invitation and without warning. So maybe the question that needs to be asked here is who do you think *you* are?"

"Young lady, I have never been addressed in this way, and by a human, no less." She's acting all shocked and awed. Vander has not relaxed at all—in fact, his eyes are wide on me, and then wider on her, and focus back on me again.

"Well, I would say it's long past time you were. Maybe then you would have learned some basic manners and generally accepted rules of appropriate behavior."

"I will deal with you later." She glares at me, and then turns to him. "Now, Son of Thelxinoe, the only guidelines I can give you are that your pre-quest will last for twelve hours from the moment of trigger. Not one second longer. You must locate your necklace in the never grown, never growing, never will grow place in this town, which represents something that doesn't actually exist. Given your hereditary inability to find things that are lost, I have no choice but to wish you luck—you're going to need it."

With a puff of air, she's gone, and my mother immediately begins to clean up the dish she dropped upon Demeter's arrival, mumbling about her clumsiness as if nothing crazy has happened. His dad also seems oblivious to what has just occurred, lazily typing away on the laptop. It's just like when Taylor and Lissy were charmed; they didn't remember any of it taking place. Meanwhile, Vander is wildly grasping at his neck to try to find the now-missing necklace.

"What did she mean—" I start to ask, but Vander holds both hands up in the air, stopping me.

"I need paper, a pen, and complete quiet until I'm done writing this down." Vander is looking around frantically. I reach around my mom to open the junk drawer next to the sink and hand him some scrap paper and a pencil. He starts scribbling furiously.

The longer I stand there without saying anything, the more nervous I get about his response to how I treated his (sort of) grandmother. The silence is killing me, so I decide to step back out into the living room to wait for Vander to get done with whatever he is writing down. I hate bullies, and she seems to be a big one—with lots of power to back her up. It makes me wonder if Kenzie-Grace spoke to her at all when they met.

"Okay." I guess Vander is done writing, because he's now standing next to the couch. "First of all, you are absolutely incredible. I've never seen a human talk to a god or goddess before, let alone in *that* way. I have to say, you looked hot putting her in her place, but it terrified me at the same time. Secondly, are you freaking out right about now?"

Well, I guess that answers the Kenzie-Grace question.

"Yes." I swallow. "Yes, I am. Mainly because I don't know what the hell just happened." I have questions, lots of them. When my heart settles down, I may be able to voice them.

"Well, you read *Percy Jackson*, right? So you know about the oracle who told him about his quest?"

I nod, sort of impressed that he remembers I read them.

"Well, I already mentioned my main quest next year. This pre-quest that my grandmother has assigned will try to prepare me for that."

"So it's just a trial run?" I sigh to let go of some of the tension I've been carrying. I'm relieved.

"No, it's very much a gods-sanctioned mini-quest. I have to succeed, or there will be very real consequences."

"Like what?"

"Demeter is capable of great things. She could make someone I love disappear or turn them into rat or something even worse."

Just like that, the ten-ton weight is back on my shoulders. Vander can tell, and he reaches up with both hands to massage them with his strong fingers from in front of me.

"I don't want you to worry about that right now. I have faith that we will figure this out."

"Well, I'm totally freaking out right now. You used the word 'we,' and I can't stop thinking about what she said. I'm *betrothed* to you? Is that like being engaged to be married? I'm not ready for anything like that—I'm only seventeen years old!"

"No, hold on. It's not like that. You are *my* betrothed, but you don't have one, since you are fully human. It means I have found my true promise. I have only one chance in the world to find the person selected to be with me. I told you this before. You are my true promise. That means you are the one human allowed to aid me on my journeys without interference from the gods. You must be the reason my dad and I landed in Cedar Rapids, Iowa—of all places in the world for a sailor to live. You are *it* for me, the one I've been looking for. But—" he pauses, and my panic starts to rise to dangerous levels.

"I don't like the sound of your 'but.'"

Vander lets a chuckle slip out before I glare at him. I'm on the edge of a major panic attack right now.

"Julia, I was just going to say, *but* you don't *have* to help me. You are human and have free will; you will always reserve the right to walk away. You are free to choose who you want to be with and just the thought that it might not be me, scares the hell out of me."

Wow, no pressure.

"But I heard her, she said we can 'never be apart.' Never is a really long time from now."

"Listen, if enough gods wanted to keep us apart, I never would have ended up here with you. They have the power to make sure of it. The fact that we are together just assures me that Demeter doesn't have the right kind of alliances to continue her mission to ensure our separation."

This is too much for me to think about when we are talking about always and never. *Screw that!* I can't handle this.

"Did you know about the water thing?"

"No, I didn't know that would cause a pre-quest. I swear." He's still reaching for his necklace, which I've only ever seen him do when he's nervous or hiding something.

"Okay, so what did you know?"

"I noticed after the first practice last week that I had more energy than usual, and didn't need as much sleep. That's all. I can only hope it had the same effect on you, because if you go with me, we could be up all night."

"Like my mom will let me go out alone with a teenage boy, even one she seems to like, all night." I laugh at the thought.

"That's not a problem—Demeter took care of that, I'm sure. She is required to eliminate those kinds of obstacles for me, since she is responsible for this pre-quest."

"What do you mean? Did that witch mess with my mom's mind?"

"I don't know how she does what she does, but if we need to stay out late your mom will probably believe you are staying with Lissy or Taylor. As for Demeter, I wouldn't ever refer to her as a witch again. She is a Greek goddess, and has the power and the contacts to become your worst nightmare, potentially literally. Just trust me—you can't even imagine what she's capable of if you get on her bad side."

He shivers as he finishes speaking and it reminds me how much is weighing on his shoulders. He's only seventeen years old, but he has been putting up with her abuse of power for every single one of them. Makes my problems seems minor, and doing this may even help me discover what is going on with me and why I can resist his charms.

"Okay, okay, okay. How are we actually going to look for your necklace when we have nothing but a riddle as a map? We should definitely start trying to figure this out."

"Are you saying you're in?"

"Hell yeah, I'm in! Any chance I get to show that wi—*woman*," I clear my throat, "that I am truly a force to be reckoned with, I'm going to take it. In fact, I'm going to make it look easy! Come at me!"

The sudden kiss he lays on me is so passionate I think my socks melt off. My heart starts pounding in my chest and my hands grasp at him to pull him closer. Part of me is shocked by his action, but if I'm honest with myself, I was kind of expecting it.

When he reluctantly pulls away, he searches my eyes. I refuse to divert my attention from him. I need him to understand that I'm with him on this. If I am this uptight and I have nothing to lose, I can't imagine how stressed he is. We don't actually know what's on the line for him specifically, but it has to be bigger than being grounded, which is the worst punishment I've ever received.

He smiles when he sees my determination. His hand slides down from around my neck and reaches into his pocket to pull out the paper with the riddle on it. We sit looking at it for a minute until he sighs.

"What does that sigh mean?" I'm not sure if he's frustrated or bored, but to me, it seems like most of the riddle is missing.

"It means I have no idea where to start. And I don't know how much time I have to figure it out."

"Yeah, what is this trigger we are waiting for?"

"I don't even know and that may be the point, to throw me off. This thing could start at any time and we might not even know it."

Vander rubs his forehead with his hand, and then grabs his cell phone. He punches at it for a little bit. I'm not sure if he is doing a web search for the riddle, or calling in reinforcements, but I just sit and continue to stare at the paper, hoping that something will come to me, or more words will appear before my eyes.

How in the world can something exist that has never grown, is not growing now, and never will? "This makes no sense."

"Ah, but it will eventually to someone on our crew."

"Crew? I thought we had to do this on our own." This is so confusing.

"We do, but I am not yet eighteen, and therefore am allowed an advisor." He's grinning now.

"Who is *our* advisor?" I squeeze his hand to emphasize our team status.

"You're not going to believe me." He has a shit-eating grin on his face.

"Why would I not believe that, out of all the things I've had to believe since I started hanging out with you?" I match the look on his face with my own.

"Most girls at our school would feel privileged to be asked to spend this time with me. And then they would really flip when they learned who our advisor is."

Just like that, the self-righteous jerk inside of this guy who I can no longer resist rears his ugly head. I try to let go of his hand and back away from him, but I can't. He's laughing, and that makes me realize that at least he knows he's being awful.

"Who is it?" I ask. But before he says anything, I know. I know that Wes is too young to be an advisor, and the only other male at our school that girls would go so gaga over is, "Mr. Daniels?"

He smiles rewardingly at me. "See? I knew you would figure it out."

"Taylor and Lissy would die."

He shrugs. "Probably."

We spend most of the rest of our time together researching the history of Cedar Rapids, hoping to find a clue about this town and something that doesn't exist. In my head, the idea of researching something that doesn't exist is asinine as can be. When Vander finally kisses me goodnight, he reassures me that everything will work out fine.

I'm not so sure.

CHAPTER TWENTY-ONE

I've been lying in bed for close to two hours, and sleep won't come. Knowing that tomorrow I could be up all night, and that I potentially could have narcolepsy, doesn't seem to be a very good combination. I can't seem to wrap my head around what's happening, and yet, I am trying not to think at all so sleep will come. Instead, I am stuck watching this wheel of anxiety spin behind my closed eyes.

What if we don't solve the riddle?

What if Mr. Daniels is no help?

What if we don't find his necklace in time?

What if I receive the punishment, too?

Whose life is this, are these things are actually happening?

How am I Vander's troth?

How does Vander have these powers?

If his mom's tears can make people see mirages, what do his tears do?

How come his powers can't help him with this riddle?

What if we don't solve the riddle?

What if Mr. Daniels is REALLY no help?

"*Aggghhh*!"

My phone's vibrations on my bedside table scare the crap out of me. I grab it and look at the time. *Great, it's been two-and-a half-hours now.* There is a text waiting for me. I must have forgotten to put it on airplane mode to go to sleep.

Vander: I can help you sleep.

Me: How did you know I wasn't already and you just woke me up?

Vander: If you were sleeping, that text wouldn't have woken you up.

Me: Touché! How can you help? My mind is racing.

Vander: I can sing to you. It should take about 3 seconds if I recall.

Me: I hate it when you mess with my brain.

Vander: A Siren song is naturally lulling, there is no mind charming involved.

I can't endure a whole night of tossing and turning, thinking over and over about all of the things causing me anxiety. It only takes a second for me to decide to press the phone icon. He answers before the first full ring has sounded on my end.

"Are you sure about this?"

"Well, I might need to be up for all of tomorrow night, so staying up tonight would create a real disadvantage."

"Is that a yes?"

"Yes." I take a deep breath and let it out slowly. I position the phone under my ear and get comfortable, making sure it's not going to come unplugged. I hear him take in a slow breath. The first words of his song make me smile from ear to ear.

"Twinkle, twinkle, little star, how I wonder..."

CHAPTER TWENTY-TWO

The sun is shining brightly through my windows. I have school today, and then I have a quest with my boyfriend and my teacher. *Or does Mr. Daniels just advise over the phone?*

"Good morning." Vander's voice is soothing to my anxious heart and mind this morning. At least it was, until I open my eyes and realize he isn't here. His voice is coming through the phone still lying at my ear.

"Vander?"

Holy crap, I have the hugest kink in my neck.

"I didn't move all night!"

"You were sleeping like a rock anytime I woke up and checked on you."

I bet I was. I had so much going on in my mind before I finally fell asleep, I wore myself out. That reminds me of another concern I have about how this mission will go.

"Does Mr. Daniels come with us?"

I can hear the smile on his face when he answers, "No, that is not allowed."

I sigh in relief. It's not like that would be a deal breaker, but I'm glad it will just be the two of us. Two teenagers out and about town is not as scandalous as a girl, a teenage boy, and their teacher.

"Okay. Thanks for helping me sleep last night. I feel great this morning." I grab my phone and sit up to stretch out my neck.

"No problem at all. I will see you at school in a little bit."

School seems different when I walk in. I'm used to school being the location that causes me stress. Right now, it's a person doing that for me. A person who I couldn't even stand to think about two weeks ago. Taylor and Lissy can attest to that fact.

The problem is that Demeter was the cause of my hatred of all boys, and the reason I refused to participate in boy talk. I hate having my brain messed with, and I hate even more that I was different from every other girl I knew. I fooled myself into thinking I was special and simply had more self-control. The truth is, I have been tampered with, I am damaged goods, and I am someone's predetermined mate—not just any someone, either—Vander McMuscles Thelxinoe.

"Is it true?" Lissy's high-pitched squeal can be heard in any hall of the school, I'm sure.

"Is *what* true?"

"You were chosen to go on the overnight leadership retreat with Mr. Daniels and Ms. Johnson? I didn't even know you applied."

Until this very moment, I had never even heard of such a thing. It dawns on me that this could be part of the cover-up Demeter is responsible for giving me. Maybe this means Mr. Daniels *is* going to be with us. I try to smile convincingly to Lissy and Taylor, who has just joined us in the hall. I hate Demeter even more than I did a minute ago, because now I am trying to convince my friends of something that isn't true.

"Um, where did you hear that?" I pretend to dig through my backpack to give my hands something to do.

"It's posted on the school website with the announcements. So, it must be true, isn't it?"

"Yeah, I guess so."

They both start bouncing up and down, giving me hugs and squealing like a small pod of dolphins that has just been released from captivity. Not for the first time, I smile when I hear the bell signaling that we are going to have to make our way to our first classes. I can't even imagine how the rest of this day is going to go if this is just the beginning.

When I walk into European literature, I'm not surprised by the fact that we have a substitute teacher. Mrs. Skaggs is a pretty popular sub in the area, because she makes sure we get the work done, and then lets us play on our phones. There aren't any bad stalker photos of her on Twitter or anything—in fact, she will take selfies with us if we ask. She's badass like that. Anyway, I wasn't expecting to see Mr. Daniels after I put two and two together this morning. He has to get prepared for the mini-quest as well, and I don't even know what that entails. What actually does surprise me is that Vander isn't here either.

I take out my phone to text him, but the bell rings and Mrs. Skaggs makes me put it away until our lesson is done for the day. She has eyes like a hawk, so we don't try to get away with anything.

Class seems to pass by slower than ever since I have read all the assignments plus more about Greek Mythology, not to mention considering what was going on with Vander and me. I know all the answers, and near the end of class I offer up a topic of conversation.

"What do you believe about the myth of the Sirens, Mrs. Skaggs?" After our lively class discussion the last time this topic came up, I'm sure people are anxious to hear what she has to say.

"Everything I know about Sirens, I learned from watching *Percy Jackson: Sea of Monsters.*" She proceeds to look up a video to share of the Sirens from that movie. As it starts to play, I take the opportunity to text Vander to find out where he is.

Me: Where are you?

Mrs. Skaggs makes her way around the desk, comes up behind me, and takes my phone from me just as it buzzes a reply. She's part hawk, I just know it.

"I'm disappointed that my response to your question wasn't entertaining enough for you to pay attention to." She gives me that mom look all good teachers can use to make me feel as tall as a troll doll.

"I'm sorry, Mrs. Skaggs." I look her in the eyes to let her know I mean it.

She nods and returns to her desk with my phone. The best I can hope for is to get it back at the end of the hour. More likely, I will be without it until the end of the day.

By lunchtime, I am pissed off. Vander could have told me he was planning to skip his classes today. I firmly remember him saying that he would see me at school in a little bit.

When I go to collect my phone from Mrs. Skaggs after school, I am livid. He could have gotten a message to me somehow, even if it meant coming to school himself, like he said he would.

I focus on having a polite and apologetic look on my face when I walk back to European Literature to see Mrs. Skaggs. There are a few stragglers from the seventh period class making their way out of the room. Maddie smiles at me and looks like she wants to talk, which is a switch from our last interaction. Stopping in front of me, she says, "Hey, I'm sorry about the Vander thing, I really didn't know."

"It's okay."

"Thanks again for helping me out with the flag contest. Did you hear what they did with the flag we made?"

"No problem, Maddie. And no, I hadn't heard."

"The Home Economics teacher asked if she could hang it in her room for her creative quilting unit." We both bust out laughing.

She walks away, and I take a second to appreciate her apology. This school is big enough for us to avoid each other if necessary. I'm glad that it wasn't.

I make an effort to put my bad puppy dog look back on my face for Mrs. Skaggs. But she isn't here. There are two people in the room, and one of them is Mr. Daniels; the other is a new science teacher in the building, Ms. Johnson.

"Mr. Daniels? I didn't know you were back. Do you happen to have my phone?"

Ignoring my question he turns to me and says, "From this moment until after Thanksgiving break, I want you to call me DJ. Okay?"

I nod, but it's not enough for him. He turns his head at me and waits. "Okay, DJ," I offer.

"Well done. This is Jerika. She is your guide."

"Hi, Ms. Johnson." I turn back to Mr. Dan—*DJ*, but he has that look on his face again, and I receive the message he's sending. "I mean Jerika, sorry. Now, can I please have my phone?"

"You can't have your phone until after this quest has been completed. It is an unacceptable advantage," she answers for him. With that answer, Ms. John—*Jerika*—has just moved to the top of my shit list. How is this going to work if I can't get a hold of Vander? We are supposed to be together for this.

"Yeah, okay. I just need to find out where Vander has been all day. I will give it back to you before the quest begins, tribute's honor." I raise three fingers for effect.

"What do you mean, 'before the quest begins'? It already started, the moment you relinquished your phone to a squire of the royal court." And just like that, DJ joins Jerika on my list.

"Don't you think you were burying the lead a bit there, DJ?" His name tastes like poison in my mouth. "You're telling me that Vander is out there on his own, trying to figure out the riddle and find his necklace, while you are busy telling me your first names, like that's the most important part?"

I'm yelling at a teacher, but he deserves it. My blood pressure is rising as my heart rate skyrockets. I take a seat and try to focus on taking deep, slow breaths.

"Listen, you and Vander were the ones who decided to declare that you would be attempting to complete this quest together, without consulting your guides first, I might add. So now, it is your responsibility to not only solve the riddle and collect the necklace, but you must also do so without your phones, without his powers, and you absolutely *must* complete it together."

There is too much information to process now, and I don't even know what to think first. Mrs. Skaggs is a squire—*whatever that is*—Vander is alone, we can't have phones, his powers aren't working on anyone, and I have a guide, who is presently sitting next to DJ on a throne at the top of my shit list.

"Well, guides," I put a nasty spin on that word for effect, "what am I supposed to do now?"

"First thing you need to do is find Vander. What was the last thing you talked about?"

Before I have a chance to respond, Jerika adds her own two cents. "Well, not necessarily the last thing you talked about, but did you make any plans for where to meet today?"

My mind races with thoughts of how today was supposed to go. The last thing we talked about was seeing each other at school, but I think it's safe to assume that since he isn't here, school is not the location where he is meeting me. We talked about hunting too, but we didn't address where. The only other thing was…

"The bowling alley! We talked about going to karaoke before the quest started tonight."

"Sounds like a great start to me." Jerika smiles. DJ is smiling too, but nobody makes a move toward the door.

"Are we going there, or what?"

"You need to do this on your own," she spits out with a little laugh, like I should have known better. *The truth is, I know nothing.* "I will be where you need me, and I'll be watching."

What the heck ever, I don't need them—I need to find Vander. I march toward the door and push it open. I turn to tell them that I will see them later, but they are both gone—the room is empty. *Who are these people?*

As I walk out to the parking lot, I reach in my bag for my phone. I groan when I remember I don't have it, and I won't have it until this is all over. I wonder if Vander knew our phones would be confiscated, because he did write the riddle down instead of just recording himself repeating it. If he knew and didn't tell me, I am going to be so pissed off. Also, why did I think we got to choose when the quest started? There is no way either of us knew it would start without our knowledge.

"Where is my car?" I laugh at the absurdity of my present circumstances. "Great, I've lost my phone, now my car is gone, and I'm talking to myself."

"It would be an unacceptable advantage to let you have that kind of transportation." Jerika appears next to me, as if we have been walking together this whole time. There is no puff of smoke or *poof* sound—I was just walking alone, and then here she is. The word *bizarre* doesn't even begin to cover it.

"Are you telling me someone took my car?" I'm trying to remind myself that she is the only help I have on my side, at least until I find Vander. I am really in the mood to yell at someone, and she is the perfect target for my anger, but if I let myself start, I don't know if I will be able to stop. There has never been a more important time for me to keep it together.

"No, Julia. Your car is safe, and will be made available to you at the completion of this quest." She looks to the parking spot behind her where I could have sworn I parked my car in this morning. It looks empty to me, but maybe it's not, and my brain is being charmed. I would rather have someone take my car than to have them mess with my mind. It's so invasive and wrong.

"I don't know what I'm doing, I don't know the rules, and I don't understand the riddle or the quest. I don't even know what's at stake—can you help me with *any* of that?" I'm pleading with her as tears fill my eyes. I refuse to let them fall for the same reason I can't allow myself to get angry—they may never stop if I let them start now.

"I can't answer all of your questions, because the whole point is for you to learn as you experience things. What I can tell you is that things aren't always what they seem." With those words, she leans back in what appears an unnatural way, and holds herself aloft like she's leaning against something.

My car! She can't tell me it's actually there, but she is showing me that it is. I can't see it, but it's there, and that confirms the one thing I wish weren't true—someone has charmed me. I hate that. I clench my jaw closed and fight the tears threatening to fall. With a firm swipe of the back of my hand across my face and a deep breath, I brace myself for the challenge ahead.

"Can I ask people for rides, or do I need to take the bus? Can I call a cab?" I'm staring at my shoes, trying to see if I can make out my car in my peripheral vision. *It doesn't work, damn it.*

She shakes her head. "Knowing when to depend on others and who you can trust is vital to success. Be careful not to ask for help unless you *need* it."

She sounds like a damn fortune cookie. I look up to tell her that, but she's gone. Again. Or at least she appears to be gone. I can't even trust my own sight right now. I just hope that the city bus is right on schedule, and that the money in my bag is not considered an unacceptable advantage. I'm really starting to hate those words.

As I make my way to the bus stop near campus, I notice that there aren't a lot of people around. I open up my ears to listen. I wonder if Jerika is following me with some kind of invisibility cloak on or something. I don't hear any footsteps, though she said she would be watching. *Does this mean I can't trust my hearing, either?*

There is only one guy waiting at the bus stop when I cross the street. "Can you tell me what time it is now, and what time the bus comes?"

He doesn't respond, and I begin to conclude that I can't trust my voice, either. But then I notice his eyes are closed, and two wires are hanging down beneath his beanie. I tap him on the shoulder, and he jumps a little bit in surprise. He takes out one of his ear buds and presses a finger to his phone.

"Sorry, I didn't mean to scare you. Can you tell me how long until the bus gets here?"

He glances at his phone and looks away with squinty eyes for a second, certainly doing some calculations. He checks his phone again and then says, "Seven minutes."

I want to ask to borrow his phone, but it would probably disappear, and I believe this guy could take me so I don't do that. Just as he reaches up to put his earbud back in place, I remember that there's one more thing I need to know. "How much does a one-way ticket cost?"

"Seventy-five cents with a student ID." He sighs, as if utterly put out by my two questions as he turns his back on me. This conversation is over. I internally rejoice at the fact that I asked two questions and got two straight answers. Time to dig through my bag for change.

It's weird how quiet everything is, and how it seems like nobody is around. I wonder if that is part of the charm—how I am made to feel isolated. I have no phone, I haven't seen my friends or Vander recently, my car is invisible, and nobody else is around. Of course, maybe this is how quiet it gets after school every day when I drive off, or stay back at the pool.

Oh, shit! Swim practice.

I completely forgot about it. Maybe that is where Vander is, and for sure Lissy will be there, too. I take off jogging back toward the school. I have no idea what time it is, but I am absolutely late, and Coach will definitely notice. When I get back to the parking lot, I decide to test out my sense of touch by moving through the parking spot where my car is—*was*—located. I walk hesitantly, but then I make it through effortlessly with no restrictions. *This is such a strange situation.*

I make my way into the school at the gym entrance and walk briskly to the locker room, where I look at the clock to note the time. When I arrive on the pool deck, Lissy grabs me around the neck.

"We were so worried about you." She says this out loud, and then whispers to me, "I told Coach you were feeling lightheaded and needed to lay down for a few minutes. Play along."

Lissy doesn't let go of me as she walks me over to one of the deck benches that line the walls. Coach waves and gives me a salute. I guess that's her way of thanking me for making the effort to be here even though she believes I am feeling unwell.

"Where have you actually been?" Lissy asks while she continues to treat me like an invalid, patting me on the leg and smoothing my hair.

Keeping up the charade, I lean against the wall and try to figure out what to even say. Lissy still doesn't understand that Vander is different. *Vander!* I sit up straight and look in his lane.

"He's not here either." Lissy grabs my knee and squeezes, reminding me that I am supposed to be sickly. I put my head back against the wall.

"Mrs. Skaggs still has my phone, and my car won't start, *and* I don't know where Vander is." Once again, I am cursing Demeter for making me lie to my friend.

"That sucks! Maybe one of these guys can get your car started." She looks around, suddenly interested in the idea of going around to ask each and every one of them what their knowledge of car problems is.

"No, that's okay. I think my mom is going to have it towed or something. I may not make it to karaoke tonight. I have to wait and see what's going on." Her mood sinks a little bit, but what else can I say?

"Edmonds!" Coach bellows at Lissy from the top of the freshman lane. We both look up in time to hear her shout again. "Water bottles!"

"You are so going to owe me." She blows me an air kiss as she gets back to work. I watch her blue and green ponytail bounce away while trying to appear as pathetic as I can.

"Wright! Go home!" I don't see any reason to stay here if I'm sick, and, evidently, neither does she.

I'm careful to keep a hand on the wall and move slowly to the locker room door. I don't want anyone to doubt my well-being—or lack thereof, in this situation. I make my way through the locker room, take another glance at the clock, and decide to inspect my parking spot again. It still looks and feels empty to me.

When I arrive at the bus stop, the guy from before is gone, but two girls are waiting where he stood. I choose to just wait with them. The bus runs every hour, except during peak times like after school and around rush hour, when it runs every half-hour. That's about how long I was at the pool for, so it should be here any minute.

Once the bus arrives, the ride to the downtown depot takes about ten minutes. I can't believe there isn't a way to ride from one side of town to the other without doing a transfer downtown. I spend every single one of those minutes trying to breathe through my mouth, so I don't have to smell the strong odor of marijuana coming from the man behind me. At the depot, I look around, testing my eyes. I want to try to figure out how to think beyond the mirages being placed in my brain.

Things aren't always what they seem. Obviously, my car was where I had left it, because she could still lean on it. Then when I walked through that space, there was no resistance. So, not only are things not what they seem visually, but there is something tricking my mind physically, too.

My life was so much easier before Vander came into it—it's hard to believe boys are worth all this trouble.

The clock in the depot tells me I left school about twenty minutes ago. I grab a seat near the front of my second bus and set my bag on the seat next to me. I hope I don't have a smelly passenger sitting next to me for this ride. My eye keeps catching on a *City of Cedar Rapids* poster with its funny-looking tree on it. Outside, all the leaves have fallen and things look pretty bleak around town, but the green of that poster makes me happy. We cross the river to the west side, and I start to get anxious. *What if Vander isn't at the bowling alley? What if he is somewhere else, looking for me?*

Breathing in through the nose and out through the mouth, just the opposite of when I'm swimming, helps to keep me calm. I need to stay cool, calm, and collected if I am going to be of any help to Vander in successfully completing this quest. Which brings me back to trying to solve the riddle. *How can we find something that doesn't exist?* That's the only thing I remember off the top of my head. It's a good thing Vander wrote it all down as soon as he heard it.

This is all so messed up. I hope Vander is off to a better start than I am. It feels like the city's tree is mocking me now. Looking all green and happy, not a care in the world, while I struggle with what will probably end up being a simple puzzle.

By the time I can see the strip mall in front of the bowling alley, I have calmed myself down. I realize that I have returned to breathing normally, just in time to get worked up again at the possibility of not finding Vander here. Fortunately, I see him leaning against the bank building on the end of the strip mall watching the bus carefully. I wave, but he doesn't seem to see me. I really hope the tinted windows are the issue, because if he is charmed not to see me, this day will be an utter mess.

I stand up when the bus arrives, and then race down the steps as soon as the driver opens the doors. Relief floods through me when I see Vander wave. This part of the quest was stressful, but at least we are together now. I decide that I'm going to keep a running tally. Demeter now owes me one dollar and fifty cents for two unnecessary bus rides.

"Julia! I've never been so happy to see you in my life!" Vander picks me up and swings me around. I put my arms around his neck and squeeze my eyes shut. The last thing we need is for me to start blowing chunks from motion sickness.

"I know the feeling. Sorry it took me so long. I thought you might be at swim practice, so I checked there before I caught the bus. Why weren't you at school today?" He sets me down and looks at me, puzzled.

"Of course you wouldn't get my text. Did you know cell phones work best when both people involved actually use them?" It's a good thing he's laughing so I know he is joking. "I had an idea about where my necklace might be and wanted to check it out as soon as possible. But I was wrong. Then DJ showed up saying you triggered the start of the quest. He took my phone, my car, and my powers, or at least he told me they would be useless until we completed this mission. Also, he said time would be taken away for breaking any rules we've been given."

He reaches for his missing necklace with one hand and laces our fingers together with the other. A chill runs down my spine, sending shivers up my arms and launching a smile on my face.

"Well, we have the first part of this mission complete—we are together now. Do you have the paper with the riddle on it? I don't remember it exactly."

I squeeze his hand before I let it go so he can search his pockets for the paper he wrote on in my kitchen last night. He flattens the paper between his hand and his abs. A fleeting thought of *lucky paper* goes through my brain. *Geeze Louise.* I shake it out of my head and refocus as Vander begins reading.

"I will find my necklace in the never grown, never growing, never will grow place in this town that represents something that doesn't actually exist. Given my hereditary inability to find things that are lost, she has no choice but to wish me luck."

"What does she mean by the last part?" I didn't think it was part of the riddle, but the fact that he wrote it down might mean something.

"I'm sure it's a dig at my mother and her friends for not finding Persephone, even though we know now that she was kidnapped and taken to the underworld."

I'm shocked to silence at how bitter that woman must be to carry on about it so many centuries later. Vander can't handle the silence and adds, "Demeter certainly has a way with words."

"Do you have any idea how little I like that woman?" I grab his hand again and squeeze it.

"I'm betting it's not a whole lot. *Anyway,*" he drags out the word, effectively changing the subject, "want to know what I think the first part has to do with?"

"Of course I do." I rub my hands together in anticipation.

"Well, I have been so focused on finding you, I haven't really put much thought into it today. But before my phone and car went missing this morning, I did some research on Cedar Rapids, as an outsider might. Our city is known as the City of Five Seasons. As there are only four seasons, maybe that explains the part about celebrating the thing that doesn't actually exist. What do you think?" His hair almost hides his eyes, but I can see the hope in them. He is nearly bouncing on his feet.

Living here my whole life, I never gave too much thought to that "five seasons" thing. I remember asking my dad about his idea of what it meant.

"What is the fifth season here?"

"Happiness," he answered simply, smiling at me.

Man, I miss my dad.

"Hello? Where did you go?" Vander's finger on my cheek brings me back to this moment. When he pulls his finger away, I can see the moisture on it. I feel his other hand has moved up my arm. He wraps me in a hug, and I take a moment to gather my thoughts as I squeeze him back.

"*It's happiness,*" I whisper over his shoulder.

"What is? That tear I wiped away? It looked more like sadness to me," he replies gently.

"No," I chuckle, backing away to wipe my eyes with the back of my hand. "The fifth season. It's happiness."

"Well, how do we find where *that* grows?" he asks exasperatedly. It's a good question, but I have to start a new train of thought for my own sanity.

"Hey, did you know Jerika Johnson is *my* guide? Did you know that they took my car, too? But I think it's still where I left it, and I just can't see or feel it. What did they take of yours, other than your phone and car? Have you seen DJ?" I take a breath, but realize it is far too shallow. If I were swimming, I wouldn't be able to continue for much longer with as little oxygen as I'm currently getting.

Vander pulls me back into a protective side hug and shushes me quietly. He rubs my back and says, "Julia, we have a lot of time. There is no need to panic. Just breathe, deep and slow."

Oxygen in through my nose, carbon dioxide out through my mouth. I repeat that a few times, and then nod. I start to think about how I had to breathe through my mouth on the first bus due to the smell, and an image from the bus ride comes to mind.

"There's a tree! The Tree of Five Seasons, downtown! That has to be it!" I'm still gasping for air due to my near hyperventilation.

"There are a lot of things in town having to do with the five seasons, though," he points out warily.

"Yes, but only one that might have anything to do with growing—or not growing—as the case may be." A hopeful smile appears on Vander's face, reminding me how handsome he can be when he's not trying to be a world-class jerkhole.

"Okay, it's definitely worth checking out. Should we take the bus?"

His question makes me scream, "*No*!"

"Okay? Let's not check it out?" His brow furrows and he looks at me questioningly.

"I was so excited to see you, and to know that I actually did something right today, I flew out of my seat and hopped down those bus steps and into your arms. Then you spun me around, and we held hands, and got right to work on this mission. The one thing I didn't do was grab my backpack from the seat next to me. I now have no money, no ID, no phone, no car, and no books! Oh shit! How am I supposed to do my homework without my books? If I don't get my homework done, I'll never be able to sleep."

"You're going to hyperventilate again if you don't calm down. It's not the end of the world—we will call the bus company and have them hold your bag at the depot for you. Maybe one of your friends could pick it up for you on their way here?"

"Wait, why are my friends coming *here*? Are they mixed up in this quest thing, too? What happened to them?" I fall to my knees, because I can feel the panic rising in my system, threatening to take my breath away entirely, until I see nothing but darkness. Vander is rubbing my back with one hand as he crouches beside me.

"Julia, I just need you to breathe with me, deep and slow." He demonstrates and I follow along, since he is the reasonable one at the moment. After a minute, the shock wears off his face and he speaks calmly to me. "That's it, good. There is a reason we met at the bowling alley, remember? It's karaoke night."

I sigh in relief. We aren't completely stranded here without hope. With nowhere else to go right now, I take a seat on the ground. Then, I reach in my pocket for my phone—that isn't there—to see the time. It's a force of habit. *This day sucks.* "Do you have a watch?"

Vander sits next to me and pushes back the sleeve of his brown V-neck sweater to reveal a fancy sports watch. I bet that baby is waterproof, and knows when he does a flip turn using GPS or something. That damn thing could probably make him coffee in the morning, too.

"It's about ten 'til five. Why don't we find a phone and call the bus depot, then we can call your friends about picking up your bag, and we can grab something to eat. I haven't had anything since I left my house this morning and now I'm so hungry." His stomach growls in agreement with his words.

"That sounds like a good plan, except I was supposed to be my friends' ride tonight." I take a deep breath to help keep the panic at bay.

"I'll call Wesley. Have no fear." He puts his arm around me and pulls me close. "Do you think they'll mind riding with him?"

I smile at the thought of Lissy's face when she finds out Wesley is picking her up tonight instead of me. Taylor will not object either, especially if there is a chance to ask about his brother. I laugh a bit as I reassure him, "I am sure they will consider it a deluxe upgrade."

Vander helps me up off the ground and asks which I would prefer, "*B-Dubs* or *Genghis Grill*?"

"Either one works for me." My appetite is completely not picky, and I won't deny the active athlete the right to choose which meal we have, even though he did skip practice today. As we walk across the parking lot to the restaurant, Vander trips over a curb and catches himself against a handicap parking sign. The corner of the sign rips a hole in the arm of his shirt.

"Typical," Vander mutters as he shakes his head in disgust.

"What do you mean, 'typical'?"

"It's the whole reason I wear that evil eye necklace to begin with—to ward off bad luck. It's why I fell asleep after waking you up this morning, why you left your bag on the bus, why I stepped in a huge puddle on my way here, even though it hasn't rained in over a week. It's why I just tripped and ripped my shirt, why I didn't think to meet you at swim practice, and why my powers aren't working on the day I need them most. Why else would all this bad stuff be happening?"

"Maybe you should have had a V-8 for breakfast?" I ask sarcastically. I can't believe how superstitious he is being. "I don't know. I was going to blame all that stuff on the excitement and stress of our quest. Are you sure that's the 'whole reason' you wear that necklace? I mean, why take it? Why would Demeter know how important it is to you?"

"Because my mom gave it to me. Well, my dad gave it to me because my mom told him to, but you know what I mean." When he mentions his mom, his eyes fall. Understanding strikes, because we have that missing parent thing in common. Knowing what Demeter has done to his mother is bad enough, but the consequence if we fail this quest could negatively affect his dad, too. The pressure is mounting; it's time to rally the troops and get to work.

"Regardless, we need to figure out a way to not only make it through the task at hand, but to do so with some happiness. It is the fifth season, after all. We have too much to accomplish to waste time worrying about our bad luck. Can you do that?"

"I'll try, that's all I can say." His sad eyes become hopeful once again. I will take what I can get.

"Me too." I give him a quick squeeze and I feel the sigh he releases. "Hey, Vander?"

"Yeah?"

"You didn't lose your wallet, did you?"

He taps the back pockets of his jeans and smiles. I'm smiling too, thinking how nice it would be to tap those pockets myself (*holy shit, what's wrong with me?*) when he winks. "No, it's right here, and I can't wait for this date."

My heart flutters at the word *date*, but this is the first time we've been in public together outside of school. Since I have been so anti-relationships for so long, it takes me a minute to get used to the idea of us being a couple—*at least, I think we are a couple now, aren't we?*

By the time we're seated at a table inside the Mongolian grill joint, it's after five, but practice isn't over yet. We won't be able to reach our friends until after we eat, so we decide to call the bus depot first. They found my bag, and are holding it for Lissy. That's a little bit of weight off my shoulders.

The next step is to enjoy our meals and try to figure out the best route to the Tree of Five Seasons' sculpture, in case we end up needing to walk. As soon as the waiter brings our ice waters and bowls, we make our way to the food area. I follow Vander's lead because I have never been here before. We both dig in to the chicken and pile on the veggies. Vander takes his time laying out a thin layer of spinach over his entire bowl and then presses down on it with both hands. He grins when he catches me watching, and goes back to piling on some pineapple and peppers. It's a genius move, now that I think about it, but I'm not as hungry as he seems to be, so I skip that step. He chooses our sauces, and we carefully carry our food to the big grill.

Even though Vander's bowl is piled high, he sets it down carefully without spilling a thing. He places the sauce down next to his bowl, and I do the same.

The prep cook hands Vander and I each a number and asks, "Starch?"

"Fried rice, please," Vander answers for both of us. Then he turns to me and whispers, "I always ask for tortillas from the waiter at the table as well."

The cook dumps the food on the grill, and I can hear the sizzle and see the heat rising above it. He separates the veggies from the meat, pushing the meat closer to the heat with two big sticks. He keeps chopping at it with his sticks, flipping it to make sure it cooks evenly. This is thrilling for me. My mom's skills in the kitchen don't even come close to this.

I catch Vander looking at me watching, and then I see him throw a couple dollars into the tip jar. The cook yells for him to bang the gong on the counter, and Vander motions for me to do it. I've never done it before so I shake my head, but he insists.

"Lightly tap the mallet on the surface, to get it vibrating a bit, before you hit it." He reaches from behind me and helps me do it just right. The sound makes me laugh—or maybe it is just the joy of this moment—and I realize I am happy. There might be something at risk for me with this quest, after all.

Vander sets the mallet down at the same time the cook calls out our numbers. He turns too quickly, and the mallet crashes to the floor. He bends to pick it up just as our waiter walks by with a tray of drinks. This is a catastrophe in the making.

"Stop!" I yell, as I can clearly see the chaos that's about to erupt if these two collide.

The sharpness of my tone halts our waiter in his place, but Vander reacts defensively, looking around for the attacker I've just yelled at with the mallet now raised in his hand. *Thank all the Greek gods he didn't make contact.* That could have ended disastrously.

We make it safely back to our table, and I can't wait to dive in. This place made our food so quick. I probably eat a little too fast, but I can't believe how delicious it is, and we are on a tight schedule. Man, Vander really knows how to fill a bowl and pick sauces at this place.

After our quick dinner, Vander asks to use the restaurant's phone again to call Wesley, and I use it to call Lissy. She squeals when I tell her that Wesley is picking her up, and has no problem getting my bag along the way. While we make our way over to the bowling alley with full bellies, I have the chance to ask about some of what's been on my mind today.

"I still don't know what's at stake if we don't do this in time. Did DJ tell you what would happen if we fail? What's our deadline? I don't even know when this quest started."

"Whoa. Slow down." Vander takes a deep breath. "DJ said Demeter will take my dad."

I gasp. He puts his arm around me and pulls me close before continuing. "The point is I'm not worried about it, because we will not fail. We can't. It's simply not a realistic option. Besides, we have until 10:16 tonight, that's nearly five more hours. We can do this." He squeezes my hand.

"Do you have any more questions for me?" He pulls us to a stop so he can look me in the eye.

"I'm sure I do, but none are coming to mind at the moment. I reserve the right to ask more as they come to me."

"Noted."

It feels like he can sense my pulse picking up again, because he takes a deep breath and nods for me to do the same. We let them out together and repeat. I feel like I owe him an explanation for the increasing frequency of my fledgling panic attacks.

"So much has changed for me so quickly. I'm in this with *you*, a guy who

I thought hated me for years. What's more, I thought I wanted nothing to do with you at all." I can't let the hurt look on his face stop me, or I'll never get it all out. "I've learned that Greek Mythology is not really a myth, and someone has been messing with my mind, taking away my free will. My favorite substitute teacher is a clerk of some royal court. My new boyfriend is the son of an actual Siren, and her tears cause everyone but me to see a convincing mirage in a painting. And I know you might think this next thing is wrong, because love is a beautiful thing and all, but the idea of being with someone for the rest of my life, starting at this age, gives me heart palpitations. Letting anyone new into my life means opening myself up to the possibility of great pain, like how we lost my dad, and I'm not sure I am strong enough to go through that again right now."

Somewhere in the middle of all of that, I found myself being held up by Vander's strong arms around me. The tears are flowing right through the hole in his shirt, but he doesn't seem to mind as he holds me, and...

Is he humming?

I pull back to look at him, and he wipes the tears from his shirt and presses his hand gently to my face. I lean into it, enjoying the comfort that seems to radiate from his touch.

"*Mmm...*" Am I moaning? *Shit, I am!* How embarrassing. "I'm sorry."

"Listen, Julia, you don't need to apologize for anything. And you certainly don't need to feel bad about any of those things you mentioned, either. Only, let me clear something up for you."

I lift my eyes to meet his. Afraid to speak, I just nod.

"I never hated you. I was drawn to you, and sometimes that caused me to be extra nice to your friends to try to get close to you. I was the immature one to try to pick fights with you for your attention, and I really wish I could take that back, but I can't. Moving forward is our only choice. Can you forgive me?" He has his hand on my face, smoothing my cheek with his thumb. I can feel his energy warming me up where his wet finger is touching me.

"Vander, I was mean, and didn't even realize it. If you can forgive me for that, then I can forgive you for far less." I can feel the smile take over his whole body through the touch on my face. I look up into his eyes before he leans in for a soft kiss. I lightly clear my throat. "Why do you hum?"

"Huh?" He grabs my hand and we continue our journey to the bowling alley.

"When you helped my headache, soothed my sore throat both times, and just now, you were humming."

"I do that, really? I never thought about it. I guess it's just what my dad did when I was little and needed soothing. He never knew he was doing it, either, and he certainly didn't know what it sounded like, but I just associate humming with healing now, I guess." He shrugs.

"So, it's not part of the process?"

"Not that I'm aware of." He winks at me again, and for the first time, I don't cringe at the sight.

"Thank you." I squeeze his hand.

"I'm glad it helped. I wasn't sure if it would, but I had to try sharing my energy with you. We have a mission to be happy now, right?"

"Right. But can I just say something? I'm not sure you actually shared any energy or if your touch just made me feel better." Smiling is becoming a consistent habit around this guy. *I like it.*

"Either way, I'm happy to help."

He pulls open the door to the bowling alley and allows me to enter first. I hear several thuds of a ball hitting the lane, and the impending thunder as it rolls to its crescendo, crashing against the pins. After my eyes adjust to the dimness, I look around and find my mother standing at the shoe counter. I've never known my mother to bowl.

"What in the hell is she doing here?" The smile falls from my face, my heart rate picks up, and the sounds go silent as my brain races to come up with a story to explain what I'm doing here.

"Don't worry," Vander murmurs near my ear, and then I see why. DJ and Jerika are making their way over to her. My breathing slows a bit as I watch them interact with her. After a minute, she looks past them and sees me.

"Hi, Julia. I just wanted to bring you this." She heaves my backpack off the floor and hands it to me. "They had a change in shifts, and the new crew didn't know if you had been contacted, so they called home. I ran down and got it, but when I got there, the lady explained the note she found, saying that Lissy was coming to get it. When I called Lissy, she said she was to bring it to you here, so I just brought it instead. Mr. Daniels explained that handling a crisis situation is part of the leadership training for the night, so I've messed that one up for you. I'm sorry about that. But then again, I have never doubted your skills as a leader."

I don't think my mom has stopped to take a breath. I can tell that she is super nervous, which is very unlike her. Makes me want to add the cost of the gas money to Demeter's tab for the sake of my mother's sanity. It's almost like her subconscious is figuring out that two and two aren't four.

"Thank you, Mom."

"You're welcome, sweetheart. Vander, what crisis are you dealing with?" She turns to him with doubt in her eyes, and his charms won't work on her today. I turn to watch him gaze up and to the right, like he's looking for a memory, not down like when he's thinking up a lie.

"Well, I left my phone in a bathroom, and I have to get it back." That could be the truth—it must have been taken while he was getting ready this morning.

Jerika and DJ step up to join the conversation, or to lead my mother away so we can continue our mission. I'm not sure which it is, but I am grateful. I won't lie to my mom, no matter what the consequences are. She would know I was lying for sure, and who knows what Demeter would do to her brain should I let it slip what is actually going on here. It's not a risk I'm willing to take.

As our guides lead her out the door, I call out, "Thanks again, Mom." Waving with a smile on my face. I move to a table so I can search my bag and make sure nothing is missing or damaged. Vander sits next to me.

"Guides to the rescue, huh?"

"I guess steering my mother away is a 'when I need them' kind of situation. I was beginning to wonder if they would be any help to us at all."

Jerika speaks next, and it makes me jump. "You both seem to be doing fine on your own."

"Well, except for the clumsiness," DJ points to Vander's ripped shirt, then to my bag, "and forgetfulness. You've been getting along pretty well."

"Now, we will let you get back to it. With only three hours left to go, we won't want to take up your time."

"*Three* hours?" I turn to Vander. "I thought we had until 10:16 tonight, not 8:16."

"I set my watch, I swear."

"Yes, Vander," DJ replies, "but did you take an hour away for every human you called to ask for help?"

"No! I didn't know that was a rule."

Jerika lifts her chin at me. "I specifically told Julia to be careful about who she trusted."

"Hey, thanks for throwing me under the bus, Jerika." I rely on sarcasm to keep from screaming in frustration. "For the record, I trust our friends, and evidently, I was right to do so, because they did exactly as we asked. That's what help looks like, in case you were wondering, since you are so bad at being helpful yourself. What you didn't say was that asking for help would cost us time—or did you conveniently forget to mention that part?"

"Why would one of you tell her the rule and then tell me the consequence, DJ? Be straight with me, man." Vander has a vein popping out of his neck above his collar.

The response we receive is both of them poofing out of existence—as far as I can tell, anyway.

"Well, that's pretty messed up, Vander. A lot of help these guides are, huh?"

I'm trying to keep my anxiety down by letting my anger rise a bit. Pulling Vander along with me to fight a common enemy seems to be a strength for us.

"We have to get out of here before our friends arrive." Vander turns to the door, just as my favorite person with green and blue-dyed hair bursts through, with other familiar faces in tow.

"Too late."

CHAPTER TWENTY-THREE

Lissy is smiling from ear to ear as she nearly knocks me down with a hug. It's only been a couple of hours since I saw her last, but I understand her zealousness when she whispers in my ear.

"Julia, he picked me up first, so I got to sit in the front seat! I was inspecting the shifter thingy when he needed to change gears, and he ended up holding my hand for a second! I died."

I laugh at her dramatics as I pull her away from me so I can hug Taylor, too.

"Sorry you stopped at the bus depot for nothing." I tap the strap of the bag on my shoulder.

"Yeah, they said your mom had already picked your bag up," Lissy replies.

I see a sparkle in Lissy's eye before she whispers, "I think Wesley checked out my ass when I got out of the car." She waggled her eyebrows and added, "I'm wearing my special jeans!"

Giving her another quick squeeze, I turn to see Vander pat Wes on the back. Behind them, I see a few employees setting up the stage for karaoke, and some teenage regulars sipping on *Starbucks* cups while they wait. When I turn back to my friends, an exit strategy reveals itself to me.

"Hey, Vander, remember how you promised to go get a salted caramel mocha with me before everything starts?"

A brief look of confusion passes over his face before he realizes what I'm telling him, but then he joins in on the charade. "Right! Hey, guys, we will be back in a little bit."

I put my hand in his proffered one, and we make our way to the door. Before we take two steps, I hear Taylor behind me. "Coffee sounds good. Can I come with you?"

Vander squeezes my hand to let me know that he has this under control. "What would you like, Taylor?" He pauses to wink at her, and nods toward me. "We'll bring it back for you."

She stops in her tracks as understanding crosses her face, "Oh. Um—actually, never mind, I think I will just get a pop."

"Are you sure?" I offer.

"Yeah," Taylor replies with a blush coming on her face. "I'm all set."

"Okay, well, we'll see you all a little later." We walk toward the exit, but I turn my head and mouth, *sorry*.

Taylor pushes her two index fingers together and makes a kissy face at me. The others just wave, with knowing grins. If they really knew what was happening, they would have a far different look on their faces.

We are out the door and in the parking lot when Vander says, "Quick thinking."

"Thanks. The thing is, I really just have to use the restroom. Do you mind if we actually do stop at *Starbucks* on the way?"

"We can stop wherever you want," he says, dangling a set of keys in my face. I drop his hand and face him.

"You asked for more help?" I reach for my phone, which should be in my back pocket, but isn't. So I grab Vander's arm to look at his fancy watch.

He shows me the time, but then explains himself. "No, I didn't ask—I just took his keys. Do you think that counts?"

"If only our *guides* would appear and actually tell us something useful."

"I'm kind of glad they haven't, because I'm sure they would not approve of stealing."

"Well, you are right about that." Naturally, DJ would reappear at those words. "However, it doesn't count as asking for help, so you won't lose any more time."

"See? It's all good." Vander shrugs.

I'm still pissed at both of our guides for being less than helpful, so I keep my eyes on the ground.

"Of course," DJ starts, bringing my gaze up to him, "the consequences of your actions are on you. I don't have the power to stop them, and must I remind you that you can't charm anyone until this quest is complete, either."

With those words, he is gone. I look to Vander, and he looks from me to Wesley's car and back to me.

"I can't put you at risk. If Wes realizes that his keys are missing and discovers that his car gone, he will call the police. And knowing that my luck is gone with my evil eye necklace, we will get pulled over, be questioned, and who knows what else."

"Careful, Vander—you're starting to sound like me when I get anxious. Just take a deep breath and relax your shoulders." I smile at him and rub his arms reassuringly. "Listen, we have time to think this through. But I do need to use the bathroom, like now. Why don't we walk over to *Starbucks*, grab a coffee so I didn't just add another lie to the list of things I blame your grandma for, and figure this out?"

"That sounds like a good plan. Can I just put his keys in your bag and we can 'help him find them' when we come back after we complete this quest?" His use of air quotes makes me laugh.

❍ ❍ ❍

The smell on the inside of *Starbucks* is life. I sigh and take a deep breath in, inhaling the caffeine as I make my way to the restroom. After I wash my hands, I meet Vander coming out of the men's room. He must have decided to go while he has the chance, too. But as we exit, I realize something isn't right; the only thing I hear is the music playing overhead. I look down the short hall toward the register, and find two people sitting under a table with their knees hugged tightly to their chests. The lime-green hair on one of them is so familiar, it stops me in my tracks. Before I can figure out what's going on in this place, I realize the people are Kenzie-Grace and Miles Udell. Vander gets down next to them and motions for me to stay low and move closer to him.

I bend down, take two steps toward them, and quietly sit. I don't know what's happening, and Vander has his finger over his lips, encouraging me to be quiet. Kenzie-Grace is clinging to Miles, and his arm is protectively around her. Moving as little as possible, I glance around. There are coffees left on a table, and a few people are crouched beneath it, hugging the table's legs. The only thing I hear is Jack Johnson crooning. There's no hiss from milk being steamed, or any conversations taking place.

Then I suddenly understand why. Near the counter, a man dressed in all black is holding up a gun. On his head he has a beanie and a ball cap pulled down low, casting shadows over his features. He starts pacing at the front of the store.

"Now, fill these bags with everything in the registers. If nobody tries to be a hero, nobody gets hurt. If anybody moves in the next five minutes, just remember, we're not afraid of going *back* to prison!"

I fight the urge to stand and look where the man is, because *holy shit*! The place is being robbed, with the very real threat of someone being shot in our midst. Vander wraps his arms around me, squeezing gently. My heart starts racing, and my breathing begins to pick up. I push down my anxiety with all I have in me, because this is no time to lose my ability to think clearly. Natural adrenaline starts to kick in, my senses perk up, and I hear sirens in the distance. Not the singing on an island kind, of course. Rather, the police are on their way variety.

Get it together, Julia. It's going to be okay—it has to be.

I watch the exit that I can see from here, to try to catch a glimpse of the robbers as they leave. However, the only person I see leaving is the same man with black clothes and black hair, long enough to touch the top of a black sweatshirt, yet mostly hidden beneath the black ball cap. The robber said "we," but I only saw one guy leaving. *Maybe the other robber is still in the store?*

Nobody moves for a few minutes. We all just sit quietly and listen to the sirens getting closer and closer to us.

The door flies open suddenly, and two police officers enter with their hands on their guns, the snaps on their holsters already undone. They start to do a visual sweep of the place, looking at us on the ground. I let out the breath I've been holding.

"Is everyone all right?" one of the officers asks, while he continues to case the environment.

Slowly, we all begin to look around and make eye contact with one another, as if checking in on our fellow victims. After a few nods, the group under the table makes their way back up into their seats. Kenzie-Grace is trembling as she stretches out her legs and lets go of Miles. We all wearily make our way to our feet, brushing ourselves off. Kenzie-Grace starts crying, and before I can comfort her with more than my attempt at a reassuring smile, Miles grabs her, holding her tight.

Vander takes my hand and squeezes it twice. I look at him and notice how uncomfortable this situation is making him. It takes me a second to decide that it's the witnessing of a robbery and not any issue with his ex-girlfriend that is the culprit, because he is watching an ambulance pull up outside.

This day just keeps getting worse. He squeezes my hand again, and then points to his watch. *Shitcicles!* We don't have time for socializing or a debriefing or a bunch of questions. If that happens, we will never finish this quest before our time runs out.

The taller officer makes his way around the counter to check on the employees, while the female one makes her way through the tables to the bathroom area. As she walks past, I read the name *Hanson* on her uniform. After walking through the back kitchen area, the male officer returns to the counter and shouts, "Clear!"

After checking both bathroom areas, Hanson finishes her sweep, and shouts, "Clear!" before snapping her holster closed.

"Can we just tell you what we saw, since we were only here to see the end of it?" Vander offers, before anyone else speaks.

"What do you mean by seeing only the end of it? Did you walk in on the crime in progress?" Hanson has her notebook out and pen poised above it, quick as a whip.

He glances at me before he starts. "We stopped in to use the restrooms before we got our coffees to go. When we came out, everything was quiet, and everyone was on the ground. The bad guy said to be cool and no one would get hurt. Then, he took the money and left."

There were a few inaccuracies in what he said, to say the least, and it must have shown on my face. But before she could ask me anything, Hanson's radio starts chirping about a "10-32" and "a possible 10-33" in the cell phone store next door with the mention of some kind of "squad." She holds up her hand with the notepad in it while turning her radio's volume up with the other hand. I don't know why she does that, because we can all hear it in stereo. It's the officer at the front of the store speaking, and he's doing so urgently.

Hanson motions for us to head to the door. "Ladies and gentlemen, please make your way to the exit. Don't make any sudden movements. It's important to stay calm." The way she is speaking makes me think of the way my mother talks to me when I first wake up in the morning—firm, but gentle. Someone up front must have mentioned the confusion about the number of robbers. I never saw any other robber, only the guy who was holding the gun. But of course, the police would have to take such a threat seriously.

"They're looking for the others," Vander whispers to me. "I was trying not to mention that so we could get out of here."

My adrenaline causes me to react harshly, though I try to keep my volume down. "You can't withhold information about an active investigation! Are you crazy?"

"I gave the highlights. Besides, I never *saw* anybody else, did you?"

"No, I only saw that one guy. But he said 'we.' I know he said 'we.'"

We step out into the parking lot and see that several more squad cars have arrived on the scene. We are ushered away from the store by Hanson and her colleagues to the soundtrack of sirens wailing and the sight of lights flashing around us. Pretty soon there will be a camera crew on the scene. *This could definitely ruin our chances of making it to the tree in time...*

Then again, maybe not.

"I have an idea."

I squeal as I slip my arm through his. With my other hand, I draw a curtain down over my face to show him that I am putting on a show. I allow the extra power rushing through my veins to let a fresh batch of tears build in my eyes. Vander shows concern, and I squeeze his arm and tell him, "I'm fine."

I pull him toward the squad car farthest from the store. The officer standing near it looks like he could be my cousin, if I had a cousin who was nearly seven feet tall and lifted weights a few hours every day.

"Officer Towns," I read the name off of his uniform, and try to display my shakiness from the adrenaline rush, "we were talking to Officer Hanson in there before we were sent out here. I don't see her anymore, so we want to tell you everything we saw. But I'm thirsty—we never got to place our order or anything—and I'm a bit cold. Also, I think I should sit down. I bet it's warm in your car." I'm careful not to ask for any help. The last thing we need is to lose even more time here.

"Why don't you take a seat," he offers, opening his rear door for me. "Let me get you the blanket out of my trunk," he adds as he steps to the rear of his vehicle.

"The station is right across the river from the tree," I whisper to Vander, who is sliding in next to me with a massive look of confusion on his face. It's like a light bulb moment, the way his eyes dance when he understands what I'm doing. We have less than three hours left to complete this mission, and since at least an hour of that would have been spent walking to the tree, we can get that time back by catching a ride, all without asking.

"Here you go, Miss—?" Officer Towns is trying to figure out what to call me.

"I'm Julia, and this is Vander." My voice sounds shaky, without even trying.

"Well, here you go, Julia—" I know he wants my last name as hands me the blanket and a bottle of water.

"It's Julia Wright," I reply as I twist the cap off. "Thank you."

"Can I get anything for you, Vander—?" Again, he leaves the end of his name dangling so that we will fill in the blank.

"Thelxinoe. Vander Thelxinoe," he answers, and then grabs the blanket to cover my shoulders. "And no, not right now, but thanks for asking."

Towns leaves the door ajar so we aren't locked in as he uses his radio. Vander starts to say something, but I shush him so I can eavesdrop on Towns. I hear words like, "debrief" and "safety," and finally I hear the one I've been listening for.

Downtown.

"Here's the deal," Towns starts, poking his head inside the vehicle. "The safest place for you to be right now is down at the station. There's no sense trying to talk over all this—"

The sound of a fire truck pulling noisily into the lot makes his point. Behind that big vehicle is another one, with Linn County Sheriff markings on it and a matching trailer attached. The bomb squad is officially on the scene. Why, was there a bomb in there? Suddenly, everyone seems to scatter to make way for them.

Towns continues, "As I was saying, it will be best for me to take you guys down to the station to get your statements, if that's okay with you."

I nod, and Vander comments, "Probably the best course of action at this point."

Towns sits down in the driver's seat and tells us, "Be sure to buckle up. I'm going to let them know we are on the way."

He proceeds to radio in our names and give some more ten codes to the dispatcher. I look around to see Kenzie-Grace and Miles being escorted to the back of a different police car. Past them, I see the *KCRG TV-9* news truck parked in the lot near where the bus dropped me off a couple of hours ago. So much has happened in that short amount of time, it seems surreal.

The way things have been appearing and disappearing today has me wondering if *any* of this is real. Come to think of it, where were our guides when we needed them in there? Ugh, they are not much help at all, practically worthless really.

I put my head down on Vander's shoulder, and he raises his arm over my head. I snuggle into him and can feel his warmth. *At least I know this part is real.* I place my hand on his heart just to feel it beat. He grabs it and holds it tight against him. The perfection of this moment causes me to sigh. When I do that, Vander bends down and places a gentle kiss on the top of my head. That is a good feeling, and, young or not, I never want it to stop.

CHAPTER TWENTY-FOUR

The ride downtown seems to pass in a blur—or maybe I just fell asleep in the car. Either way, I can smell the river when the squad car's door opens. We are right where we need to be. Before I step out of the car, I see DJ leaning against the entrance to the station. I nudge Vander to make sure he sees him, too. Jerika must be close, because someone will have to vouch for me as well, or else I will have to call my mother again.

Huh, I thought they weren't going to help us get out of trouble? I guess that doesn't apply to potentially life-ending, dangerous situations, like being involved in a robbery with a possible bomb threat, but getting us out of a police station without calling our parents they can handle. *Whatever.*

I roll my eyes at the lack of concern I see on DJ's face. *Some guide he is.* I completely ignore him and walk right past, following Officer Towns. Vander slows to chat with DJ, but quickly joins me inside. We are escorted through the public waiting area to a small office and directed to sit in the two chairs opposite a messy desk. Towns offers us water again while rifling through some documents, but I still have half a bottle in my hand.

"Can we get a recorder or whatever in here so we can get this over with?" Vander seems annoyed when he speaks. Officer Towns is about as surprised as I am with his tone. He stops shuffling papers to look between us. I can't blame him for the curious look on his face.

Vander softens, "I mean, I just want to put this terrifying experience behind me as soon as possible."

I reach over and pat his knee, offering him a supportive smile.

Suddenly, there is a big commotion in the lobby of the police station. I'm sure this kind of thing probably happens all the time here, but I'm spooked by it. Towns seems to be ignoring it as he settles in behind his desk, which is not an easy task with legs as long as his are, I'm sure. He clicks his mouse a few times and speaks into a microphone.

"Testing one, two, three," he states, and then clicks again before we hear his echo coming from the machine. After a few more clicks, he starts listing off the date, his name, and badge number before he turns the mic toward us. He grabs a pen and hovers it above his yellow legal pad.

"Please state and spell your name." He nods to me. Then the door to his office bursts open and Jerika is standing there in a suit, carrying a briefcase and wearing glasses I've never seen before as she looks at us.

"Don't say another word," she says to Vander and me before she points to Officer Towns, who is on his way around his desk to step in front of her. "And you'd better have a good reason for questioning my underage clients without notifying their parents or offering them proper representation."

Officer Towns laughs before explaining, "Ma'am, I think you watch too much TV. These two are witnesses to a crime. They are not under arrest, and are free to leave at any time. However, they expressed their desire to share what they saw in hopes of finding the criminal responsible. If they want to speak to their parents, they have every right to do so." Towns turns to us. "Would you like to contact your parents before we continue?"

Over his shoulder, Jerika is giving us the shushing motion with her finger over her lips as she shakes her head. Without saying anything, I shake my head as well. Then DJ pops up behind Jerika and starts signing something to Vander, and gesturing at Jerika along with it.

"I think I would like to talk to our attorney in private," Vander suddenly suggests. Officer Towns steps through the door and motions for Jerika to enter. DJ is gone, but I know that doesn't matter. I'm proven right when the door closes and DJ appears behind the messy desk, even though he didn't walk through the door.

Vander puts both hands up and leans across the desk. He looks at the computer and maneuvers the mouse to shut off the recorder. I bet Towns didn't think we would know to do that and hoped he could just replay our conversation later.

"Okay," Vander starts, "are you actually going to give us some useful information here, or are you just trying to stall us?" I'm glad to hear that the annoyance in his voice matches mine.

"There is too much at stake here for us to let you talk to him. What were you thinking? You can't charm him."

"So what? All we plan to tell him is what we saw, which wasn't much, and then we would be out of here." My irritation is growing with each word I speak.

"No, you wouldn't, because then they will set you down with a sketch artist, and then do the next thing and another after that. Demeter's reach has no end."

My stomach drops out of my body, like I'm on some roller coaster ride and we've just breached the peak. I turn to Vander and whisper, "She doesn't play by any rules, so why should we?"

I grab the legal pad and pen from the desk and begin writing down everything that happened, from the moment we left the bathroom until the moment Hanson came on the scene. When Jerika or DJ open their mouths, I stare daggers at them, and Vander clears his throat. Every few sentences, Vander suggests another detail, or a different description of the order of events.

After we settle on our full witness statement, I sign it, date it, and write my contact information down as well. Vander does the same, and when he sets the pen down, Jerika and DJ vanish.

We open the door, but Officer Towns is not standing outside of it. Vander grabs my hand and guides me through the public waiting area and out of the station. Nobody even looks at us; it's like we are invisible. I wonder how the guides did that.

The tree is about five blocks north and across the river from here. We walk about two blocks before either of us says anything, and it is me who breaks the silence first.

"Thank you."

"For what?" Vander asks. He must not realize how well he voiced my own frustration earlier.

"For being upset on my behalf. I know you think DJ is some awesome miracle guide for you. But he hasn't done much actual guiding, nor has he been there when things were really challenging, like when we were being held hostage. I don't think you need him anymore, if you ever really did at all."

He nods so I know he heard me, but then seems to consider what I've said, weighing it carefully. We walk another block quietly before he replies, "I am afraid of Demeter. I can't charm her, and she has a lot of power. Of course, she has a lot of enemies, too. Maybe it's time we made friends with some of them."

Vander has always been under her control. He's never known life without her hovering over him. His official quest is bound to be full of obstacles, and the last thing he needs is a guide playing technicality games with him, or giving him someone to lean on when he would do better standing on his own two feet.

After another block, I fill him in on my thoughts. "Maybe for now, try to reject the idea that you aren't capable of doing this on your own. *Ow*!"

I fall to my butt, grasping my ankle. It hurts like it has been set on fire. The damn pothole I stepped in is the size of a volleyball. Vander takes the half-empty water bottle from where I stored it in my backpack and dumps some of it in his hand. He starts humming as I carefully fold the hem of my jeans up my calf and roll my sock down past my ankle. I bite my lip to hold back the cry of pain gathering steam in my throat.

I feel warmth transferring from Vander's hands to my body. It radiates up and down his fingers and swirls around my ankle. His humming has a calming effect on my nerves, but nothing else is happening. I remember his tip about relaxing my shoulders, so I let the tension go and try to breathe circularly, in through my nose and out from my mouth. What feels like only a minute passes, and he pours more water into his hand for a second round of his warm, healing touch. My ankle doesn't feel any better, though—just hotter.

I look away and notice how dark it has gotten. I steal a glance at Vander's fancy watch and then take a second look because it reads eight o'clock. "There are sixteen minutes left."

Vander doesn't look at his watch, he doesn't stop humming, and he doesn't seem to share my distress, so I repeat myself. "Vander, we only have sixteen minutes. We've got to go."

He shakes his head. "Not until you're ready."

"Vander, it's not working."

The look of disbelief on his face is quickly followed by one of anger. "I'm sorry. It's Demeter, she took my powers. But I have an idea."

"What kind of idea? Time is running out."

"I don't know if it will work," he preambles absentmindedly, while taking his wallet out of his back pocket. He pulls a flat vial from a credit card slot and presses it to his lips before uncorking it. "But it's worth a shot."

"What is that?" I inquire.

As if he is afraid to change his mind, he carefully pours the contents of the vial, a single drop of liquid, on my ankle. The heat is immediate and intense.

"Whoa!" I gasp.

"Are you okay?" He reaches over to wipe it off, but I stop him.

"It feels so much better! That was just like your touch, times a hundred."

I try lifting my foot, and it doesn't hurt at all. I hesitantly twirl it in a circle, waiting for a twinge of pain, but none comes. I feel brand new.

He gently rolls my sock into place and unties my shoe, only to retie it a bit tighter to help support my ankle, just in case. Then he unfolds my jeans and slips his head under my arm to help me get up and finish this journey.

"I should have been watching where I was going." We start moving again, and I realize I can put all of my weight on my foot without it hurting now.

"You know it's my fault that you fell."

I take another step forward and try to reconcile myself with the fact that some mysterious liquid has healed my ankle. "No, Vander, the reason I fell falls squarely on the city of Cedar Rapids, and its love of polka-dotting their streets with pothole decorations." I chuckle at my attempt at lightening the mood. "I think I can walk, Vander. Let me try it on my own."

"Under one condition—you have to let me carry you if it hurts."

"Okay." I can give him that promise. He steps back, taking hold of my hand, and watches as I make a show of stepping gingerly down on my foot. My speed increases until we are moving along at a normal pace. I'm watching where I put my foot down, every single step. I have to know what was in that vial.

"It's amazing that you can do that. That injury could have taken weeks to heal on its own. Thank you."

"Julia, it's the least I can do for dragging you into this whole thing."

"You didn't drag me into anything. It was my choice to join you." I squeeze his hand to emphasize my point.

"I know, and you're so amazing for choosing to do this with me."

Some heat comes to my cheeks at the compliment. "So, what exactly was that?" I point to my ankle to show him what I'm talking about.

"The last tear I have from my mom. My dad told me to save it for when I found something I cared about enough to use it on."

"And you used it on me?" It's merely a whisper, not the shocked yell I was going for. I can barely hold back the emotions threatening to overtake me at the thought of what he has done.

"Of course I did. And I would do it again in a heartbeat."

I'm speechless. Vander takes my hand and squeezes it.

We round the corner onto the bridge, and we can see the tree from here. The rush of water in the river matches the blood pumping through my veins. We don't have any more time to waste. Our pace picks up as we get closer, and we hustle past the courthouse and onto May's Island, in the middle of the river. The cars driving past us don't even register in my brain, though we stop and look both ways before crossing the street.

I begin to search the tree as we get on the path that leads to it. There is a tire hanging from one of the metal branches of the sculpture. Someone must have hung it as a prank—I've never seen it there before.

"Look at the tire swing. I'll push you, if you want a ride." Vander laughs at the idea, but I think it has merit. Though first, we have to find the necklace.

I start looking around.

Vander starts looking around.

We walk around the tree in opposite directions, and meet back at the tire swing.

The tree is huge, so we can't climb it. The only leverage we could gain would be to get up on the tire swing, so I do. I put a foot through the hole before lifting the other one onto the swing. Vander is holding it steady while I position myself on the upper part of the tire, to get as high as I can. I search the crooks of all of the branches around me, and then I tell him to give me a push, so I can check out the tree from new angles.

When he does, it is thrilling. I feel like a little kid on the playground when my dad would do an under doggy and run underneath me to push my swing high in the sky. I'm so high off the ground, and yet feel perfectly safe. The smile on my face must express all of that to Vander, because he starts to laugh. I look down to him, and then I see it. The blue stone that looks like an eye is as plain as day already hanging around his neck.

"What time is it?" I ask.

The handsome smile leaves his face as he checks his watch. "Eight-sixteen. Our time is up."

CHAPTER TWENTY-FIVE

"It's a good thing we found it when we did, then." I laugh as he pulls me to a stop to keep me from swinging.

"Wait. *What*? We did?" He looks around, like it might be floating next to his head or something, and he's close.

"We did," I confirm as I climb down from the tire to hug him tight. I pull back and gently tug on the necklace that is in place around his neck. "We found happiness at the never-growing Tree of Five Seasons. Together."

His eyes are glistening now, and he wears a smile that is taking over his whole face. He kisses me on the cheek, picks me up, and spins me around. We both laugh. I'm glad this day is over. I would change so many things, take out so much of the stress and worry if I had to do it all over again.

I wish I could have a do-over.

Clinging to his neck, I have a dizzy feeling that overwhelms me. "Please put me down, my head is spinning."

I try to shake away the uneasy feeling, but then, suddenly, I am sitting on the couch in my living room. Gone is the Tree of Five Seasons and the scent of the river, replaced by the familiar sights of my own home. *What the actual hell is happening?*

A light blazes out from the kitchen, brightening the living room for a few seconds, and I hear a dish crash into the sink. I'm on my feet and flying through the house in no time flat. Mr. Thelxinoe is a statue at our table with the computer in front of him. I find my mother standing in front of the sink with her mouth agape and eyes wide. *Holy Mother of déjà vu!* I follow her gaze and find a tall man standing there. I am so glad it's not Demeter this time, but my hackles are still raised at the idea of another stranger welcoming himself into my home.

"Good job on your quest. I'm sorry to intrude, but my hands are tied. I have to enter your sequence in the same way and at the same time that the wicked witch of the fields has set up." The lilt in his voice assures me he is not from around here, but I can't place the accent. He may be taller than Vander, but he's very thin. And it might be the lighting, but it looks like his skin has an almost green tint to it. "I'm Calab, and I can honestly say, it is so lovely to meet you." He sticks out his hand, and I shake it out of habit. Though, I am inclined to give him the benefit of doubt because of how he described Demeter.

"I'm Julia," I offer, and pull my hand back to my side.

"Oh, we all know very well who *you* are. Good job performing your first redundancy." I look around for a second, trying to decipher why he is referring to more than one person. I feel Vander's arm pushing me back behind him, protectively.

So far, this is going much better than the first time my mother dropped that dish, but I understand his concern. My thoughts are swirling, trying to figure out what the hell is going on. *How can I be back in this moment? Oh shit, are we going to have to do the quest over? Wait, did he say that he knows who I am? Good job on what, exactly? I mean, what the what?*

"Calab, have you been sent here, or are you here by choice?" Vander's question is a good place to start, since my mind is reeling.

"I'm here of my own volition. I've been waiting for an opportunity to show Demeter what I think of her. And until your actions of late, I had no reason to hope that I could throw her mistake back in her face. Turns out, you aren't as big a fan of hers as we previously believed." Calab looks past Vander to me before continuing. "Now that you've discovered your abilities and harnessed your power, Julia, it seems like the present is as good a time as any."

Vander slides more directly in front of Calab, guarding me. "Before we say anything else, I expect some answers to my questions. How do you know Julia?"

"Demeter has warned us all about how your betrothed can turn back time."

"I can do what?" *This was my fault? I did this?* My small disbelieving voice isn't heard above Vander's next question.

"Who is the mysterious 'we' you keep referring to?"

"Not all of us ally with Demeter. 'We' are those Greek-aware who would like to see how much of her life Julia can ruin."

It's silent for a few seconds. Then I step alongside Vander and watch a small smile grow into one of his big grins. "How can we help you stick it to my grandmother?"

Placing my hand on Vander's chest, to slow his roll, I shake my head. "We all know I don't like that woman, but I don't even know how I did what I did. I am still trying to figure out who I am. How can I possibly be of any help?"

"Don't you see?" He grabs my hand and holds it close, looking right into my eyes. "All of this is only possible because of you. It has always been about you."

After I swallow the lump in my throat caused by the skipped beat of my heart, I nod in agreement. "What do I need to do?"

A wicked smile appears on Calab's face. There is a matching one lifting the corners of my own mouth as well. A glance at my mom tells me she still seems shocked and is completely frozen in place. I can't blame her for that, this is a lot to take in and she doesn't know the half of it.

“I have a lot to explain.” Calab rubs his hands together. “Let me start at the beginning.”

TO BE CONTINUED...

ACKNOWLEDGEMENTS

When someone loves you, they fuel your passion and battle anyone or anything that tries to douse your flames. Thank you, Dave, for stoking my fire and being my warrior. I love you, always.

When you have created something you are proud of and can't wait to show it off, you only have a taste of what it's like to be a mother. Thank you, Bridget and Will, for calling me Momma. I love you, always.

When your day job provides some of your best friends and an atmosphere conducive to creativity, you know you are working in the right place. Washington High School is full of fun staff, amazing teenagers, and an endless number of stories to be told. It's always a great day to be a Warrior; thanks for letting me be one.

When people believe in you and push you to reach your goals while supporting your dreams, that's friendship. I can't even tell you how much I love you, Angie, Rose, Emily, and Chris. You ladies are the real champions of this book. Keeping up on word counts during NaNoWriMo, reading as I wrote to press for more, challenging me to writing sprints, and being the inspiration for the story of friendship on these pages makes me love you even more. It is an honor to fangirl with you, my tribe.

When the story you've written resonates with someone else enough that they want to be a part of telling it to the rest of the world, that matters deep in your heart. Thanks, Kristina and everyone else at Elephantine Publishing, for taking a chance on me and helping me share the best version of Julia and Vander's journey possible.

When you have been raised in a loving family and married into one, too, who could ask for anything more? Lots of love to Dave, Bev, Nancy, Paul, John, Heidi, Sam, Sophie, Jim, Monica, Mason, Logan, Jill, Brian, Kyle, Ruth, and Scott. I wouldn't be who I am today without each of you in my life.

When readers who encourage you with their reviews express their excitement for the next book, it makes you want to write more. Thank you to my beta readers and especially to Kyla at Missed Period Editing for making Trial By Charm better than I could have on my own.

When the list of friends to thank seems too long to manage, you are blessed. I know I am. To my Utopia Con friends, fellow authors, future readers, all fangirls and fanboys, kindred spirits, and to God, who has blessed me with all of these, many thanks and much love always.

ABOUT THE AUTHOR

As a substitute teacher, Jolene spends her days in high school classrooms harvesting material for her Young Adult novels. She also uses it as an outlet for fangirling by showing upcoming book-to-movie trailers at the end of class, or discussing vital issues like whether Katniss should have picked Gale or Peeta.

She is committed to helping Special Education teenagers become independent adults and helping them find a way to focus on the positive especially when life gets hard. At home, Jolene loves to cuddle with her husband, two kids, and three cats—sometimes all at once—while reading Young Adult books or repeatedly watching movies based on them.

Sign up for her newsletter to stay updated on her latest releases and to discuss your favorite YA love triangles!

61782693R00131

Made in the USA
Lexington, KY
20 March 2017